COMING IN HOT

JENNIFER BERNARD

1

THE MAN SITTING AT THE BACK OF CAROLYN MOORE'S CLASS looked nothing like her usual students. Starting with the fact that he was male, since most of the students in Renaissance Art History 201 were women. Then there was the fact that he was a full-grown adult male, not a kid who'd barely reached drinking age. Not to mention the additional facts of his size and appearance, which were big and imposing. Attractive, one might even say, if broad shoulders, intense dark eyes, and black leather jackets were your thing.

A peaceful art history teacher like herself should certainly not find someone like him attractive. But he actually reminded her of a painting she loved, a Bronzino portrait of a man aiming his smoldering gaze directly at the viewer. So to be completely honest with herself, the mystery man did push a few of her buttons.

But she could deal with that kind of unsettling stare a lot better in an oil painting than in the back of her classroom. He'd slipped in midway through her lecture on the technique of *chiaroscuro* and immediately thrown her off stride.

She cleared her throat and checked her notes. "Does anyone

here know the precise meaning of the term *chiaroscuro*? Any Italian speakers in the house?"

A few students volunteered words like "cappuccino," and "Prada," which made her laugh. The blond kid in the middle row looked lost in a dream, as usual. One student surreptitiously checked her phone.

"No Google," Carolyn said with a smile. "We can figure this one out. Let's start with the last part, "scuro." What other words contain that root?"

Again, no answer.

"I'm thinking of a common word, very familiar, not at all..." She dragged it out as a teasing hint.

"Obscure!" someone exclaimed.

"Exactly. Obscure means hidden, hard to find, because it's ... what?"

"In the dark? *Scuro* means dark!" A student in the front row bounced in her seat, thrilled that she'd come up with the answer, then slouched back down. They were always so anxious about playing it cool, sometimes it made Carolyn sad. Was there something wrong with getting excited and passionate? She always tried to encourage that in her students.

"Yes!" She stepped away from the podium where her laptop was set up with slides and high-fived the student. "You're correct, *scuro* means dark. So you can probably guess what *chiaro* means as well."

A brief silence followed, interrupted by the man at the back of the class. The man in black.

"Light," he said in a voice so deep and resonant it sent a chill down her spine. It brought to mind the image of the last dregs of black coffee in a pot that had been left on overnight. Late nights, rough times, danger, adventure, somehow it was all there in that one softly spoken word.

In the middle row, the blond boy—Aiden something—craned his neck to see who had spoken. Then he wheeled back around and slouched deep in his seat. The girls in the class looked too, so Carolyn found herself responding to an array of turned heads.

"Correct. *Chiaro*, in this context, means light."

She pretended to check her student roster, but she certainly had no need to. There was no way this man had enrolled in her class midterm. "I'm sorry, are you a student here?"

"I'm just visiting the campus." He moved his jacket to show his stick-on visitor's badge. "I'm sorry to interrupt."

"No problem." Although, eyeing him more closely, she wasn't entirely sure that was true. She could spot several potential problems, or at least distractions. The width of his shoulders. The sensual fullness of his lips. And most especially, the way he was looking—or glaring—at her. Wary. Suspicious. Curious. Hot. Or some heady, confusing mixture of all of the above.

"If you were a student, you'd get a high five." She smiled at him brightly, determined not to allow a dangerously attractive visitor to disrupt her class. Tapping her laser pointer on the podium, she brought her students back to attention. Or tried, anyway. Several were too fascinated by the stranger to get back into Renaissance painting mode.

"Chiaroscuro is the treatment of light and shade. It's a technique that uses strong contrast between light and dark to create a three-dimensional effect. It was developed during the Renaissance by masters of oil painting like Leonardo da Vinci and Rembrandt. They were looking for drama, for impact—we might call it the 'wow' factor today. These masters figured out how to manipulate the effect of a light source falling against a solid dark object. I'm going to show some slides now, and I want you guys to look for where the light is coming from and how it helps illuminate the subject of the painting."

She tapped a button on her laptop to play her slide show. Then she looked up and realized that the person closest to the light switch happened to be the solid dark object of the man in black.

"Sir, would you mind hitting that light behind you?" she asked him.

He twisted around to locate the light switch. Her eyes widened at the sight of his powerful torso and big hand reaching for the wall. He turned his head at the last minute, so the last thing she saw before the room went dark was that intense gaze of his. Wowza. It really packed a punch. Everything about him did. He was like a truckload of TNT plopped into a meadow of college-student flowers.

With the room in darkness, she let out a long breath, calling on some yoga breathing to regain her cool. Just because she spent most of her time with kids under the age of twenty didn't mean she couldn't handle an adult. Even if it was an intensely male sort of adult.

She too was an adult, after all. Granted, an adult who'd gone quite some time without any intimate contact with a man. Also known as sex.

Sex. Bad thought. Don't go there. Look at the slides. Talk about Caravaggio. Yes.

"Notice how you don't really know where that light comes from or what's producing it? It doesn't matter. It's only there to create the dramatic contrast that enables us to get the full impact of this portrait. In case you were wondering, this technique isn't confined to Renaissance oil paintings. Can anyone tell me who else uses *chiaroscuro*?"

"Black-and-white photography?" someone suggested.

"Yup. Exactly." She drew in another deep breath. Thank goodness, she was back in the groove now. The stranger was just a minor, temporary glitch. This was her class, she was in control.

She switched to the next slide. "Now not everyone was in favor of *chiaroscuro*. This portrait of the Queen of England is set in an open meadow with no sources of shade anywhere nearby. As you can see, the effect is serene rather than dramatic. Does anyone have any theories about why *chiaroscuro* would be controversial?"

Silence while the students gazed at the pleasant portrait of Queen Elizabeth I. She looked at the back of the class. The stranger, head tilted, was surveying the slide with a thoughtful expression. Talk about chiaroscuro ... his eyes were deep pools in the minimal light cast by the projector.

Suddenly she wanted to hear what an adult man would say instead of a twenty-year-old. It wasn't really fair. He was a visitor, not a student paying for his education. But no one else seemed eager to step up with their thoughts. So she addressed the man in black.

"You in the back, by the light switch. Why do you think chiaroscuro would find opponents in the art world at that time?"

His gaze flicked to her, as if in surprise. But he didn't hesitate. "Some people would rather not deal with the shadows. You might even say most people."

A shiver passed through her. That was exactly why she'd wanted his reaction, to hear someone with experience speak. But at the same time, his words hit close to home. Unintentionally, of course. He knew nothing about her. But still, it was enough to give her a little chill.

"Right. Here's a quote from the artist who painted this portrait. "Seeing that best to show oneself needeth no shadow of place but rather the open light...Her Majesty chose to sit in the open alley of a goodly garden where no tree was near, nor any shadow at all. So..." She turned back to the students. "What say you, young members of the twenty-first century? Do you prefer the more open lighting in this painting, or the chiaroscuro effect in something like this famous Rembrandt portrait, An Old Man in Red? Are the subjects revealed more by direct sunlight or by the use of shadows?"

Finally the students seemed to get it. Discussion erupted as they looked back and forth between the two examples.

Carolyn grinned happily. There was nothing she loved more than when her students stopped daydreaming or looking at their phones and actually engaged in the material. And really, she had to thank the man in black for that. He'd been willing to dive in with an answer despite not even being enrolled in the class.

She looked toward the back of the room to offer some kind of "thank you" to the mystery man.

But he was gone.

2

TOBIAS KNIGHT STRODE ACROSS THE PRETTY PASTORAL CAMPUS OF Evergreen, picturing himself like some kind of ogre trampling through a magical fairyland. He felt about a foot taller than everyone else here, even though there were plenty of football players and the like wandering around the central landscaped area called the "quadrangle." Maybe his extra years made the difference, or his time in the army, or his naturally fiery temperament.

Whatever it was, he felt about as alien to these students and this environment as a warrior at a tea party.

Weirdly, he hadn't felt that way in Carolyn Moore's class. Something about the way she looked at him, as if she really wanted to know what he thought, had gotten to him. Plus, she was beautiful, with all that ash-blond hair and luminous gray-blue eyes under delicately arched eyebrows. He didn't normally notice eyebrows. But she had the kind of face you just wanted to stare at forever and figure out what made it so appealing.

No wonder his little brother Aiden was in love with her.

"A golden goddess," he'd called her in his letter explaining his decision to transfer from Evergreen. He'd quoted some poem--

"Like the first evening star bright against the infinite sky." He'd even confessed to staying up late writing her love letters.

Good God. The poor kid was hooked harder than a trout. And if Carolyn Moore chose to, she could reel him in and get a small fortune for her trouble. Aiden, like all of the Knight brothers, had a trust from his share of their father's life insurance. Will had used his to buy a house and raise Aiden. Tobias and Ben had used theirs as the startup capital for Knight and Day Flight Tours, their new flightseeing business. Aiden, still only nineteen, needed Will's permission to access his trust.

He'd asked for exactly that in the letter that had sent all the brothers into a panic. Aiden wanted to transfer to Jupiter Point Community College, and use funds from his trust to win over his "golden goddess." The kid had lost his damn mind.

So far, Aiden had refused to identify the "golden goddess." The fact that he refused to give any other details pointed in the direction of someone they wouldn't approve of. So Tobias had combed through his schedule and located all the female professors on the list. One was nearly sixty and sported a gray braid down her back. Another was a proud-and-very-out black lesbian. That left the blond and lovely adjunct professor Carolyn Moore as the only potential "golden goddess."

A little more research had revealed the fact that Carolyn Moore was on staff at JPCC, and was only teaching at Evergreen for one semester.

Bingo.

Tobias had volunteered to come to Evergreen and rescue Aiden from making the worst mistake of his life. He hadn't planned to participate in Ms. Gold Digger's class on Renaissance art, but every mission had its unexpected moments.

Footfalls came pounding after him, and someone grabbed the back of his jacket. Good thing he knew it had to be Aiden, or his unknown accoster would have gotten a shock. Special Forces training died hard.

"What the hell are you doing here, Tobias?"

Tobias turned to see his youngest brother glaring at him. His blond hair stuck up in bedhead spikes. He wore torn jeans and a t-shirt that said, Ride the Wave, with a picture of a surfer wearing headphones. For a moment, just a brief one, Tobias wondered what his life would have been like if he hadn't joined the army, if he'd gone to college the way his counselors had urged him. But life had sent him in a different direction. Once a warrior, always a warrior, he supposed.

Aiden, on the other hand, was a sunny, sweet-natured kid. He was naive, and this was his first time entering the big bad world. Granted, Evergreen College didn't really fit the "big bad" description, but appearances could be deceiving. A beautiful, soft-eyed blonde could well be a scheming gold digger, and how would Aiden have any clue about it?

He wouldn't. That was Tobias's job. He had one mission— save his brother from squandering his future on a con woman.

"Good to see you, kid." Tobias reached out to squeeze his brother's shoulder. Aiden looked too pissed to risk anything more than that, like an actual hug. "You don't look too happy to see me, though."

"That depends. I mean, yeah. I'm kind of happy." Aiden eyed him with blatant suspicion. With his blond good looks, he resembled their mother, whereas Tobias had gotten his darker coloring from their father. "But if you're here to talk me out of leaving Evergreen, you can forget it."

"I don't know why you'd want to leave." Tobias shoved his hands in his pockets and gazed around at the sweeping lawns and winding pathways shaded by oak and pine trees. "It's a nice campus."

"I told you all why I wanted to leave." Aiden lifted his chin and shifted his backpack, which he'd slung over one shoulder. "And I'm not changing my mind."

Tobias surveyed his younger brother and thought about the

last time he'd seen him. Aiden had come home for a long weekend and the four brothers had held a family meeting. Even though Will was a deputy sheriff and Tobias and Ben had both recently left the armed forces, Aiden had been the one who had fearlessly confronted the elephant in the room—the murder of their father.

Aiden might look young—he was young—but he was no pushover.

"Hey, you're over eighteen. You can make your own choices," Tobias told him. Of course he hoped to talk him out of this choice, but he couldn't do that if Aiden got stubborn right off the bat. "Can we go somewhere and talk? Do you have another class now?"

"No, I have a break until my Geology class." Aiden glanced around the quadrangle. "Do you want coffee? We could go to the Caf. It's your basic cafeteria, but not too bad."

"Works for me."

As they walked toward the Caf—which had a paved courtyard dotted with tables—Aiden peppered him with questions. "Do you want to see my dorm? How long are you here for? When are you going back to Jupiter Point?"

"No specific plans yet, young blood." Tobias ruffled his hair affectionately. "Just thought it would be cool to see you living the life. My little goofball brother, a college student. What do you know."

Aiden grinned at him. Now that Tobias had acknowledged his sovereignty over his own life, he'd apparently relaxed his guard. "College is pretty cool, Tobias. There are students from all over here. My roommate is from India, how cool is that?"

"Very cool. How are the parties?"

"I hardly ever party because I'm studying so much." He plastered that innocent smile on his face, the one Tobias remembered well from his younger years.

"Busted," he said good-naturedly. "But don't worry, Will doesn't have to know."

Will was the one who had raised Aiden after their father's murder. He'd done a great job, of course, but if you asked Tobias, he'd held the reins a little too tight.

"Does Will know you're here?" Aiden asked.

"He does. He said to give you a hug. So here you go." Tobias pulled his brother into a one-armed side hug from which Aiden emerged with his hair even more mussed.

"Jeez, Tobias, you're like a two-ton truck." Aiden grumbled as he adjusted his backpack. They'd reached the edge of the outdoor patio of the Caf. Students filled the tables, laughing, eating, chatting, checking their phones, listening to their headphones. Tobias felt about a thousand years old compared to the youthfulness of these kids.

"You know what I feel like right now?" Aiden complained. "I feel like one of those kids who hires a bodyguard to scare bullies away. Do you have to scowl so much?"

Tobias relaxed his face. He hadn't realized he was scowling. "I'm not trying to scare anyone. You've heard of 'resting bitch face?' I figured out that I have 'resting fuck-you face.'"

Aiden howled with laughter. The sound lightened Tobias's heart. That was the sound of life, right there. Young, innocent life. Protecting that innocence was his job here.

Aiden spotted a table being vacated by a group of girls. "You go claim that table and I'll get the coffee."

"I can get the coffee," Tobias protested. He was the big brother, wasn't that his job?

"Nope. I got it. I prepaid a hundred dollars so I can come get a drink whenever I want. This is my turf, Tobias. My treat."

Tobias gave in and went to claim the table while Aiden disappeared through the glass doors into the Caf's inner workings. He sank into a chair and stretched out his legs. Since he and Ben had started Knight and Day Flight Tours, he didn't get nearly as much hardcore exercise as he was used to. Maybe he ought to hit the gym when he got home, or go for a trail run in the hills, or—

His brain momentarily short-circuited when he caught sight of the woman crossing the quadrangle, the sunlight catching her hair as she passed between two oak trees.

Carolyn Moore.

Except now she wasn't hidden behind that lectern, bathed in hideous fluorescent light. No, she was in full, glorious view. She wore a knee-length skirt and suede boots, along with a soft pearly sweater that clung to her long and elegantly curved torso. She was chatting with one of the students from the art class as she walked; she kept smiling at the younger woman, also a blonde, as if to encourage her. Tall and lithe, she moved with a sensual grace that sent a message right to his cock. His body responded with annoying eagerness. *You want her,* it said. *You're attracted. Possibly fascinated.*

Except that his body wasn't in charge here. He was. And he wasn't here to get involved. In fact, he was here to stop his *brother* from getting involved. And one thing he absolutely wouldn't do was upset Aiden.

So he determinedly dragged his gaze away from Carolyn Moore and stared at the tips of his shoes. A working-man's boots, designed to help him fly planes and traverse the tarmac. That's what he was—a working man, a warrior, a brawler, a brother. He had no business lusting after a refined art history type who would probably faint if he took off his shirt and showed what eight years as a Chinook pilot in the 160th Airborne—also known as a Night Stalker—did to a guy.

"You still like your coffee black, right?" Aiden said as he appeared at the table with a cardboard tray holding two steaming paper cups. Recycled paper, Tobias noticed. College campus style. Piled in the middle of the tray were a variety of snack bags ranging from unhealthy to utter crap.

"Sure, sounds good." Actually, he'd been adding sugar and

cream to his coffee lately. Just one more of the changes he was experimenting with since leaving the army. But it didn't really matter. The coffee was just an excuse. "Hey isn't that the teacher from the class we were just in?" he asked, feigning innocence.

Aiden's head shot around so fast it could have made sparks. He zeroed in on the two women, teacher and student, like a laser beam. "Yes," he said in a strangled voice. He plopped down on the chair next to Tobias and sighed. "That's Ms. Moore. What did you think of her class?"

"Interesting," Tobias said, referring to both the class and Aiden's reaction. "What inspired you to sign up for a class on art history?"

Aiden turned red and avoided his gaze.

Bingo again.

So Carolyn Moore was the woman who could ruin Aiden's life. The question was, would she do it? Teacher-student relationships were against the rules at Evergreen College. She could lose her job if she crossed the line with Aiden. But if she'd figured out that Aiden had a substantial fortune in the bank, she might not care.

He shouldn't jump to conclusions yet. He had to talk to her. Face to face, he'd be able to get a feel for what her intentions were, and what kind of person she was. Until then, he had to keep Aiden talking.

"I'm not sure I agreed with her interpretation of that Rembrandt painting. You know, how she said the guy was trying to bring out the shadow side of his personality? How'd she get all that just from the angle of his head?"

Aiden blew on his coffee. "So now you're the expert just because you know how to kill people and fly planes?"

"Mostly helicopters," Tobias pointed out gravely.

"Whatever! Rocket ships, I don't care. You're a pilot, not a professor, so you should really give Ms. Moore a lot more respect."

"Oh, I give her a lot of respect." You always had to respect the enemy. Otherwise you might get caught with your pants down.

"What does that mean?" Aiden went on full alert. "Why did you show up in her class, anyway? Why didn't you tell me you were coming?" He narrowed his eyes. "Is this some kind of ambush?"

"Dude. Would you take it down a notch? I gave up ambushes when I left the army. This is a pop-in, not an ambush."

Aiden ripped open a bag of cheese puffs. "Just a random pop-in. And these are meatballs wrapped in solid gold." He brandished a puff before popping it into his mouth.

Tobias closed his eyes with a sigh. He should have stayed out of sight in that class. Chosen his moment more carefully. Now Aiden was full-on suspicious, and the only way he could throw him off the scent would be to lie. And he didn't want to do that. His brother would lose trust in him if he lied. Besides, he despised liars and deceivers of all sorts.

"Okay, you're right. I came here for a reason. We got your letter about leaving Evergreen and obviously we're worried. This is a great college, Aiden. You worked hard to get in and you're pulling good grades. It doesn't make sense to leave after one semester."

Aiden fixed his wide gray eyes on him. Those eyes always reminded Tobias of Mom, and the reminder was fricking painful, like a serrated knife to the chest. "What do you care? You've been gone for twelve years."

The note of betrayal in Aiden's voice took Tobias aback. "I came back during my leaves. I kept in touch."

Aiden, unimpressed, popped another cheese puff in his mouth and offered the bag to Tobias. He waved it off. After so many years of relying on his strength and fitness, he didn't like to pour junk into his body. "Fine, you kept in touch. Yay Skype. I just don't get why you care now. I can get a good education in Jupiter

Point. And I'd be around you guys, too. All the Knight brothers could be together again. What's wrong with that?"

"We'll be together at Christmas. We can be together all summer. But Jupiter Point Community College doesn't compare to Evergreen and you know it."

Aiden shrugged, looking mulish. "I have other reasons too. And they're important to me. Maybe I don't want to be here without—" He broke off.

"Without the golden goddess?" Tobias said gently. He didn't want to push Aiden, but it would be easier to have this discussion if the kid came out and named his mystery crush.

"I don't want to talk about it." Aiden surged to his feet. "Just... just go. Go home. My life is *my* business. You shouldn't have even come here."

Tobias pushed his chair back, sloshing black coffee all over his pants. Damn, he'd screwed this up. He didn't want to alienate his brother; that was the last thing he wanted. "Shit, Aiden. Come on. I'm not trying to run your life. We're just having a conversation, right?"

"Not anymore. This is some kind of army Jedi mind trick you're pulling, isn't it? You're going to get me to talk about...*her*... and then you'll twist everything around and make it seem like she isn't the most amazing, incredible, amazing..."

"You already said that," murmured Tobias.

"Gaaah!!!! !" Aiden tossed his bag of cheese puffs in the air, so a neon-orange shower of fake cheese cascaded around them. "I'm done. I said I wasn't going to talk about it and I won't. Goodbye, Tobias. I'll see you at Christmas. Maybe."

He grabbed his backpack and stormed away from the table, crunching cheese puffs onto the courtyard pavers as he went.

Tobias ran a hand across his nearly bald scalp. He'd stopped shaving his head when he left the army. New start kind of thing. His hair was just beginning to grow back in a soft baby-like fuzz.

Man, he'd fucked up. Aiden was furious with him now. He was going to dig in and refuse to listen to reason.

But at least he was pretty darn sure who the golden goddess was.

He looked at the cheese puffs scattered across the pavers. The sight offended his clean-freak sensibilities, which had been honed in the orderly living quarters of military barracks. The least he could do was clean them up. He dropped to his knees and swept the orange runaways into the bag that Aiden had left behind.

He worked quickly, already thinking about his next step. Clearly he couldn't go back to Jupiter Point yet. He didn't want to leave on a bad note with Aiden. At the very least, he had to patch things up with his brother. And he still had to have a talk with adjunct professor Carolyn Moore. But before he did that, he wanted to do some research. He wanted to find out everything he could about her. And he wanted to look up the exact wording of the rules forbidding teacher-student relationships. Were there any loopholes she might try to slip through?

There was another possibility. Maybe she was unaware of Aiden's crush. In which case, his job was pretty simple. Point it out and make the rules perfectly clear to her. Also, let her know that he'd be watching. Maybe that would make her extra cautious about stepping over any lines.

A suede boot the color of red wine stepped into his field of vision. Then another one. He looked up, an act that seemed to take longer than it should, because his gaze had so far to travel. Hot sexy boots, skirt molded around long thighs, slim hips, trim waist, cashmere sweater with buttons running between perfectly curved breasts, the soft shadow at the base of her throat, the long line of her neck, the tilt of her face looking down, the quirk of her lips, the shine of her eyes.

Jesus. She *was* a goddess.

3

"Need a little help there, man in black?"

"Excuse me?"

"Sorry, it was a Johnny Cash reference. I tend to assign students little monikers because I'm bad at remembering names. When you visited my class, you became the Man in Black, at least in my head."

"Big Johnny Cash fan here too," he said stupidly.

"Well, that settles it. Us Johnny Cash fans have to stick together. Let me help."

She crouched next to him, and suddenly they were face to face, and he was having a little trouble with his heart rate.

"Let me guess. Snack attack?" She smiled at him as she scooped up a handful of puffs and dumped them into the bag he still held.

"Something like that."

With all the cheese puffs back in the bag, he rose to his feet. She followed suit and they stood facing one another. He still felt tongue-tied, almost as if he were a student in the presence of a much smarter authority figure.

"So what do you think of Evergreen so far?" she asked patiently, almost as if she were talking to a student.

"Pretty campus. Good reputation. Still a few questions I need to resolve, but I'm impressed so far." Was he referring to Evergreen or to her? He wasn't completely sure.

"Well, if there's anything I can answer, go ahead. I'm not the best source, since I'm only a guest lecturer here. But I'll share what I know, and I can point you to the people with the real answers."

He tried to get his head back in the game. *Drag out the conversation. Seach for confirmation.* "Where do you normally teach?"

"Jupiter Point. It's a little town on the coast with a very high-quality community college."

Should he mention that he was born and raised there? No. He didn't want to tip her off to his hidden agenda.

"So do you have a kid considering Evergreen?" She gave him a swift up-and-down assessment with those soft blue eyes. It damn near gave him the chills. "You don't look old enough to have a college-age child."

"You're right, it's not for any kid of mine. No kids. Not married. Or ever likely to be." Why'd he go mentioning that? "I'm here for someone I care about," he added.

She nodded, her eyebrows arching. He must sound like a moron. He had to get it together before she decided he had a screw loose and refused to talk to him. When she surreptitiously checked her watch, he knew his time was running out. "I do have a few questions, as a matter of fact. Any chance you have some time later?"

"I have office hours this evening from five to seven. You're welcome to stop by." She gestured toward a building adjacent to the quadrangle. "First floor, last office on the right. But I suggest you talk to the Admissions people first. They're much more informed than I am."

"I'll do that. Thank you." She nodded politely and turned to go. He added, "See you at seven."

"Office hours are over at seven."

"Exactly. You'll probably be hungry by then."

She opened her mouth to object.

But didn't.

Instead she gave him a confused smile and hurried away from the Caf.

Sweet Jesus. Did he just come on to Aiden's crush? Did he just arrange a semi-potential date-ish meeting with her? Whatever it was, she hadn't turned him down flat. Did that mean she wasn't involved with Aiden? Did it mean she was toying with his little brother? Or did it mean he'd taken her by surprise and she didn't quite know how to react? She didn't even know his name. He ought to give her some dating safety tips. Could anyone just walk onto this campus and go to her office and talk to her? That didn't seem right.

He caught himself up. This was a peaceful college campus, not Afghanistan. No threat existed here, except from pissed-off older brothers of innocent kids who thought they were in love. *Get a fucking grip.*

The Man in Black kept popping back into Carolyn's brain as she moved through her day. Something about his banked intensity and smoldering good looks made him hard to forget. She realized, in the midst of a lecture on religious themes in the Venetian school, that she didn't even know his name. He'd become the Man in Black in her mind, and that was that.

If he came to her office hours, she would definitely ask him. Certainly, if he wanted to have dinner with her, she'd have to know his name. She pictured that square-jawed, dark-grained, fierce-eyed face across a dinner table, with a bottle of red wine between them. Would he switch the black leather jacket to something else? A dinner jacket or a dress shirt? Or did he always stay casual? Why was she so fascinated?

Actually, she knew why. It was that response that he'd given in her class. "Some people don't want to deal with the shadows."

She knew from personal, firsthand experience just how true that was. Why else had she taken refuge in this sweetly pretty campus filled with smiling faces and controversies no bigger than who should be the commencement speaker?

But when she unlocked her office door shortly before five, she was immediately reminded that even Evergreen College wasn't immune to the darker side of life. Another anonymous letter had been slid under her door.

She hesitated, then bent to pick it up. Lately she'd been getting unnerving anonymous messages. Four of them had been slipped under her door so far, all in the same style. Same block handwriting on the same kind of basic, difficult-to-trace paper. Something about the way they were written made her think they were from a student, but she couldn't be sure. They all conveyed basically the same threatening message.

This one read, *I know who you are and where you're from. Did you think no one would figure it out? Pretty soon everyone's going to know the truth because the light is going to shine. But you can save yourself. Be ready.*

She shivered as she picked apart the letter for clues. *Creepy.* That phrase "the light is going to shine" proved that the mystery letter-writer did know who she was. Or at least who she used to be. "Save yourself. Be Ready"—was that some kind of extortion attempt? Was she about to get blackmailed?

Or—was the writer hoping to drag her back to the Light Keepers compound? He or she was welcome to try. There was no way in hell she was going back. When she'd turned eighteen and left the group, they'd banned her anyway. She hadn't seen her family or anyone else from there since.

She slid the note into the manila folder where she kept the others. Technically, she ought to report it to the campus police. But she didn't want anyone knowing about her past, so that option was out. If the anonymous letter writer wanted her to react with fear, she refused to give him or her the satisfaction. She'd wait it out and see if they followed up their words with action. Otherwise, the threats were just pen markings on a piece of paper.

Since she had a few minutes before her office hours were due to start, she rolled out her yoga mat and did a few moves that always calmed her down. Breathe long and deep, in through the nose. Release all the tension. This was her life now. Peace and tranquility. The crazy armed paranoia of her childhood was in the past. Just breathe.

Between the yoga and the distraction of students complaining about their grades or asking for advice about their personal lives, she'd nearly forgotten about the Man in Black when he walked into her office a few minutes before seven.

Immediately her heart did a weird twisting move, possibly inspired by one of her yoga poses. He'd taken off his jacket and carried it draped over his arm. Under it he wore a simple black t-shirt that displayed the hard rippling muscles of his forearms. No tattoos, no statement of anything on his t-shirt. On campus, she was used to college kids going crazy with self-expression in the form of piercings, markings, words on t-shirts, hair color, really anything.

But this man didn't wear any part of his inner self on his sleeve, so to speak. Neither did she, so she supposed they had that in common. She preferred to reveal herself slowly, once she felt comfortable with someone. Not even her closest friends— such as Merry Warren—knew the full story of her upbringing. She worried that it would create a barrier between them, so she just avoided talking about it.

Avoiding the shadows. Yup, that was her.

She rose to her feet and came around to the front of her desk with her hand outstretched. Time to get a name out of this man. "We haven't met properly. I'm Carolyn Moore, Professor Moore to my students."

He took her hand. "So cheese puffs don't count as meeting properly?"

His hand was rough and powerful and warm. The contact made some deeply hidden part of her respond with a flare of heat.

But he still hadn't said his name. "No, and neither do Rembrandt slides. You are?"

"Tobias Knight." He watched her closely as he spoke. The name registered only distantly because she was trying to pin down the color of his eyes. She noticed, with her eye for artistic detail, that they weren't black. They were a very, very deep blue, the kind of deepest indigo that Caravaggio might use in a night landscape, shot through with lighter glints of gray. "But you can call me Tobias."

"Tobias. Okay." She shook herself back to attention and went to sit behind her desk. These were office hours, and even though he wasn't a student she should be professional. She waved him toward the chair facing her desk. "Have a seat, Tobias. So what would you like to know about Evergreen?"

He lowered himself into the metal folding chair, his powerful frame dwarfing the poor thing. "Well, let's start with the student body. What's your take on the caliber of students here? What sort of student does best at Evergreen?"

She picked up a pen and tapped it against her palm. She needed something to occupy her hands. It irritated her that she found this man so attractive. Was it thanks to some kind of residual childhood attachment to strong aggressive men willing to fight?

"I've only been teaching here one semester, but my take so far is that it's a pretty harmonious campus. The kids seem to take their studies pretty seriously, although there's certainly some partying. Underage drinking is highly discouraged. The administration is very hard on date rape, that sort of thing. Is the student in question male or female?"

"Male."

He could have been summing up himself in one impactful word. *Male.* Amen. One thousand percent male.

"Well, to tell you the truth, I deal more with female students. Art history seems to draw the ladies more than the gentlemen. That's probably because the boys don't know how badass Renaissance artists actually were. Did you know that Michelangelo painted the Sistine Chapel while standing on a wooden scaffold, working over his head, living on onions and stale bread? It took him years. Maybe I should tell the boys he did it on a skateboard."

Tobias smiled, his firm lips curving in a devastatingly sensual manner. "So is skateboarding a big thing here, based on the male students you know personally?"

Puzzled, she frowned at him. Clearly, this guy had some kind of hidden agenda behind his questions. She had no idea what. "I don't really know any of the students *personally*, unless you count problems in their lives that interfere with turning their papers in on time. I know a lot about those."

"Really? None of them? No apples for the teacher?"

Suddenly a horrified thought struck her. Was it possible this was the man who'd been sending her the anonymous threatening messages? She'd assumed they came from a student, but maybe she had it wrong. Had the Light Keepers sent this man? He looked like the paramilitary type. "What are you after, Tobias?"

"Excuse me?" But from the way his expression shut down, she knew she was onto something.

"You're here for a reason, and it's not to talk about skateboarding or ask me to dinner."

"You're wrong about that part," he murmured.

The idea that the person sending her nasty letters might ask her to dinner made her ill. She opened her desk drawer and pulled out the manila folder with the letters. Grabbing one at random, she brandished it in the air. "Why don't you just cut the crap and tell me what this is all about?"

He narrowed his eyes at the letters. "You saved them all."

"So it was you!" Her stomach dropped in a sickening plunge. All her little fantasies about the Man in Black seemed stupid now. "I thought these were bad coming from a student, but from an adult? That's a whole different story. If you don't want me to call security, you'd better tell me right now why you're doing this."

He opened his mouth, then closed it again. She couldn't read his expression, but the predominant emotion seemed to be confusion. "Is it really such a mystery?" he finally asked.

"Of course it is. I left over ten years ago and that ought to be the end of it."

She held his gaze, refusing to back down no matter how intimidating he was. This was her turf. Her office. His dark eyebrows drew together. The air between them pulsed with tension.

"Can I see those?" he finally asked.

"Need to refresh your memory about what you wrote? These are copies, by the way."

She thrust the folder at him. He leafed through the letters quickly, then looked at her sharply. "What the hell is this?"

For the first time, her certainty faltered. Maybe Tobias wasn't the letter writer, in which case she'd just handed over a little window into her past life. "That was my question, too."

"Who sent you these letters?" he demanded.

"If it wasn't you, then I have no idea."

"*Me*?" His face turned into one big, astonished scowl. "Why would I send you these? I've never even seen you before today. I have nothing to do with this."

"Then what are you here for? You knew about the letters. You weren't surprised when I pulled them out."

"I thought they were..." He rubbed the heel of his hand into his forehead, then rose restlessly to his feet. Not wanting to be at a disadvantage, she did the same, though she kept the desk between them. He paced back and forth around her small borrowed office. "You should give those letters to the police. You could be at risk."

"Don't change the subject," she snapped. "You thought they were what?"

"A different kind of letter," he muttered, as though deathly embarrassed. "Love letters."

She gaped at him in astonishment. *Love* letters. "Does anyone write love letters anymore? I'd like to meet that person."

As he gave her a fierce frown, she spotted a hint of a blush under the dark scruff of his five o'clock—now seven o'clock —shadow.

"So tell me what's really going on here, Tobias Kni—" She broke off as she recognized the name.

Tobias *Knight*. Didn't she have a student with the last name Knight? For the hundredth time, she cursed her bad memory when it came to names. Roster. She needed the student rosters from all her classes. *Think, Caro.* Who has the last name Knight?

There was Will Knight. Merry's new fiancé. But Tobias looked nothing like Will, who had much lighter coloring and gray eyes—

Her eyes flew to meet Tobias's. "Aiden. He's in my Renaissance class. The one you visited today."

Tobias was watching her so closely it was uncomfortable.

"Are you related to Aiden?" She called up an image of Aiden Knight from the middle row, the one with the dreamy gaze. Was he the one sending love letters to someone?

"He's my little brother. And I'd do anything to protect him."

Bewildered, she blinked at him. "Okay. That's nice."

Then it clicked. "Wait. Are you here to...what...protect your brother from *me*?" Furious outrage made her voice shake. "Get out of my office."

"Wait." He threw up his hand. "Can't we just talk? I have the feeling we're on the same side here."

"We are not on the same side. You're on the side that came here to lecture me about something that's none of your business."

His eyes narrowed dangerously. "Are you saying my brother is none of my business?"

"I'm saying get out of my office." She marched from behind her desk, ready to push him out if need be. He took a step backwards but otherwise didn't seem very worried. Over six feet of pure muscle didn't intimidate easily. She snatched the manila folder from his hand.

"I checked the college rules," he told her. "Fraternization between students and teachers is grounds for dismissal. And if you mess with Aiden, dismissal would be the least of your problems."

Heat rushed into her face. How dare this man insinuate such a thing? She would never cross the line with a student. Their psyches were in her care. She considered that a sacred trust never to be violated. "Do I need to call security?"

One corner of his mouth quirked up. "You can if you want. My point remains."

His point! His point was apparently that she was an unethical corrupter of students.

"You can take your point and shove it where the sun don't shine." He was still blocking her way, that slight smirk on his face. At the Light Keepers, she'd been drilled in martial arts, like everyone else. She hardly used that training anymore, but this seemed like an appropriate moment.

In a quick surprise move, she swept his legs out from under him. He would have toppled onto the floor if he didn't have such quick reflexes. But he managed to twist and roll, then come into a crouching position.

He was a trained fighter too, clearly. Probably military.

Oops.

But he made no move to fight her or defend himself. "Can I take that as a commitment that you'll stay away from Aiden?"

"You can take that as an invitation to go to hell." She shoved the folder into her bag, along with her sweater, Tupperware lunch container and cucumber-infusion water bottle, and stepped past him, out the door. "The door locks when you pull it closed. Nice meeting you."

4

OF ALL THE WAYS TOBIAS HAD PICTURED HIS MEETING WITH AIDEN'S crush, getting knocked on his ass didn't make the top five. For the second time that day, he got an upfront view of Carolyn's suede boots—this time as they walked out the door.

Well, apparently she wasn't too worried about leaving him alone in her office.

Maybe because she has nothing to hide, his conscience whispered. Anything related to students was probably under lock and key, or maybe in that big bag of hers.

Slowly he rose to his feet. Damn, he was getting out of shape. He needed to get back into the gym. No way should a delicate-looking art history teacher get the jump on him. Carolyn Moore was more than she appeared.

What the hell had just happened?

He hauled a long breath into his lungs and followed her out of the office, pulling the door closed behind him. As he strode down the hallway, he pulled out his phone and did a quick search for hotels near the campus.

He was still confused about a few things, but one fact he knew for sure. This wasn't finished. He was going to stick around Evergreen for a little while longer.

ONCE HE'D CHECKED into the nearest Embassy Suites, he called Will. Will didn't answer—probably snuggled up with Merry at this hour—so he tried Ben.

"Hey bro," his second youngest brother answered. In the background he heard the unmistakable sounds of a bar.

"Where are you?"

"Barstow's. It's Tuesday, man. Burger and beer for five bucks. Where else would I be?"

"You sure know how to live."

"Live until you die," Ben countered. "Are you back in town yet?"

"No. I'm going to stay a little longer. Can you handle things there for a couple more days?"

"For Aiden, of course I can. How is the kid?"

"Right now he's not speaking to me. But I'm sure we'll get past that. Overall, he seems good. Defensive, but good."

"Did you track down the evil golden goddess?"

Tobias uncomfortably shifted his position on the queen-size bed. Now that he'd gotten to know Carolyn a little better—if getting knocked on his ass counted as getting to know her—he didn't like calling her names. "I think so. Her name's Carolyn Moore and she teaches art history. But I don't think she's involved with him. I think it's just a one-sided crush."

"Well, that's good. I mean, not for poor Aiden. He must think he has a chance with her. I hate to break the poor kid's heart, but maybe this art history teacher could let him down easy. Can you talk to her?"

"She's not speaking to me either."

Ben let out an amused snort. "We sent the right guy out there, didn't we?"

"Okay, I fucked it up right off the bat. I can fix it. That's why I need to stay a few more days. Can you cover my flights?"

"Yeah, yeah. But maybe it would make more sense for us to switch places. I'm a lot more charming than you are and I hardly ever piss people off within the first ten minutes of meeting them."

Tobias ground his teeth together. "I got this, Ben."

"All right. You're the boss. I'll see you in a few days."

"Wait. Before you hang up, how's Will doing? Any progress yet?" Will had recently left his deputy sheriff position to hunt for their father's murderer.

"Not that I've heard. For now he's re-interviewing all the original police investigators to see if they might have missed something. When he gets back, he wants to interview you."

"Me?"

"You found his body."

An uncomfortable silence followed. The topic of their father's murder had been forbidden territory for so long. They'd all coped with the trauma in their own ways, but as a group they'd completely shut it down. It wasn't just the murder, either. Afterwards, their mother had left Jupiter Point, where everything reminded her of her husband. She'd taken Cassie, their sixteen-year old sister, with her. To this day, their only communication with Cassie was through the postcards she sent. Apparently Mom was still so fragile she couldn't handle any talk about Jupiter Point or the family she'd left behind.

"The Jupiter Point PD has all the transcripts of my interviews. It was fresh back then. I don't remember anything new."

"Hey, tell it to Will. He's the private eye. All I know is that he thinks it's worth a try."

"Okay, I'll talk to him when I get back to town." One more reason not to rush back, honestly. Finding his father's dead body had been the single most horrifying moment of his life, and that included everything that he'd witnessed as a pilot for the 160th

Airborne, also known as a Night Stalker. It had changed him forever. The worst thing was that he'd had a huge fight with his father just the night before, when Dad had bailed him out of jail.

He heaved himself off the bed and went into the bathroom, where he stripped off his clothes and stood under water so hot, it stung like needles. Once he started thinking about his father, it was hard to make himself stop. That last fight lived on, a taunting loop in his mind.

"You're wasting your life, Tobias. Wasting your God-given abilities. I never thought I'd see the day when I had to spring my own son out of jail." His furious father had been ranting the entire drive home. Never paused to hear Tobias's side of the story.

"Dad—" he tried again. But when Robert Knight got on a roll, nothing could throw him off. Not even Tobias, his most hard-headed son, the one most like him.

"I'm ashamed of you, Tobias. You're twenty years old. You ought to be in college, not wasting your time doing manual labor. You have a brain inside that thick head, you know. But you won't if you keep brawling with those lowlifes."

Some drunken assholes had been beating up a kid he'd known from school. A gay kid. The hell if he was going to stand by and watch that happen. "But they were—"

"I don't want to hear it. Whatever they were doing, it wasn't worth sacrificing your future for. What college is going to take you with a police record?"

"The charges will get dropped, those guys aren't going to—"

"The charges will be dropped because I'm good friends with the police chief and the DA. That doesn't mean you can go around playing vigilante. Jesus, Tobias. Your mother just about had a heart attack when we got the call. It took me an hour to calm her down. I figured you could use the extra time in jail to talk some sense into yourself."

"Should have just left me," Tobias muttered. "I don't give a shit."

"Next time I will. And the next time after that, don't bother coming back."

"Asshole," he muttered even lower.

He didn't know whether Dad heard that last word or not. They reached the house, where his mother was fluttering back and forth in the driveway. Instantly both father and son switched into containment mode. No matter how much they battled, they knew better than to get Janine Knight upset. With her volatile emotional states, it could take days for her to recover.

They got out of the car, all smiles and good cheer. Tobias played off the bruises on his face, claimed he'd had a run-in with a tree. His dad threw an arm around his shoulders, as if he hadn't been yelling at him two minutes earlier. Tobias went right to the loft he'd hammered together for himself in the barn, and that was that.

The next time he saw his father, he was dead on the kitchen floor.

Which meant the last word he'd spoken directly to his dad was "asshole."

And that—he still wasn't over that. Maybe he never would be. If he'd known that would be the last night he ever saw Dad alive, he would have done everything differently. He would have thanked him instead of arguing. He would have told him he loved him. He would have promised to get his life together and stop wasting his potential. He would have told him that he'd already talked to an Army recruiter and was trying to decide if he should actually sign up.

Instead his dad had died never knowing that his most difficult son had followed in his footsteps.

The guilt shadowed him wherever he went. He couldn't change that night. But he could take care of the only family he had left—his brothers.

After a long time under the shower, Tobias wrapped a towel around his hips and went to call Aiden.

"Let me buy you a burger, dude. Come on. We're family here. I came all the way from Jupiter Point," he cajoled.

"Yeah, you came all the way to mess things up for me."

"Come on, kid," Tobias said gently. "That's not why I'm here. I'm just performing my brotherly duty. Watching out for you."

"Then you can keep your burger."

"What about the fries? I know how you are about fries. I heard there's a great greasy spoon right around the corner. I'll even throw in a game of pool. I bet you haven't played pool since you got to college. Can you still do that triple bank shot I taught you?"

The long pause told him this tactic was working. Aiden had been raised by Will, for the most part, but the other brothers had contributed what they could during their leaves. Tobias took special pride in the pool techniques he'd shared.

"Okay, I'll have burgers with you and I'll whip your ass at pool *if...*"

"If?"

"If you promise not to come to any of my classes anymore."

"Absolutely. I've had all the education I need for one trip."

"Not even Ms. Moore's?"

Tobias's mouth twisted. He heard the anxious tone in his brother's voice. Maybe the boy hadn't written those letters, but he still had a crush.

"I promise I won't do anything that will embarrass you, interfere with your life, or make you look bad to any of your teachers, including Ms. Moore. How's that?"

Aiden chewed on that for a moment, then said, "Fine. Are you going to pick me up?"

"Be there in ten."

Tobias hung up and ran a hand across his scalp. He'd framed his promise very carefully. He'd stay away from Carolyn's class, but not Carolyn herself. He no longer suspected her of messing around with his brother. Now that he'd met her, he couldn't imagine her breaking the rules like that.

But the letters with the weird threats, those were different. He couldn't leave Evergreen until he was confident she was dealing with the situation appropriately. He couldn't leave until he felt sure she was safe.

It was a purely altruistic, good Samaritan kind of impulse, the kind of thing instilled in him during his service. Protect the innocent.

Then again, based on that lethal move she'd executed, maybe Carolyn Moore wasn't as innocent as she appeared. For sure, he intended to find out. He crossed to the jacket he'd tossed on the back of a chair and rummaged through the inner pocket. It was an envelope snagged from the wastepaper basket in Carolyn's office—an electric bill. With an address. Maybe he'd swing by there after dinner and pool with Aiden.

5

Since Carolyn's guest lecture gig would only last one semester, she'd sublet a house from a math professor on sabbatical. He lived in a large two-story Colonial made of brick, with a glossy black door. He'd offered her a break on the rent in exchange for taking care of his gigantic Newfoundland. She'd eagerly agreed, with no clue what she was getting into.

The professor had an obsession with Hong Kong martial arts movies, so every time she walked through the door, a life-size cardboard cutout of Jet Li greeted her. Not that she was complaining. Jet made an attractive and uncomplaining housemate. Especially compared to the Newfie, Dragon.

Dragon had a habit of leaving pools of slobber on the gleaming wood floors. Whenever she got home, her first act, after giving Dragon some affection, was to crawl around the floor on her knees wiping up drool.

As soon as that was done, she poured a mammoth pile of dog food into Dragon's bowl. While he was consuming his mountain of dinner, Carolyn unzipped her boots and wriggled her toes in relief. If she could teach barefoot, she would. She changed into comfy yoga pants and a tank top, then checked on Dragon again.

Still eating.

She pulled a box of crackers from a cupboard, some cheddar cheese from the fridge, and a jar of pickles. Standing at the kitchen island, she munched her way through a satisfying number of salty, crunchy cracker sandwiches. She'd been raised on a strict diet prescribed by the Light Keepers, so the act of eating whatever the hell she wanted at any given moment always felt like sweet rebellion.

She checked Dragon again. *Still* eating. Even while he gobbled down food, the big Newfie was flinging slobber in all directions. She sighed and got a wash towel from the drawer. Ten minutes later, Dragon finally finished his meal. He looked up at her, his droopy, wise eyes weeping as if in gratitude.

"I know. I know," she murmured to him. "I'm the queen of the world, the bringer of food, the slayer of hunger. Want to go for a walk? Will that make you love me even more?"

Dragon's ears twitched at the word "walk." She pulled on her cross-trainers, found his leash and some plastic poop bags, and together they trotted into the crisp, starry night.

She jogged down the quiet street, Dragon keeping pace at her side. He was such a big, comfortable presence that she often found herself talking to him as she jogged.

"I nearly injured a man tonight, Dragon. Can you believe it? I mean, he had it coming, but you know me. I'm all about peace and harmony. I'm not exactly sure what came over me. Would you still love me if I beat someone up?"

Dragon panted, a stream of drool flying into the breeze.

"Don't bother trying to deny it. You'd still love me because I've got the keys to the dog food bag. And because you're a lovey-dovey-sweetie-patootie, yes, you are, aren't you?"

The big dog sensibly ignored her.

"Fine, be that way." Carolyn jogged in silence for a moment, finding her groove with a long, easy stride. The gracious homes of professors and other upscale members of the Evergreen community slid past. While she loved this neighborhood, she often felt like an imposter here. How many of these residents would be able to recite the complete Old Testament? How many would be able to break down an M-15 in under thirty seconds? How many would be able to disable an attacker in one move?

Of course, that was all in the past. She'd renounced that part of her life when she'd defied her father and the Light Keepers and left for college. She had no family anymore. She was alone.

Which made her think of Tobias and the way he'd shown up to defend his little brother. It was sweet, really. Way off base, but sweet.

That name, Knight...

She settled her Bluetooth in her ear and clicked the speed dial button on her phone to call Merry.

"Hey, girl," her friend answered. "You aren't dialing and running again, are you?"

"How else am I supposed to pass the time? Dragon and I already ran out of topics of conversation."

"Listen to music like a normal person. Didn't I make that playlist for you? My Power Play Workout, have you tried it?"

"Yes. It's definitely energizing. It makes me want to punch random things like every telephone pole I pass. Can you make me something more Zen-like next time? And less deafening? I like to remain aware of my surroundings."

"Picky, picky," Merry grumbled. "And you know I don't do Zen unless it comes with a disco ball."

"Funny. So listen. I remember you mentioned once that Will has a couple of brothers."

"Yup. Three."

"Any of them named Tobias?"

"Yes, he's the second in line after Will. Tobias, Ben and Aiden. They have a sister, too, but I've never met her. Why do you ask?"

Carolyn turned the corner onto a street that circled a city park. Floodlights lit up a basketball court at one end. Well-lit pathways wound through the park, but she stayed on the perimeter street. She knew from experience that a jogger accompanied by a dog the size of Dragon was better off away from other dog-walkers.

"I just met Tobias. And it turns out that Aiden is in one of my classes."

Merry didn't answer for a second, then a peal of laughter rang into Caro's Bluetooth receiver. She winced.

"Wait a second. *You're* the golden goddess?"

"Excuse me?"

"Aiden's crush, the one they're all freaked out about. Oh my gosh, this is hilarious. I have to tell Will right away."

"Wait! Please don't go yet. And *please* don't say anything to Will. What makes them think Aiden has a crush on me? And why is this such a big deal?"

"Because Aiden's talking about following you back to Jupiter Point when you leave Evergreen. He's saying he wants to use his trust fund to, I don't know, set up house or something. The boy's in over his head. Personally, I think it's a reaction to being away from home for the first time. Also, his mother basically abandoned him. He probably needs counseling. But the brothers are all at DEFCON five trying to keep him from going off the rails."

Carolyn sidestepped a pile of dog poop no one had cleaned up. "That's crazy! Aiden Knight has barely ever spoken to me. I had no idea about any of this."

"Of course you didn't. And I had no idea you were his mystery crush! I could have saved Tobias a lot of trouble. He went there to find you and make sure you didn't have designs on Aiden's money."

"Oh my God. This is so insane." Carolyn's breath was coming faster now, a combination of exertion and indignation making her heart pound. "I didn't know Aiden had any money, and I definitely don't care. He's a *student,* for Pete's sake. I let Tobias off easy with that kick."

"Excuse me? You *kicked* Tobias?"

"No! I didn't kick *him.* I just knocked him on the ground."

"*Tobias?* Are we talking about the same guy? Big, lots of muscles, kind of intense, extremely attractive to most women?"

"Most? Really? I don't know about that." A weird feeling of jealousy snuck through her. Apparently she wasn't the only one to have noticed Tobias's sexual charisma. "But yes, in other respects your description rings true. I'm sure it's the same person. Lots of muscles is all you needed to say."

"Don't be fooled, though, babe. Tobias is a lot more than muscles. Will says he's super-smart, that he never studied in school but aced the SATs. Will said that once he brought home one of his law books and Tobias read the whole thing in one weekend. He won several service awards in the Army, too. I think he did a bunch of counterintelligence ops. He's brawn and brains. Don't underestimate him."

Carolyn checked on Dragon, then slowed her pace when she saw the dog was starting to lag. "So he went from counterintelligence to tracking down a college professor? Seems like a big downgrade." On the other hand, the thought that he might be some kind of super-spy made her a little uncomfortable. What if in his zeal to help Aiden he uncovered things about her, about her past?

She needed to get him off her back as soon as could be.

"Listen, Merry. Now that you know it's a big fuss about nothing, can you let Will know there's no reason to worry? I have no designs on Aiden or his trust fund. I would never get involved with a student under any circumstances. I shouldn't even have to say it, but I understand their concern. Can you relay that to the whole Knight family? They have nothing to fear from me."

"Of course. I'll definitely do that. I got your back, Caro. But it sounds like you're handling Tobias just fine on your own." The teasing laughter in Merry's voice made her smile. "For the record, Tobias looks intimidating, but he's got a soft heart. Will says he spent most of his school years protecting kids from bullies. And he did something for me I'll never forget."

"What's that?"

"Remember when I got fired from the *Gazette*? The Knight brothers more or less got my job back by giving me the exclusive about their father's cold case murder. But it was hardest for Tobias because he's the one who found his body. It was a very bloody and horrible crime scene and Will said Tobias still has nightmares about it. But he let me ask him as many questions as I needed. I could tell it was tough because his knuckles were pure white, he was clenching his fists so hard. But he wanted to help me out. So go easy on him. No more beating his ass, okay?"

"All right. Anything for you, Merry."

They hung up. Carolyn reached the far end of the park and made the turn toward home. Her friendship with Merry was so precious to her, but it wouldn't have been possible if she hadn't left home. The Light Keepers didn't allow non-Caucasians. Someone like Merry, who'd grown up biracial in Brooklyn, would be horrified by the belief system Carolyn had lived with from age ten to eighteen. Would she still be her friend if she knew? Would anyone?

"Ready for the final sprint, big guy?" she asked Dragon. He'd recovered his energy and was now trotting briskly next to her. He was such a smart dog, he knew the drill. She liked to leave it all on the field during the last hundred yards.

As she pounded toward her sublet house, she picked up the pace. Her breath sawed through her lungs and sweat dripped into her eyes.

Which was why she almost didn't see the figure kneeling surreptitiously at her door.

She wiped the sweat away to see better—sure enough,

someone was crouched on the top step of her front stoop, barely illuminated by the porch light.

"Hey!" she called as she sprinted closer. "What are you doing?"

But then she saw exactly what he was doing. Using a can of orange spray paint, he was painting something on the black front door of the house. A circle with five rays radiating from it and a triangle within. The logo of the Light Keepers.

The vandal jolted around and sprang to his feet. She saw he was a young man wearing a hoodie. He bolted down the front steps, stumbling as he hit the sidewalk. She nearly caught up to him then, but he scrambled upright and launched himself down the street. She followed, panting, but her energy reserves were used up and she couldn't summon enough extra speed to catch up.

She stopped, breath coming in ragged pants, watching the fleeing figure. Another man was approaching with long, confident strides, his broad shoulders momentarily blocking out the light from someone's street lamp.

Tobias. The Man in Black.

She didn't stop to wonder what he was doing here. It was almost as if she knew she could trust him. "Hey, Knight!" she wheezed as loud as she could. "Stop him!"

Tobias didn't hesitate. He grabbed for the runaway, who tried to veer past him. But Tobias was too quick for him. Even though he was wily and tried to wriggle out of his hoodie, which Tobias had snagged, he didn't stand a chance against the bigger man's superior strength and skill.

With the boy in a firm arm-lock, Tobias marched him toward Carolyn. "What's going on here? I assume he did something wrong and that I haven't just manhandled an innocent passing stranger."

Carolyn looked closely at the sullen young man. Blond and wiry, unfamiliar to her. Maybe he was one of her students, but she didn't think so. "Are you the one sending me those letters?" she asked him.

He stared at her defiantly and didn't answer.

"Why did you paint that on my front door?"

"Wasn't me," he mumbled.

"Of course it was you. I saw you. Look, there's orange paint on your hand and you smell like fluorocarbons. What is this all about?"

He cast a look in Tobias's direction. Tobias still held him confined in a tight lock. "Tell him to let me go. If he leaves, I'll talk."

Carolyn considered. She had complete confidence in her ability to handle a college student with a grudge and a spray can. But a little backup wouldn't hurt. She shook her head. "No, sorry. He's staying put. And I don't mind calling the police. You vandalized private property. If you're a student at Evergreen, that's grounds for expulsion. Your best option right now is to tell me what you're up to. You aren't in any of my classes, are you?"

"No. I'd never take a class from a pariah."

She snapped her mouth shut. If this youth was a member of the Light Keepers, what the heck was he doing at Evergreen? Maybe he was one of the few young people—always male—who were allowed to attend college and remain part of the group. But how would he know about her? And why would he care? As he'd said, she was officially dead to them. A "pariah."

The bigger question right now was whether or not she wanted Tobias Knight to be part of this conversation. Could she trust him?

She met his impassive gaze. He was watching her with those deep dark-as-night eyes, waiting for her next move. He had the air of someone who'd seen a thousand terrible things, who shouldered burdens most people would shy away from. She thought about what Merry had told her—that he spent his school years fighting bullies. He'd come here to protect his brother. Granted, she was the one he wanted to protect Aiden *from*. But that was beside the point. He was most likely a trustworthy person.

Besides, if she let this young man slip away, she might not get another chance to pin down what was going on.

She took a deep breath and spoke the name that hadn't left her lips in years.

"Are you from the Light Keepers?"

6

TOBIAS HAD NO CLUE WHAT WAS GOING ON, BUT HE PAID EXTRA close attention as Carolyn spoke to the runaway he held pinned in an arm-twist lock. Her giant dog, who had to be the worst guard dog ever, slouched to the grass and collapsed on a long, snuffling exhale.

"I don't talk to traitors," the vandal snarled.

"Hey. Show a little respect here," he told his prisoner. "She's giving you a break. My advice would be to call the cops, and I will if you don't behave yourself."

He felt the guy deflate, as often happened once you called a hyped-up kid on their bluster. In his experience, very few bullies actually had the guts to follow through if you isolated them and confronted them. And anyone who left anonymous letters and vandalized doors fell into the category of a bully, in his opinion.

"What's your name?" Carolyn asked him.

Tobias tried to keep his focus on her sweat-dampened face rather than the gleaming upper curve of her breasts revealed by her tank top. Her chest was still rising and falling from her run, which made it even harder to ignore. Damn. She was really something.

"Joseph," the vandal mumbled. "Joseph Brown."

"Is your father Ethan Brown?"

He nodded. Tobias's curiosity intensified. What was going on here? Carolyn seemed to know all about this person. And who were the Light Keepers?

"You know I'm not part of that anymore," Carolyn said. "So why are you harassing me? What's with the letters?"

"It doesn't matter anymore. It's over. Done."

"Did someone ask you to give me those letters, or are you doing that all on your own? I'm not sure what their purpose is, but you're welcome to explain it to me."

"You want me to tell the whole college where you came from?"

Carolyn's eyes lifted to meet Tobias's. In them he saw a kind of shame, as if she was embarrassed that he was witnessing this. He schooled his expression to show nothing but neutral support. Whatever was going on here, he was in no position to judge. He sure was curious, though.

"Look, I'm not going to say any more, so you might as well let me go. It's not going to happen again." Joseph struggled to free himself. Tobias loosened his grip. He didn't have any right to detain him if he wanted to leave, unless Carolyn wanted to call the police.

He shot her a questioning look, and she gave a slight shrug of her shoulders. "Fine, you can go. Just tell me what you were after in the first place."

"It was dumb," Joseph muttered. "I thought you could get Coach Driscoll to let me on the track team."

"Seriously? That's what this is all about? I don't even know Coach Driscoll."

"No, but he thinks you're hot. I heard him say so one time when you were running around the track at school."

The color rose in Carolyn's face. "Oh for heaven's sake. This is ridiculous. I couldn't help you if I wanted, and it's not something

I would do in any case. If you want to make the track team, I suggest you practice running. Right now might be a good time."

She nodded to Tobias. He released Joseph, who quickly stepped away from them. But he didn't take off right away, his gaze darting from the sidewalk to Carolyn's shoes.

"Listen, Joseph. I know how it is there. If you ever want to talk, I mean, *really* talk, my door is open to you," she said gently.

Joseph blinked at her. For a moment he seemed to hear her words, hear the kindness in them. Then he spat onto the sidewalk. "Whatever, pariah. Too late." And he ran away into the darkness.

Carolyn stared at the spittle on the sidewalk. She appeared frozen in place, temporarily stunned into paralysis. Tobias hesitated, wanting to offer some comfort but unsure if it would be welcome.

"Kids," he finally said. "You never know what crazy thing they'll get in their heads."

She snapped out of her trance and looked at Tobias. "What exactly are you doing here, anyway? How did you just happen to be walking down the street at that exact moment?"

Damn. Busted. He decided that complete truthfulness was his only real option at this point. "Well, the exact moment part was pure coincidence. But I was coming to see you, see where you lived."

"You were stalking me?"

"*Reconnaissance.*" He shoved his hands in his pockets. "Among other things."

"You couldn't just Google me?"

"Oh, I did," he admitted. "But you know the Internet. It's filled with bad information along with the good. And there's no replacement for visual observation."

She put her hand on her stomach. "I'm very confused."

"Listen. For what it's worth, it's not about Aiden anymore. I just spent the evening with him and I can see it's a one-sided crush. My suspicious nature got the best of me. I'm sorry."

"Oh." She tilted her head, causing the lamplight to slide across her hair, giving it a ghostly sheen. "So let me get this straight. You thought I was some kind of cougar gold-digger, but now you see that's wrong, so you came to my house to apologize?"

"No. I mean, yes. I am apologizing. This is an apology." He grinned ruefully. "Can't you tell?"

She laughed a little.

"Mostly I came by because I was worried about you and those letters. You might call it an instinct. I learned to trust my instincts in the army. And it looks like I was right. So can we call it a truce? Will you accept my apology?"

She chewed on her lower lip while she gazed at him for a while. He stood patiently under her scrutiny. He couldn't blame her for being cautious. She'd never laid eyes on him before this morning when he crashed her class. Then he'd shown up at her office, and now her home. Plus, he didn't exactly present the most welcoming appearance. Especially when he forgot to smile.

Do it, asshole. It wouldn't kill him to look a little less terrifying, now that he knew for sure Carolyn wasn't the enemy here.

He stretched his mouth in a grin.

She peered at him, squinting in the dim light from her porch, and burst out laughing. "Is that the best you can do?"

"Excuse me?"

"I see what you're doing there." She circled her index finger in the general direction of his mouth. "You're forcing yourself to present a warm and fuzzy appearance so I'll relax and forgive you for stalking me."

"I wasn't—"

"Reconnaissance. Whatever. Can you deny the rest?"

He gave an unwilling laugh. "I've been told I can strike terror into the hearts of innocent maidens."

"You're no ogre, sorry. And I'm not exactly a maiden." He

caught a hot shimmer of a look from under her eyelashes. It rocked him back on his heels, at least internally. On the surface, he managed to keep his cool. "And I'm definitely not terrified of you. I already know I can get the jump on you."

She grinned at him.

"You don't want to throw down a challenge like that. You caught me unprepared. And you're a woman. It wasn't fair."

"It wasn't fair because I'm a woman?" She blinked at him and tucked a sweaty strand of hair behind her ears.

"A civilian woman," he corrected. "If you were military, that would be different. How could I go a hundred percent against an art history teacher?"

"Oh, you are asking for it, Mister." She put her hands on her hips and cocked her head. "On the other hand, I did just run several miles and this poor dog is exhausted." He glanced at the big black Newfoundland who was stretched on the lawn, his dripping jowls resting on his enormous paws. "So I guess any kind of rematch is out."

A sharp pang of disappointment shot through him. He didn't want to part ways just yet with the beautiful Carolyn Moore. It was after ten, and she probably had classes to teach, and he had ... well, he wasn't really sure what he had to do tomorrow. Spend some time brushing up on his defensive martial arts moves, for one.

"It's a date," he said.

"Excuse me?"

"You said rematch. You're on. If I lose, loser buys dinner."

"What if you win?"

"Then winner buys dinner." He grinned at her, a real smile this time, instead of the stiff "don't look like a jerk" version. She blinked, looking surprised that he was actually capable of such a thing. "I'd like to buy you dinner no matter what. If you're willing. I won't twist your arm."

She laughed at that, but shook her head. "I don't think dinner is a good idea. You're related to one of my students, who you're obviously worried about. I'm happy to talk with you about counseling options and that sort of thing. But I don't think that socializing in any way is helpful."

He gave a quick jerk of a nod. Of course she was right. Besides, he'd promised Aiden. Had he temporarily lost his mind?

Yeah, probably, and it was the fault of those leggings she wore, and the way her skin glowed in the lamplight.

"You're right. My bad. I won't bother you again." He gave her another nod, of the formal "goodbye" kind, and turned to go. Then paused, and turned back. "There is one more thing. I feel that I owe you something for all this trouble."

She started to object, but he shook his head.

"Not dinner or letting you kick my ass or anything like that." He gestured toward her front door, with the weird symbol painted on it in garish orange. "How about I get rid of that for you? I have nothing too important to do tomorrow. I'd be happy to pick up some paint and take care of your door."

"Now that, I wouldn't mind at all." She gave him a brilliant smile. "But I'll get the paint. I have a light schedule tomorrow. Come on over around lunch time. I'll make you a sandwich and you can play handyman."

"You don't have to feed me—"

"I did use physical force against the brother of a student. I feel a little bit guilty about that. And you helped me catch my anonymous letter sender. I think gratitude and guilt add up to at least a sandwich, maybe a cup of coffee too."

"Deal." He nodded again, then walked away before he was tempted to say anything dumb, like "it's a date." Carolyn had made it perfectly clear that she wasn't interesting in anything of the sort. He shouldn't be either.

Key word: shouldn't. But when had he ever avoided the shouldn'ts of life? Ask anyone in his family. Never.

Back in his rental car, Tobias waited until Carolyn had disappeared inside her house. Then he grabbed his iPad from the backseat and snapped a quick photo of her front door. He drove in the direction of the Embassy Suites, but then his curiosity got the best of him. He pulled over and did a quick Google search for the image that the vandal had painted on her front door.

Since the orange paint had dripped a little, and Carolyn had interrupted Joseph before he'd completely finished, the search results were confusing. A Sumerian sun god. A store in Beverly Hills. A motorcycle manufacturer in Italy. None of those seemed to fit what he'd heard Joseph and Carolyn talk about.

Then he remembered the first phrase she'd mentioned— Light Keepers. Even though it was a generic term, like a scented candle or a yoga studio, it was worth a shot. He typed that in along with the image, and finally hit something useful.

The Light Keepers Brigade was located in a rural area of northern California. There wasn't much reliable information about it. It seemed to be part militia, part survivalist, part end-times cult, part back-to-nature wholesome living. It didn't operate under the auspices of any particular religion, but it did follow Old Testament beliefs like women's subservience to men and unquestioning obedience to the group's founder, who called himself The Ray.

But what did an art history teacher have to do with such a crazypants organization? From that brief interaction with Joseph, it sounded like she used to live there. That could explain why she had that karate move down. As a militia group, they probably trained their members in all sorts of battle skills.

He thought about Joseph, and how hard it had been to wrangle him into an arm-lock. That kid was tough and wiry and fast. Guaranteed, he'd have no trouble making a cross-country team on his own. He didn't buy that explanation for a second. Something else was going on.

He clicked around for more recent information, and landed

on an article from a small local newspaper in Humboldt County.
"The popular farm stand operated by the Light Keepers has been
shut down in the midst of the fall harvest season. In past years, it
was the only stand to stay open year-round, selling a mix of root
crops and winter greens. No one from the compound would
explain why they've closed the farm stand, or whether they might
reopen at all. The group has recently gained increased attention
from the federal authorities amid reports of illegal arms dealing
and other suspicious activities. Said one neighbor, 'they've always
been 'keep-to-yourself,' 'live-and-let-live' folks. But lately, no one
ever sees them. It's like they're circling the wagons or something. I
feel especially bad for the kids, because that farm stand was the
only time they came out into the rest of the community.'"

Huh.

Something unusual was happening up there. But what did it
have to do with Carolyn? And what business was it of his?

Shrugging it off, he closed up his iPad and tossed it in the
backseat. Maybe he should just go back to Jupiter Point. Carolyn
wanted nothing to do with him. Aiden wanted him out of his
hair. The crisis was still a crisis, but short of sticking Aiden in
quarantine until he fell out of love with Carolyn, there wasn't
much he could do. Besides, now that he'd met Carolyn, he had no
real advice on how to stop thinking about her.

Decision made. He'd cover up the spray paint on Carolyn's
door and then he'd head home.

7

BETWEEN THE VANDALISM AND THE THREATENING LETTERS, Carolyn had trouble getting to sleep. It unnerved her that all this time a member of the Light Keepers had been right under her nose. At least he hadn't been in any of her classes. The expression on his face when he'd called her a pariah—it gave her chills. Obviously the community hadn't completely erased her from their memories. She wondered if her father and stepmother still talked about her, or if the name Carolyn was strictly off-limits.

The thought made her so sad that she called to Dragon. "Come on up here, big guy. I know it's against house rules, but they'll never know. It'll be our secret, okay?"

The big Newfie hauled himself off the dog bed in the corner and trotted to her side. His nails scrabbling on the shiny surface of her comforter, he hauled his lumbering body onto the bed. He looked somewhere between guilty and triumphant as he surveyed the room from his new perch.

"I know, I know, breaking the rules is hard, isn't it? I know the feeling. I swear it's okay." She patted his haunches until he sat, then collapsed into a furry pile of doggy bliss at her feet.

She lay back, finally relaxing. Dragon wasn't trained as a

guard dog, the way the Light Keepers' dogs were. But he would certainly let her know if any strange sound or movement occurred in the night.

When she finally did sleep, she had a nightmare. A man dressed entirely in black strode into her office. He swept all her papers off her desk—students' essays on the significance of Leonardo da Vinci went flying. Books flew out of the shelves and landed in a big mess on the floor. A wild wind rushed through the room like a hurricane. Her hair whipped out of its knot and swirled against her face. The wind was tugging her out of the room toward a window that suddenly opened up. She was going to be sucked into a void, disappear forever...

But the man in black—Tobias—reached out his hand and grabbed her wrist. He held on tight while she battled the force of the howling gale.

And then she woke up, sitting bolt upright. Poor Dragon uttered a reproachful howl.

"Sorry, boy," she whispered. When her heart rate finally approached normal, she lay back down.

Wow. For a man she'd only met yesterday, Tobias Knight sure took up a lot of space in her brain.

THE NEXT DAY was her lightest teaching day. She usually used the hours between classes to catch up on grading or assemble slides for her next lecture. But today she went first to the hardware store, where she picked up some black gloss paint, then home.

Tobias was already busy cleaning off her door with a damp cloth. He wasn't wearing black this time. Instead he wore jeans and a green plaid long-sleeved shirt with a hole at the elbow. Painting clothes. He wore a bandanna tied backwards on his head, maybe to keep off the sun.

In black or out of black, he looked like pure, unrefined, one hundred percent sin. So male, so strong, so lethally attractive.

She shook off her momentary trance and walked up the steps to join him. "It's a good thing the door is black," she told him. "Easy to match. How are you today, Tobias?"

He paused in his work and glanced at her. The shadows in his eyes made her wonder if he'd had trouble sleeping too. Maybe he was worried about his brother. "Just fine. And you?"

His formal tone made her smile. "Oh, ducky. No letters arrived at my office today. It was kind of a lonely feeling, actually. I might need a pen pal if I want more mail. That was a joke," she said quickly. "My sense of humor can get a little morbid sometimes."

He lifted his eyebrows. "I bet I can beat you in that department. Black humor is the official language of the Special Forces."

"I can well imagine." Her father had an obsession with the various branches of the military, none of which had accepted him because of his psychological profile. The Special Forces had been a particular dream of his. "What made you leave the army?"

"It was time," he said simply. "My brother Ben had this idea about a pilot service. He couldn't do it alone. So I came home and we started Knight and Day Flight Tours. Just had the grand opening recently."

She cocked her head at him. "First Aiden, now Ben ... Is it always about your brothers with you?"

He reached for a spot at the top of the door, causing his shirt to stretch tight. "Do you have brothers?" he asked instead of answering.

"No, I never had any brothers or sisters. Just the other kids at —" She broke off, not wanting to get into a discussion of her weird childhood. "Are you hungry?"

"Let me finish cleaning the surface, then I'll have a quick bite while it's drying."

"Sure."

He stepped back so she could unlock the door. In order to slip inside, she had to pass within a few inches of him. As she did so, their sudden closeness made her nerves go haywire. The whirlwind sensation of her dream came back to her. Her heart skipped and raced, her breath fluttered in her throat like a trapped moth.

She practically bolted inside. Dragon trotted to greet her, and she crouched down to bury her head in his shaggy coat.

Sweet lord in heaven, what was this? Being around Tobias was like sticking her finger in a light socket. It was a good thing he didn't live here. She petted Dragon and forced her breath to ease. Good old Dragon. She was going to miss this dog when she went back to Jupiter Point next semester.

Jupiter Point.

Where Tobias lived. Will Knight's brother. Merry's future brother-in-law. Oh God.

She muttered a curse into Dragon's coat and rose to her feet. She'd have to get used to him, that was all there was to it. That meant spending time with him, like a normal person.

Starting with lunch.

She went into the kitchen and pulled sandwich makings from the fridge. What kind of sandwich would a guy like Tobias Knight like? Something hearty, to maintain all those muscles. Roast beef, perhaps. Also, something that packed a punch. Horseradish. Horseradish was the testosterone of condiments. He'd probably like lots of that. Cheese? The guy didn't have an ounce of fat anywhere on him, at least that she could see.

That might require closer inspection, however.

Jarred by the thought, she accidentally squirted mustard onto the counter. As she was wiping it up with a paper towel, Tobias walked into the kitchen.

"All clean," he told her as he went to the sink to rinse off the cloth he was using. "Should be dry in a few minutes with this sunshine."

"Mmm-hmm." She tried hard not to watch the flexing of his muscles as he wrung out the cloth. What were those muscles at the back of the arm called? The ones that ran in a firm line between shoulder and elbow and made her mouth water? "What kind of sandwich would you like? I have roast beef, ham, cheese, I can make some tuna, whatever you like. Are you a peanut butter jelly man?"

He turned, grabbed a dish towel to dry his hands, and leaned his rear against the enamel of the farmhouse-style sink. "I'm easy. You learn not to be picky in the Army."

"Yes, but you're not in the Army anymore," she pointed out. "Now you can you eat whatever you want. That's what I do. Every single meal, I give serious and extensive thought to what I actually want to eat. So, what do you want?"

He stared at her, lips quirking up in a half-smile. "Really? Every single meal? What did you eat last night?"

"My favorite guilty secret snack. Ritz crackers, cheese, and pickles."

"I'll have that," he said promptly.

"What? That's not lunch. That won't hold you through painting the door."

He waved that off as he hung the dish towel back on its rod. "I could paint that door on no food. It won't take me long. The only question is how many coats we need to cover up that ugly orange."

She shuddered as she pictured it. This morning she'd sent an email to the math professor letting him know about the vandalism, though she hadn't included any details—like the fact that it was directed at her.

"Well, I'm sorry, but I'm not ready to share my guilty secret snack with you," she teased, half serious. "We barely just met."

"Guess you have a point there." He grinned at her. "So what do you want to know so you can decide if I'm worthy or not?"

"Let's start with what kind of sandwich you want."

"I told you, I'm easy. Anything you put together, I'll eat." He put his hand on his belly, hard and flat as a country highway.

"Roast beef and peanut butter? With bananas?"

"You're a lot meaner than you look, you know that?"

She gave him an evil grin. "Fine, I'll make you what I originally had in mind—roast beef and horseradish. No complaints."

"Sounds perfect. Can I help?"

She startled. Even after ten years away from the Light Keepers, it sometimes seemed strange for a man to offer help with anything domestic. At the compound, women did all the housework.

"There's nothing much to do. Maybe grab some plates for us?" She indicated the cabinet where the professor kept his dishes. He retrieved two plates, then examined them closely. "I'll tell you one thing I am picky about—dishes," he explained. "I don't believe in automatic dishwashers. They don't do as good a job as a human being can. I got rid of the dishwasher at my brother's place. Do you mind?"

"Go for it." She rarely even used the dishes here. Her guilty pleasure snack didn't need them, and she usually ate on campus.

She finished making the sandwiches as he took down all the dinner plates and carefully washed them by hand. She seared the image into her brain. A studly man doing her dishes and painting her door. This was fantasyland stuff.

"So you live with your brother? Is that Ben or Will?"

He looked sharply over his shoulder at her. "You know Will?"

Oops. She'd left out that piece of information in the chaos of yesterday. "I know *of* him. Merry Warren is one of my best friends back in Jupiter Point."

He stared at her with bemusement. "No shit. Small world."

"I only figured out last night that Aiden, my student, was related to Merry's fiancé. I supposed I should have put it together before but names are not my forte."

He turned back and put the dish he'd just washed on the rack to dry. "Well, now I really feel like an ass, showing up here at Evergreen. Coming in hot with my accusations and attitude. Merry will probably rip me a new one when I see her next."

Carolyn smiled at the thought of her friend reading Tobias

the riot act. If there was anyone who could pull that off, it would be Merry.

"From what Merry said, you guys didn't know exactly who you were looking for, is that right?"

"Yes. Aiden wouldn't say. He still won't come out and say it."

"Maybe it's not me."

He set the last plate on the rack and turned to face her. "I asked him what made him sign up for your class and his face went bright red. It's pretty obvious that it's you. But he doesn't want to talk to his big brother about it. I can't say I blame him. I did all kinds of shit at his age that I never told anyone. *Especially* my big brother."

"Like what? Can you share any juicy details?"

He shut that down with a firm shake of his head. "I'm going to take the fifth on that. Suffice it to say I learned all my lessons at an early age. Now I'm a model citizen."

Maybe that smile was supposed to look innocent, but to Carolyn it suggested all kinds of naughtiness. She blocked it out and slid a roast beef sandwich toward him, then took a stool on the other side of the kitchen island. She felt a little safer with it between them.

He waited politely until she picked up her sandwich.

"Please." She waved him ahead. "You're a hard-working man, you must be hungry."

"I am. Thanks." Something in the way he looked at her as he said it made the hairs on her arm rise. He surveyed the sandwich, which she'd loaded up with extras—tomatoes, lettuce, cucumbers, mustard, mayo and horseradish. "When you make a sandwich, you don't mess around."

"I like food. All kinds of food. When I first left—" She broke off, stunned that she'd almost mentioned the compound in such a casual way. She never did that. Clearing her throat, she tried again. "When I first left home, I wanted to try everything. Every ethnic food I could find. To me it was like traveling without the airfare."

He pretended not to notice her near-gaffe, although most certainly he had. Those deep blue eyes didn't seem to miss much. He bit into his sandwich, eyes half-closing as he consumed the layers of her masterpiece. It dawned on her that making food for someone, then watching them enjoy it, was a very sensual experience. She'd thought carefully about what to make for him, she'd spent time creating it, and now he was wrapping his mouth around it in obvious pleasure.

Oh boy. She was in deep, embarrassing trouble if she couldn't watch this man eat a sandwich without lusting over him.

She shifted her focus to her own simple peanut butter and raspberry jam. They ate in silence for a while. It was more companionable than uncomfortable, although that river of awareness provided a constant backdrop.

He finished with a sigh. "That was great, thank you. I'd paint this whole house for another sandwich like that."

"If Joseph Brown gets any ideas about further vandalism, I may take you up on that." As soon as she said his name, she regretted it. It opened a door that he stepped through immediately.

"I got the impression you knew him, or his family."

"I knew his parents, but I don't remember him. It was a long time ago. Are you thirsty? I'm not sure what I have to offer, but whatever it is you're welcome to it." She crossed to the fridge, which took her to his side of the island. Again the hairs on her arm lifted. She was just so hyper-*aware* of him. It was unnerving. The cold air from the fridge's interior cooled her hot cheeks.

"I'd take an answer over a soda, if you're handing those out." His deep voice curled around her insides like chocolate.

"I did answer. I knew Joseph's parents."

"At the Light Keepers Brigade?"

She took out two San Pellegrinos and closed the refrigerator door with a sigh. "You're persistent, aren't you?"

"I'm curious. I told you those letters had me worried."

"But we caught Joseph and it should be over now. I'm not going to get him on the track team." She rolled her eyes. "Students. Life would be so much easier if their good judgement kicked in a few years earlier."

"Are you so sure it's over? You let him off pretty easy with that track team excuse."

She froze, still holding the cans of soda. He made a good point. She'd swallowed Joseph's explanation without question, mostly because she wanted to. She didn't want to believe anything more threatening was going on. This campus—her life as a teacher in general—was her safe haven.

But no place was immune from bad behavior. There was nowhere you could hide away completely.

She handed him one of the sodas, then cracked open her own. The sound broke the silence like a firecracker.

And it occurred to her that it was *too* quiet. Usually there was some kind of doggy sound every few minutes—snuffling, toenails clicking, something. She looked over at the corner Dragon usually occupied, but no sprawling black Newfie peered back. "Where's Dragon? My dog? I mean, he's not mine, but I'm taking care of him and...Dragon!" she called. "Here, boy!"

No answer. She dropped her soda can on the island and ran into the living room. The dog bed was empty. No little puddles of drool glistened on the floor. Tobias was right behind her.

"I remember seeing him when I came in. He came to the door the way he usually does. But I don't remember what happened after that. Did you see him while you were cleaning off the door?"

Tobias shook his head with a frown. "No, I don't think so. I do remember seeing him inside. I didn't notice him come out, but I wasn't really paying attention to him."

The subtext being that he was paying attention to her instead.

Which would have been flattering if she weren't suddenly terrified. "One of us would have noticed if he went outside, right?"

He screwed up his face. "I'm going to be honest. I was mostly
looking at you and the door. Not much beyond that."

Her face burned, but at the same time she felt sick with guilt.
From the moment she'd walked in the door, she'd been one
hundred percent laser-focused on thoughts of Tobias. She
couldn't even remember if Dragon had followed her to the
kitchen. She needed a freaking brain replacement!

"I'm going to look upstairs. He doesn't usually like the stairs,
but maybe he got scared because a stranger was in the house."
She ran for the flight of stairs that led up to the guest room level.

"I'll check outside." Tobias strode toward the front door.

Cursing her easily distracted self, she flew upstairs, calling for
Dragon as she went. But a quick check of all the guest bedrooms
revealed no sign of the big dog. Then a shout from outside sent
her heart pounding into overdrive.

8

SHE FLEW DOWNSTAIRS AND FLUNG OPEN THE DOOR. ACROSS THE lawn, a black shape sprawled like a spreading ink stain. *Dragon.* Tobias crouched over him. She stumbled down the steps of the front stoop and launched herself toward the two of them. "Oh my God, poor Dragon, poor baby, what happened?" She dropped to her knees next to the two of them. A weird whining cough came from the dog's chest, as if he was trying to cough something out.

"Something's stuck in his throat. We have to get it out or he'll suffocate."

Tobias manhandled him onto his side. His furry limbs sprawled awkwardly and scrabbled against Tobias's arms, leaving long scratches.

"I need you to hold him while I try to get it out. Come here and take my place."

Her heart hammering, she slid next to Tobias, feeling his iron thigh against hers. Poor Dragon was thrashing, terrified. She managed to get her arms and legs around the dog, pinning his limbs to minimize the damage he could do. She rested her chin in the scruff of fur at Dragon's neck, where he loved to be stroked.

"We got you, Dragon. We'll get that thing out. Don't you worry."

Tobias put his hands on Dragon's jaws, which were slightly ajar, drool dripping in big globs. Wild-eyed, the dog twisted in protest. "Okay, my friend," he muttered to the dog. "I'd really prefer to keep this hand, just so you know."

Carolyn held Dragon as tight as she could. "I've never seen him bite."

"Bet you've never seen him with a hand down his throat either." Grimacing, Tobias worked his hand between the dog's jaws. Dragon tried to bite down against the invading hand, scraping his teeth against Tobias's skin. But Tobias kept going, reaching his fingers toward whatever was in there.

Tears blurred Carolyn's eyes as she watched, her arms full of tense and struggling dog. Tobias was one brave human to be willing to stick his hand into the slobbery, drooling mouth of a terrified dog.

"I feel it," Tobias said after a few excruciating seconds. "It's a ball."

"Probably a tennis ball." Relief flooded through her. With all the strange things that had been happening, she'd been half convinced this was another attack by Joseph. "He likes to chase them."

Tobias grunted as he worked to dislodge it. Sweat dripped down his face. Dragon's entire body was rigid now—fear? Or was he suffocating?

"Got it." In a swift move, Tobias dragged the slobber-drenched object from between Dragon's jaws. He sat back on his heels, ball in hand. The dog thrashed his way out of Carolyn's grip and scrambled a few feet away, where he shook himself like an enormous black dust mop.

Carolyn collapsed onto the grass, her entire body shaking. "Oh my God. Thank you. Thank you. I was so scared. If you hadn't been here, Tobias..." She buried her face in her hands. "I don't even want to think about it."

"Hey, hey. Don't think like that. He's fine, that's all that matters. Dogs chase things, it happens. But this ball..." She looked up to see Tobias examining the slobbery thing. Dragon's teeth had mauled it into an unidentifiable shredded mystery lump. He sniffed it. "Smells like meat."

"Maybe that's just the smell of his saliva?"

"I don't think so." He stared at it some more, turning it this way and that. "I hate to say it, but I think someone wrapped meat around this ball. They wanted Dragon to wolf it down."

A horrid jolt of fear shook her to her core. Someone had tried to kill Dragon? Who would do such a thing? Everyone in the neighborhood loved Dragon. Everyone at the dog park loved him, everyone on campus loved him. He was one big lovable slobbery sweetheart of a dog.

She looked over at him, making sure he was still alive and well. The sun on his coat made it shine like black shoe polish. He was nibbling at one of his paws, running his big tongue over the nails.

"What if it was Joseph, the kid from last night?" she said slowly.

Tobias crouched beside her, wiping his drool-covered hands on his jeans. "I think it's time you tell me more about this situation. Who is Joseph? Why does he mean you harm?"

Right now, she was so grateful to Tobias that she'd give him anything he wanted, even answers. Besides, he'd earned her trust —and more.

"I'm not sure why he's doing all this. But I can tell you who he is. I knew his parents from a group called the Light Keepers Brigade. About fifty families live there. My mother died when I was five, and my father got kind of...lost. Eventually he met Lilith, my stepmother, at church, but regular church wasn't enough for her. She wanted something more purist, more old-school. They got involved with the Light Keepers and when I was ten we moved into their compound. It's more or less a cult, though they wouldn't call themselves that. Very traditional, very authoritarian. They do whatever the leader says. It's also a private militia. I spent more time learning how to handle weapons than I did learning math."

Dragon lumbered to his feet and came over to Tobias and licked his face. Tobias laughed, but even Dragon's big slobbery tongue couldn't distract him from his questions. "So they took you out of school?"

"Oh yes. They don't want outside influences on the kids, but in my case, it was a little too late. I was ten, and I already had my own ideas about things. I didn't like the part where women are subservient to men, or the part where you always do what you're told. Not to mention their beliefs, which never made sense to me. So when I turned eighteen I left."

"They allowed that? You can just leave?" Tobias scratched Dragon behind the ears, exactly where he liked it. Carolyn felt slightly jealous, to tell the truth.

"Of course. But you have to sever all ties to the group, including your immediate family members. You become a "pariah." No one is supposed to talk to you or look you in the face if you're a pariah. Did you notice that Joseph never looked directly at me last night? That's why. And that's the reason he left those letters under my door. The idea of communicating with me directly was probably impossible for him."

He gave her a puzzled frown over the top of Dragon's glossy head. "So why is Joseph out and about? Did he leave the Light Keepers too?"

"No, he's clearly still a member. Young men are allowed to attend college, as long as they study something useful to the group. Evergreen has a good computer engineering program, that's most likely what he's here for. Once he gets his degree, he'll go back and put it to work for the Light Keepers. He'll get a wife for his trouble and be a daddy in no time."

"That's how it works, huh?"

"Oh yeah. Arranged marriages are all the thing. God forbid a woman have a say in any aspect of her life. That's why I left, and I've stayed away, just like I was supposed to. I'm dead to them. So why is this happening?" She gingerly picked up the sopping wet ball, which was nestled in the lawn where Tobias had dropped it.

"I don't think it's a tennis ball," Tobias said. "Maybe a stress ball? I noticed a symbol on it, but it's hard to read because of all the teeth marks."

She stared at the disgusting object, recognizing the symbol right away. *The Light Keepers logo.* She'd seen so many renditions of it that she'd recognize it anywhere, even mauled by a meat-seeking dog. Someone had come here with one of the Light Keeper promotional items, covered it in meat and fed it to her dog behind her back.

A rush of anger made her surge to her feet. "It *was* them! I didn't believe it at first. Why would they go after my dog? And Dragon doesn't even belong to me! This is bullshit! I'll get Joseph expelled for this. This is attempted murder. I don't care what they want to do to me, but Dragon is an innocent dog who has nothing to do with them." Her fury rose as she pictured Tobias wrenching apart the dog's jaws. "You could have lost a hand."

"But I didn't. We're all fine." Tobias rose to his feet as well, flexing his shoulders to ease the strain of his wrestling match with Dragon. "Let's take a breath here. Let's get Dragon settled in, clean ourselves up. Then we'll figure out how to handle this."

She glared at him. "You're using that soothing voice. I remember it from yesterday."

"Oh, so you already know my voices?"

"Oddly enough, I do. A couple of them, anyway. This is the voice you use when you want someone to calm down so you can make them do what you want."

He narrowed his eyes at her. "Have you been talking to Aiden?"

She laughed, then laughed again out of amazement that she *could* laugh. Dragon had *nearly choked to death*.

But now the big Newfie was trotting across the lawn after a grasshopper that kept leaping between his legs. The dog was fine. He probably didn't remember any of it, because he lived in the moment like all dogs. *Dragon was fine,* thanks to Tobias. She wanted to kiss him for his bravery. Hard and long, deep and hot.

Stop that.

But how amazing was this man? He'd put his hand down a dog's throat without flinching. She reached over and lifted the cuff of his shirt. Long scratches ran up his wrist and forearm. "Look at you," she exclaimed. "My God."

He shrugged his big shoulders. "It's fine."

"It's not fine. We have to clean these up right away. No arguments." She lightened her tone, added a teasing edge. "Come inside so I can soap you up and douse you with Bactine, baby."

"Is that your voice to get me to do what you want? Because it's absolutely working."

9

TOBIAS FOLLOWED CAROLYN BACK INSIDE, THE BIG NEWFIE trotting alongside them. His hand throbbed from the strain of keeping the dog's teeth from closing around it. But he would do it again, to see that expression on Carolyn's face—pure, awed gratitude.

It made him feel like a hero.

But he was no hero, all he could think about was crowding her against that kitchen island and feeling her body against his.

She led him to the bathroom first, but one look at the small space and he objected. His willpower was already being tested enough. She collected the Bactine and a washcloth and they went back to the kitchen.

"Take off your shirt," she told him as she ran water in the sink.

Without a word, he stripped off his outer layer, a worn plaid shirt one step from a rag. Underneath, all he wore was a ribbed undershirt. But hey—she'd asked.

She didn't say anything as she guided his forearm under the faucet. Her hair smelled like honey. Long strands of it fell forward, blocking the curve of her cheek, but he was pretty sure she was blushing. The air between them throbbed with energy. His arm stung under the stream of water, but he barely noticed.

He cleared his throat. "I think you should consider calling the police."

"No." She shook her head. "If I called anyone, it would be the FBI. They're aware of the Light Keepers. But I doubt it's necessary. He's just a kid whose brain has been filled with a lot of nonsense."

"Not to be the doomsayer in the room, but you don't really know what's going on. Joseph might have left that ball for Dragon, but maybe someone else did."

She pulled his arm from under the faucet and grabbed a paper towel to dry it with. He let her tend to him even though he'd gotten much more serious scrapes from dirt biking as a kid. Obviously it made her feel good to help him, so he allowed it.

"I don't think you're taking this seriously enough, Carolyn. Law enforcement needs to get on this, one way or another. Police or FBI, I don't care. Hell, I wouldn't mind calling my brother Will in."

She shook her head and pulled him away from the sink. He leaned against the island while she uncapped the bottle of Bactine. She squirted the antiseptic on the long scratches on his arm.

"We need to talk to Joseph again." Tobias ignored the sting of Bactine as he came to that decision.

"I will. As soon as I get back on campus, I'm going to look for him."

"How about if I do the dirty work? You probably have classes to teach. And he might talk to me more, since I'm a Tobias, not a pariah." He smiled, hoping his little rhyme might make her laugh. It didn't.

"This isn't your problem."

He gave a growl of frustration. "I nearly got my hand chewed off by your dog. I have a stake in this now." He stared at her bent head. Her lower lip was pulled between her teeth in an anxious expression.

"I just...okay, I'll say it. Joseph's behavior was weird. He ought to be avoiding me completely. It doesn't make sense. I guess I'm worried that something's different at the Light Keepers."

"Do you keep tabs on them?"

"No. I try to avoid all mention of them. Since you got here, that's not working out so well."

She finished with the Bactine and blotted a few drops that ran down his arm.

"Thanks," he told her, trying to block out the fragrance of her hair. "I did a little Internet search last night and saw an article about some changes. A farm stand shut down?"

"Really?" She frowned as she capped the bottle. "The farm stand's a mainstay. One of their few consistent contacts with the community. That's definitely not a good sign."

"So? Will you call the FBI?"

She looked up at him, and he got momentarily lost in those luminous blue-gray eyes. "I can't believe you're wasting your time on this," she said softly. "You didn't come here to get sucked into my problems."

"As a matter of fact, I did." He grinned at her. "They just turned out to be different problems than I expected."

She worried at the cap of the Bactine bottle with her thumb. "About that..." She hesitated, looking down at the dog who suddenly flopped onto her feet with a low groan. "I was thinking...maybe I can help with this situation with Aiden."

His eyebrows lifted. "How?"

"Well, *if* he has a crush on me, which I'm still not sure about, maybe I can help. Maybe I should do something that would make him see me differently. You know, disillusion him. Make him see I'm nothing special and that he's better off with someone his own age."

"You mean, break his heart?" He scowled so fiercely she winced.

"No no. It would be the opposite of that. I know how kids that age think—if you like a band they hate, they lose all respect for you. If we find the right flaws, he'll start seeing me in a different light and his crush will just go away naturally. Tell me something he absolutely detests. Whatever he dislikes the most, I'll pretend I love it. I have a teacher meeting with him tomorrow, so it could be a good opportunity. It might be a way to let him down easy, without coming out and saying, 'Kid, I'm a teacher, this is never happening.'"

He nodded slowly. The thought of crushing Aiden's dreams didn't feel good, but maybe she was right and this would be a way to treat him kindly rather than rejecting him.

"Let me think about it. But first, make that call to the feds. If they want to see you, I'm coming with."

"You don't have to."

"I'm coming. I'm a witness. Besides, I'm a little nervous about leaving you alone. Dragon needs to recover, so I'm appointing myself your new guard dog."

Smiling, she pushed against his chest. Fire flew straight to his groin from that one touch. "Haven't you figured out that I'm my own guard dog?"

He put his hand over hers, pressing it lightly against his chest. Her eyelids flickered, and her lips parted slightly. He noticed she had a mark on her upper cheekbone, a crescent scar, and wondered if she'd acquired it while being "her own guard dog."

"I did pick up on that, yes. How about this—call it a gesture of thanks for me nearly sacrificing my right hand to your dog's molars."

Cocking her head, she opened her hand wide, her fingers splaying across his pectorals. God, if she had any idea how hard he was right now. "You're playing the dog rescue card?"

"I'm playing the dog rescue card. And the door painting card.

Whatever other cards I might have up my sleeve." The hot gravel of desire roughened his voice. She heard it too; he could tell perfectly well from the way the fluttering pulse in her throat sped up.

She nodded, swallowed, then nodded again. Cleared her throat. "Fine. I'll make the call right away." But still she didn't move, as if she were trapped in the same force field that kept him from looking away from her.

He bent his head closer, aching to kiss her. Or even just touch his lips to her hair. He wanted to revel in her fresh honey fragrance, find out if her skin was as soft as it looked.

But just then his phone buzzed, making them both jump. When he saw the call came from Aiden, horrible guilt shot through him. What was he doing, messing around with the woman Aiden was crushing on? That wasn't right, whether she returned the crush or not.

He stepped away from Carolyn and answered. "Hey, bro. What's up?"

"Where are you? Are you still in town?"

"Uh, yeah. You bet."

"'You bet?' When do ever say 'you bet'? You sound so funny. Where are you?"

"I'm...uh..." He couldn't tell Aiden he was with Carolyn. But he hated to deceive him. "I got into it with a dog."

"Shit. Are you okay?"

Deflection successful, Tobias gave a quick rundown of his wounds, then made plans to meet Aiden for a game of racquetball later on. Good reminder, he told himself savagely. No more coming onto Carolyn.

When he hung up, Carolyn was just wrapping up her phone call with the FBI. "They're going to call me back after they've located someone familiar with the Light Keepers. I know they're on a watch list, so it should be soon." Her tone shifted. "But listen, Tobias..."

He threw up a hand to forestall her. "Don't worry. I won't try to kiss you. I won't make any moves whatsoever. I'm sorry about that, I think the Bactine went to my head."

Startled, she opened her mouth, then closed it again. Maybe she wasn't talking about his near faux pas. Didn't matter. He still had to avoid her, no matter what.

"But I intend to finish this damn door, and I'm going to stick around town until you talk to the Feds. I'm pretty sure I can do that without trying to kiss you again." He tried to make a joke out of it, but his smile felt a little lopsided. "Deal?"

"Okay, sure. And if you think of anything that will change Aiden's view of me, let me know."

"Got it." That could be a challenge, he thought. So far he didn't see any fatal flaws in Carolyn Moore, except for sticking her head in the sand about her wacko former group members. If she didn't find Joseph he'd track the kid down himself.

WHEN CAROLYN GOT TO CAMPUS, her first stop was the registrar's office. To her shock, she learned that Joseph Brown had dropped out of school that very morning.

Wow. This was getting more and more intense. He must have gone back to the Light Keepers before finishing his degree. But why? She remembered that strange thing he'd said—*It doesn't matter anymore. It's over.* Had he been called back to the compound? She wished she had more information to share with the FBI. She felt kind of silly calling them, but Tobias had forced her hand.

She fired off a text to Tobias letting him know that Joseph had left the campus.

I'm going to see if I can snag him before he leaves town, he answered. *Talk later.*

Talk later...she liked the sound of that. This feeling of being in cahoots with Tobias somehow—she liked that too.

But she wound up talking to the FBI alone because they showed up at her office later that day.

The lead agent introduced herself as Special Agent Maia Turner. With her tidy helmet of hair and gleaming dark skin, she looked terrifyingly competent. The other agent, Tom Jackson, was an older man with sharp blue eyes that darted around her office as if looking for evidence that she was making the whole thing up.

She related the whole tale, which required delving back to when her family had first moved to the Light Keepers compound, as well as explaining the recent incidents, from the letters to the vandalism.

"So you're saying you think something has escalated, but you don't know why?" Agent Foster scribbled notes at a rapid pace.

"Right. I haven't been there in ten years. But Joseph Brown's behavior set off some alarm bells."

"Can we talk to him?" Agent Jackson asked.

"Well, no, I just found out that he dropped out of school. Which is also a big red flag. But he was at my house last night, so he probably hasn't gone far. I'm sure he has roommates and friends who might lead you to him. Tobias—my, uh friend who was with me last night—he's trying to find him before he leaves town."

The two of them exchanged a glance. "So what we have so far is an act of vandalism, some anonymous vaguely threatening letters, and a dog choking on a ball," Agent Foster said skeptically.

Carolyn felt heat rise in her face. If only Tobias was here. She didn't like this two-against-one dynamic. A witness, someone to back her up, would feel pretty good right about now. "Look, I just think someone should find out if anything unusual is happening there. Don't you have a local branch office in Northern California? Just send someone over there to scope it out."

"Good idea," Agent Turner said dryly. "I hear they're very open to uninvited visitors. Especially when they look like me."

Carolyn's face flamed even brighter. The Light Keepers took pride in their "pure" bloodlines. "You're a federal agent. They're not stupid. But obviously anyone who goes out there should be careful. They're big into weapons and they know their rights down to the letter."

Agent Jackson cleared his throat. "Can you contact the group yourself? Did you keep in touch with anyone there, family or friends?"

She shook her head. "No, once you're out, you're out. No exceptions or wiggle room. That's one way they keep people in the group. No one wants to lose their family. Believe me, my father wouldn't take a call from me, and neither would anyone else there."

Agent Turner made a note in her book, then snapped it shut. "Okay, I think we're good for now. We'll send this information along. If anything else happens, give us a call." The agent handed over her card, which Carolyn pocketed. "I suggest you take your own advice and be careful," she added. The two agents got to their feet.

"I will. Luckily, I have an amazing guard dog." As the agents took off, Carolyn smiled faintly, thinking of both the guard dog and the guard dog's guardian angel—Tobias.

Those moments in her kitchen were the hottest that she'd experienced in years—and they hadn't even done anything. Everything about him spoke to her on a primal level. The quiet smolder of his deep blue eyes, the smooth bulge of his chest muscles, the intensity with which he looked at her, the way he hadn't hesitated to do what it took to save Dragon.

And he'd almost kissed her. His lips had been millimeters from hers when his phone rang. Now the moment was past, and it was too late for kisses. He'd promised not to try again, and she could guess why. Obviously he was attracted to her. But as long as Aiden had this misbegotten crush, nothing would happen between her and Tobias. That was clear. No wonder he hadn't mentioned dinner or a rematch again.

Which was fine. Tobias was absurdly attractive to her, and it worried her. His strength, his military background, his intense maleness—that was exactly what the men at the Light Keepers Brigade revered most. Behind their vague religious preachings, they were kind of...bullies. They wanted their women to be subsidiaries, not equals. Some women wanted that too, so the Light Keepers was the perfect place for them.

But not Carolyn. She wanted to be in charge of her own life. What if this attraction was some kind of weird throwback to her youth? If that was the case, it was going nowhere. Because no matter how sexy Tobias was, her hard-won independence was too important to risk. She would not allow some rugged shoulders and six-pack abs to drag her backwards.

10

THIS TRIP TO EVERGREEN WAS OPENING TOBIAS'S EYES TO SO MANY things. At the top of the list—the fact that he didn't know his own little brother very well.

It wasn't surprising, since he'd spent so much of Aiden's childhood overseas. Every time he came home on leave, he'd had to get to know the kid all over again, because he'd be into different things by then. The Minecraft phase would be over and he'd be into skateboards, for instance. Never once had he managed to bring back a present that suited whatever Aiden's current passion was.

In fact, this visit to Evergreen was his first chance to spend extended time alone with his little brother. So maybe he had Carolyn to thank for that. And for all the questions he was sneaking in during their racquetball match. Cleverly disguised, of course.

"So what happened with Daisy?" Daisy was Aiden's longtime girlfriend back in Jupiter Point.

Aiden whacked the ball into the corner. "Nothing happened. We just decided that we should take a break. I'm in college, she's starting a business. It's a good time to see what else is out there."

Huh. That didn't give much information. He raced for the ball and slammed it back. The court echoed with the sound of their squeaky shoes and the impact of the ball. "I always thought you two were great together. Very compatible. Same likes, dislikes, that sort of thing."

Aiden executed a cross court slam, then shrugged. "I guess. We both like to have fun. Hang out at the beach. Hike."

"Exactly. And you both hate..." He cast around for an example. "Smoking."

Tobias had picked up a cigarette habit during his first stint in Afghanistan. Aiden had freaked out when he'd first seen Tobias smoking. That was the end of that.

"That's true, I never had to shame Daisy into quitting." Aiden grinned at him as he lunged for a shot.

"You didn't shame me. You went online and found a comprehensive list of reasons to quit. And you threatened to disown me as your big brother."

"I was hardcore."

"Yup. When you don't like something, you *really* don't like it. Such as..." He pretended to be out of breath so he couldn't finish the sentence.

"Tattoos," Aiden said promptly. "I'm like the only student here who doesn't have one. I think they're pretentious."

"There you go. Tattoos. Funny thing, half my team had tattoos but I was never tempted." He missed the next ball, signaled for a break and went to mop his face with a gym towel. Cigarettes and tattoos. Would that be enough for Carolyn to work with? "So what about the girls here in college? Anything stand out about them? Good or bad?"

"They're nice, I guess." Aiden twirled his racket in the air and caught it. "I haven't paid that much attention. I kind of got...well, anyway. They're always doing Snapchat and Instagram and I'm not that into social media. Everyone stares at their phone all the time, it's boring. But there's a girl in my dorm who doesn't have a phone, so I asked her out. This was at the beginning of school, before..." He coughed to avoid finishing that sentence. "It turned out she was super religious and wasn't allowed to have a phone *or* go out with boys. She tried really hard to convert me. Prayers, pamphlets, bible verses. She had a thing about angels. It was total overkill."

"Ah." Tobias filed that tidbit away, though he didn't know how it would be useful.

Aiden tapped his racket against the toe of his shoe. "So are you giving up, old man? You'd rather talk than try to keep up with me, is that it?"

"You kidding? I've been idling, bro. Keeping it in second gear. You ready to rock?"

"Bring it."

And they switched to the more traditional Knight brother approach, in which they basically tried to beat the crap out of each other.

Afterwards, they grabbed lunch at the Caf and Tobias managed to pry a few more pieces of information out of Aiden. But more importantly, he realized what a great kid he'd turned out to be. He disliked bullies, hated cruelty of all sorts, and, biggest shocker of all, was already thinking about the big family he wanted to have someday.

"Being the youngest sucks," he told Tobias wistfully as he popped French fries into his mouth. "We had this big fun family, and then everyone either grew up or left. It was just me and Will after that. I want like, ten kids when I grow up. I might even adopt a few. Oh, and a dog. Will never let us get a dog because he worked so much. I want a nice big dog. Maybe two."

Tobias cocked his head at his brother. "You have this all planned out, don't you?"

"Not really." Aiden grinned. "Okay, I kind of do. But I still have some details to fill in."

"You're still young. Plenty of time to get the details right."

Aiden dipped a fry in their shared puddle of ketchup. "Yes, but I don't want to wait too long and end up like you. All alone in your doddering old age."

"I'm thirty-one."

"Exactly. What are you waiting for, T? Doesn't seeing Will and Merry together make you want to hook up with someone?"

"I hook up. No worries about that."

Aiden rolled his eyes. "That's not what I mean. I know half the women in Jupiter Point are after you, and the other half are after Ben. It's not about hooking up. I'm only a freshman in college and even I know that."

"Then you're a very unusual college student."

His brother's open, innocent face sobered. "We're all unusual, Tobias. Our father was murdered and our mother left us. Don't you think that screwed us up? I mean, each in our own way?"

Tobias snagged the last fry and glanced around at the buzzing cafeteria. Aiden really knew how to cut to the heart of matters. Tobias might be the most physically fearsome, but Aiden was *emotionally* fearless.

He could learn a thing or two from his little brother.

"You're probably right about that," he said finally. "About the screwed-up part, not necessarily the woman part. And anyway, aren't I supposed to be lecturing you? How'd you go turning the tables like that?"

Aiden made a face at him. "It's called college. Suck it."

Gotta love that kid.

Later, Tobias called Carolyn from his hotel room. A part of him longed to go to her house and talk to her in person. He could probably rustle up an excuse. How's that paint drying? Is Dragon still breathing?

But a bigger part of him didn't want to take any chances with Aiden's feelings. His brother had such a big, caring heart. He wanted to protect it, not hurt it.

"So listen," he said to Carolyn once he got her on the phone.

"Before we go any further with this, you have to promise me that you won't say or do anything that might hurt Aiden."

"Of course not. That's the whole point. Maybe this is a bad idea." The doubt in her voice echoed his own. "I just thought, since I have to meet with him anyway, maybe I can use the opportunity to change his perspective."

"All right. Well, I'm trusting you here. Trusting you with my brother's heart."

"Got it." Her serious tone reassured him. Carolyn was a kind, sensitive person, after all. She wasn't looking for a way to hurt one of her students. He knew that. "Before you fill me in, I should let you know that the FBI showed up at my office unannounced today. I gave them your number and they might call you."

"Damn it. I really wanted to be there. What'd they have to say?"

"Not much." She told him about the meeting, which made his teeth grind. They'd basically brushed her off.

"If they don't pay a visit to that compound, you tell me where it is and I'll go myself." The offer came out before he even thought about it. But once it had, it seemed like the best idea he'd had in a while.

She laughed. "We'll see. I wouldn't want to send you into the line of fire. That's the FBI's job."

"The line of fire is my natural habitat," he told her. "The crunchier the better. That's when I do my best thinking, in the midst of chaos and bullets."

"Then we're complete opposites. Give me peace and quiet and I'm purring like a cat."

"Yeah, maybe, but there's a wildcat inside that cat. I've seen it in action."

"Pffft. That was a special occasion. I'm not usually like that," she said primly, though he caught a hint of laughter under her scolding.

"I guess it takes a special kind of person to bring it out, is that it?"

"You're obviously gifted."

Ten thousand naughty answers came to mind. He managed to keep them to himself only by thinking of Aiden and his feelings.

CAROLYN MET TWICE a semester with each of her students to talk about their progress and answer any questions they might have. During her first meeting with Aiden, he hadn't said much. She'd assumed that he was simply a shy freshman who was taking her course to fulfill a liberal arts credit requirement. Now she wondered if he'd been tongue-tied, not bored.

When he walked into her office, she surreptitiously looked for any resemblance to Tobias. Would her young student have any similarity to the big former soldier with the intense eyes?

Yes, she saw with a quick scan. Their faces had a similar square-jawed shape, and they both had devastating smiles, with a groove that popped up in their left cheek. Aiden's smile came more easily, but Tobias's was more lethal, maybe because it was more hard-won.

Their differences were easier to identify. Tobias was more physically imposing, his sheer presence more compelling. Aiden had a lighter manner and a more open face. The biggest difference was that she felt no magnetic tug toward Tobias's little brother.

She smiled at him and gestured toward the chair where visitors sat. The same one Tobias had occupied during that infamous encounter during which she'd kicked his legs out from under him. Hiding the smile that memory inspired, she opened Aiden's folder.

"So how are you enjoying your freshman year so far, Aiden?"

"It's...yeah, it's good. I like it."

Well...she drew in a deep breath. Might as well jump right into this performance.

"Listen, do you mind if I take a tiny break before we start?" She pulled a pack of Marlboro Reds from her purse and knocked one into her hand. The damn pack had cost her nearly ten bucks, and she'd had to practice that movement. She'd never smoked a cigarette before.

"Uh, sure." A look of surprised revulsion crossed his face as he locked onto the cigarette. "You should really think about quitting, you know."

That might have been the longest sentence he'd ever spoken to her. "You're right, I should. I keep telling myself that. I've been praying every night about it too. If I can't find the strength on my own, maybe God can take on the burden for me."

He blinked at her as she hurried out of the office. Smoking was forbidden inside the building, but there was a terrace outside where smokers could indulge. She dashed onto it, lit her cigarette, and waved it through the air around her body. Singh Dal, the grumpy chemistry professor, looked at her as if she was crazy. "How much does it take to smell like cigarette smoke?" she asked him.

"You're going to set yourself on fire. Watch that thing."

The smoldering top had nearly caught the sleeve of her jacket.

Good. She could probably use that.

The cigarette was burned about halfway through. She dropped it into the sand-filled urn for used butts and rushed back inside. As she passed the office next to hers, she popped her head inside and gave the five minutes signal to her friend Amanda, who taught French poetry. Once she'd gotten a thumb's up, she hurried to her own office.

"Whew," she said as she plopped into her chair. "Sorry about that."

Aiden coughed, forehead creased, then managed a smile. "No problem."

"Well, of course it *is* a problem, but I'm putting it in the hands of a higher power. Now, let's talk about your last essay. You did an excellent job with your comparison between the Tuscan school and the Venetian school." As she rattled off her critique of his work, she noticed, with a quick glance under her lashes, that he was...holding his breath?

Yes. The poor kid was not enjoying the aroma of Marlboros that had invaded her office. Neither was she, quite frankly. She'd have to invest in a case of air freshener after this.

She glanced down at the sleeve of her jacket. "Oh my goodness. Yet another reason to quit."

A bit of ash had burned a tiny hole in the fabric. She pulled off her jacket with an exasperated pout. Underneath it she wore a cap-sleeved shirt that left most of her upper arms bare.

She angled her body so that Aiden had a perfect view of her right arm. He squinted at it. "Is that—"

"Oh. My new guardian angel, yes. I acquired it just the other day. I'm hoping it will help with the quitting smoking, but so far, well..." She shrugged apologetically, making the fake tattoo on her upper arm twitch. It was a colorful, almost cartoonish rendition of an angel wearing a long blue robe, hands in prayer, looking soulfully heavenward. "I can't be praying all the time, you see. But with this on my arm, part of me always is."

"Uh huh. That's uh...a good idea."

She took note of his completely flummoxed expression. Not a single bit of googly-eyed adoration to be seen. "So. It looks like you're in good shape going into finals. Do you have any questions for me about the class, or about Renaissance art, or the perils of nicotine addiction?" She smiled innocently and set her forearms on the desk, so there was no way he could avoid the angel.

"No." He shook his head and scooted his chair back a little. "I think I'm good."

"Excellent." She took a surreptitious glance at her watch. Time for the coup de grace. She could already hear those toenails clicking... "Well, if that's it, then I guess I'll see you in—" She broke off. Dragon came trotting into the office. In her tiny space, he looked about the size of a small Clydesdale.

"Oh my Goodness. What is *wrong* with people? Why do they think it's okay to bring their pets to work? Especially dogs. They're revolting. They leave hair everywhere, they slobber. Ugh, I'm so sorry." Dragon had done his usual routine and sniffed Aiden's leg, leaving a string of drool on his jeans.

"That's okay, I like dogs."

"Yes, well, no one likes a big hairy beast leaving slime all over them. It beats me why would anyone want a dog like this. Come on, you." She came around the desk and took a firm hold of Dragon's collar. Out of Aiden's direct line of sight, she gave Dragon a reassuring pat.

She tugged the dog toward the door. He came willingly, trotting alongside her. Too bad Dragon wasn't much of an actor so he could pretend to resist. "I'm going to have a word with my colleague. This is completely inappropriate. Just imagine if you were allergic to dog hair! Or dog slobber. If you want to make an official complaint—"

"No! Of course not. Dogs are great."

Carolyn twisted her face into a dubious look. "If you say so. Call me unconvinced." Hiding a smile, she took Dragon back to Amanda's office and slipped him a dog treat.

When she got back to her own office, Aiden was on his feet. He looked neither adoring nor heartbroken. "I have another class to get to, but thank you, Professor Moore."

"Good to see you, Aiden. Keep up the good work."

He practically ran out of the office. When he reached the hallway, she heard him haul in a long breath of air. Had her ridiculous act actually worked? Aiden didn't seem to be at all crushed by anything he'd witnessed. She was absolutely certain she hadn't broken his heart with her goofy angel tattoo and Marlboro Reds.

If he was hurt, at least he was in the right place to seek comfort. There were probably hundreds of girls here at Ever-green who would be happy to heal his broken heart.

11

LATER ON, AFTER THE DAY'S CLASSES AND MEETINGS WERE OVER AND she was relaxing on her couch, her toes snuggled under Dragon's warm stomach, she shot off a quick text to Tobias. *Deed is done. Any fallout?*

Yep. He texted back right away. *Aiden told me he really likes Evergreen and isn't sure if he should leave.*

That's great news! She added a few celebratory emojis. *Does he seem upset? I didn't get that impression when he left.*

Nope. He seems just fine. Thoughtful. He told me that it takes time to really know someone. Said he'd gotten spoiled with his high school girlfriend because they've known each other so long.

Well, that certainly seemed like a good lesson to walk away with. *My work is done, then. Now to get the smoke out of my hair.*

He fired back quickly. *I make a great shampoo boy. You might need help with the fake tattoo too.*

She laughed out loud, even though shivers ran up and down her spine at the thought of Tobias washing her hair with those big hands of his. Oh. My. Better deflect before she got weak and invited him over.

Dragon gets most of the props. I really think that was the final blow, me complaining about the dog hair and the slobber. If he only knew how much time I spent wiping up drool.

I guess now he'll never know.

A strange sadness passed through her. *Never.* It seemed like such a final word. Aiden would never know that she actually loved dogs—because their association would be finished after this. She'd go back to teaching at Jupiter Point, Aiden would stay at Evergreen, and Tobias would have no reason to have anything to do with her anymore.

I guess your mission is accomplished then? What's next, back to Jupiter Point?

Yup, Ben's getting antsy. I need to get back to work. Next time you're in Jupiter Point, I'd love to take you up for a ride.

That's a nice offer. But what about Aiden?

What about him?

Are you planning to tell him about it? Will I have to pretend to smoke if he's around?

After a short pause, her phone rang. Texting only went so far, apparently. His deep voice caressed her nerve endings as soon as she answered. "I guess we didn't think this through."

"It's okay. The most important thing is that Aiden's not leaving Evergreen. That was your goal, right?"

"Yes. Originally."

Again, shivers went up and down her spine. "Tobias—"

"I know. I know what you're going to say. And you're right. I can't do that to Aiden. As much as it fucking kills me, I need to keep my distance. But I—" He hesitated, and she got the feeling he wasn't used to speaking so openly about his inner feelings. "I'm glad I met you. I hope we meet again."

Her throat closed up. So this was goodbye. Of course it was. It had to be. "You never know," she managed. God, how silly. She'd just met the guy a couple days ago. How could he possibly have such a powerful effect on her? It didn't make sense. "Thanks for painting my door, and rescuing Dragon and everything else you've done."

"Take care of yourself."

"You too, Tobias. And that means you, not just your brothers. You deserve some taking-care-of too."

An odd silence made her wonder if she'd gone too far. "What do you mean by that?"

She drew in a long breath. If she wasn't going to see Tobias again, she might as well express the observation that had been running through her mind. "It's just an impression I've gotten, that you seem to put your brothers before anything else. Like Knight and Day. That was Ben's baby, right? You left the army to help him. Not that I don't respect that. I do, but what about you and your wishes and dreams?"

A stiff silence followed that question. She wondered if he'd hung up, or was mouthing curse words at his phone. "I'm fine. If my brothers are fine, I'm good. That's all I wish for."

Which seemed to prove her point, quite honestly. "Hey, forget I said anything. I'm probably way off base. I just met you, after all."

"That's right. You don't know me. Or my brothers."

She expelled a long breath. "Okay, then. I guess I'll...see you around. Goodbye, Tobias."

And she hung up before things could get even more uncomfortable. Dragon lifted an eyelid and surveyed her with one weepy eye. "Well. So much for that, Dragon. I really know how to drive them away, don't I?"

He closed his eye again and let loose a long, snuffly sigh.

"You said it, boy."

She hauled herself off the couch and went to run herself a bath. If anything called for bubbles, it was stale cigarette smoke, a fake tattoo, and the sense that she'd missed out on something spectacular.

It was only later, when she'd finished her bath and was

grading papers in bed, that she remembered to check her phone again.

Tobias had texted one last time. *Sorry I was rude. You may have a point. I hope we can keep texting and/or talking.* After that he'd added a broken heart emoji.

Which struck her as so poignant it brought tears to her eyes. That was the thing about Tobias...he had a broken heart—whether he knew it or not.

12

AIDEN SAW TOBIAS OFF AT THE AIRPORT. HIS BROTHER ACTUALLY got a little sniffly when they said goodbye. "I'm glad you came, T."

"Yeah, me too. It sucks, being away from home for the first time. It's good to have a little dose of family, huh?"

"Yeah. You kind of got my feet back on the ground. I think I was going a little nuts." Aiden shook his head disgustedly. "Now that I look back, I honestly don't know what kind of crack I was smoking."

"Hey, don't beat yourself up." Tobias knew all about that crack —its name was Carolyn, and it was freaking addictive. Now that it was running through his blood, he had no idea how he was going to get rid of it. It would take a lot more than a fake cigarette habit. "So I'll see you at Christmas, kid."

"Our first complete family Christmas!" Aiden's face lit up with a huge grin. They hugged tightly. Tobias's heart welled up with love for his little brother. The poor kid's life had been completely torn apart and what had he done? Joined the army and left him behind.

Well, now he was back and determined to make up for that.

Carolyn's comment threaded through his mind as he embraced his brother's wiry frame. *You put your brothers before anything else.*

He wished he'd put his brothers first after the murder. Instead he'd run away, terrified of the guilt and anger that boiled in his veins. But now he was putting his brothers first—of course he was. It was the least he could do for Dad. It wouldn't make up for the last night of Dad's life. But it was something.

BACK IN JUPITER POINT, he swung back into his regular routine, almost as if nothing had happened. Even though Knight and Day Flight Tours was a new business, in operation for barely a month, they were already booking up fast. He and Ben split the piloting duties. They owned a Cessna six-seater, a Piper Matrix and a helicopter, which they'd added to their little fleet to assist the local hotshot and rescue crews. Occasionally someone wanted to be dropped off on one of the offshore islands, and they used the chopper for that. But mostly the tourists wanted to see the spectacular views of mountains and cliffs, and the sweeping ocean vistas that you could only experience from above.

After all his days flying missions, it was pure joy to show off the beauty of Jupiter Point and the surrounding wilderness. And he loved it, he really did. Except—he had to admit, sometimes it seemed a little tame compared to his previous line of work.

Ben had always been the one with the passion for flying. Taking over the old Marcus airstrip and reviving the flightseeing business was Ben's idea. Ben had thought of the name, he'd come up with the logo design, with the chess-piece silhouette over a sun. Ben was the one who worked night and day—pun intended —on the business, crunching numbers and taking online marketing courses when he wasn't actually piloting a plane.

Tobias was the supporting player here. He did his job, of course. He memorized the spiel Ben wrote, so he had something to say to the tourists as they flew past the observatory. He quizzed wildlife biologists so he'd know the best places to spot bears in the mountains, or dolphins riding the currents. His goal was to deliver an unforgettable experience during every tour he flew, with at least one wildlife sighting.

When it came to the management side of things, he tried to hold up his end. He sat in on interviews. They needed to hire some support staffers—a receptionist to take bookings, a book-keeper to manage the finances, a part-time mechanic to keep the planes in top condition. There was so much involved in getting the business off the ground, sometimes he missed the simple days of the military chain of command. At Knight and Day, the chain of command was more like a scramble to keep up with everything that had to be done.

Ben loved every minute. He strode around the airstrip with a piratical grin, greeting customers with a handshake and a free *Guide to the Skies of Jupiter Point*. He kept lecturing Tobias about his manner with the tourists.

"You have to smile more, dude. These are not enemy combatants. They're *customers*."

"I know that. That's why I make sure to get them back alive," Tobias grumbled.

"They might be alive, but they're afraid you're going to scowl at them again. Would it kill you to lighten up?"

"Fuck off."

"I'll take that as a yes," Ben said dryly. He adjusted the bandanna he wore to hold back his hair. He'd vowed not to cut it for at least five years to make up for all the buzz cuts he'd had in the Air Force.

"Look, I'm doing my best here. I'm not a ray of sunshine like you. I'm more of a—"

"A death ray?"

Tobias grimaced. Was he really that lacking in cheer? "I'll work on the smiling part."

"Eh, don't worry about it. I wouldn't want you to strain

anything. Besides, you freed Aiden from the evil spell of the golden goddess, so you're good for the rest of the year. How'd you do it, anyway? You really know how to complete a mission, bro."

Tobias checked the last bolt on the Cessna, to which he was giving a preflight safety check. "Classified info, eyes only, man. Can't reveal my tradecraft."

"Oh, so you're playing it that way. Did you meet the lady in question?"

"No comment."

"Dude, now you sound like Will."

"Sound like Will, how?" The man in question strode into the hangar. Will looked like a different man these days. Loose, happy, free. Tobias figured it was thanks to his new and blissful relationship with Merry Warren. Tobias had never seen two people who enjoyed each other as much as Will and Merry. Their sparks could light up a room.

"He pulled out the 'no comment'," explained Ben. "Refuses to talk about what went down at Evergreen."

Will put his hands in his pockets and surveyed Tobias with sharp gray eyes. "Can't complain about the results. Aiden seems in good shape. I just asked him if he still wants to liquidate his trust and he said 'no.'"

"Great." Tobias twirled his wrench, then put it back in the toolbox. "He's a good kid. Let's give him a little breathing room. Everyone has a right to lose their mind once in a while, right?"

"Sure." Will jerked his chin at Tobias. "Do you have a few minutes?"

"If you want me to dish the dirt about the golden goddess, it's not happening."

Did Will know that it was Carolyn? Had Merry told him? Carolyn had made Merry promise not to, but that might be a hard promise to keep. No matter what, Tobias had no intention of telling either of his brothers. His experience and connection with Carolyn felt too personal, too precious, to share.

Will held up a hand in a defensive gesture. "Not about that. As far as I'm concerned, that chapter is closed. I was hoping I could ask you some questions about..." he hesitated. "That morning."

That morning.

The morning Tobias had found Dad dead and all their lives had changed. A thick ball of dread formed in his gut. The memory never really left him, but talking about it...that was another matter. He hadn't done that at all, except with the interrogating officers at the scene, and then with Merry for her article. That interview had been excruciating.

"Sure," he managed. "Where do you want to do it?"

"Actually, I was thinking we could go back to the old house. You can walk me through exactly what you saw and where. I already spoke to the new owners. We just have to give them a head's up when we're on the way."

The old house. Jesus. Tobias hadn't been back there since he left for boot camp. Will had sold it and moved to an old farmhouse closer to town. Could he handle a trip back there? Back to the most horrifying moment of his life?

For some reason, the thought of Aiden stiffened his spine. Aiden wouldn't be afraid to go back. He was good at facing emotionally painful things.

"Yeah, let's do that. I have one more flight today, then let's go."

"That works."

Ben interrupted and dragged Will away to show him the new weather radar system they'd installed. Tobias moved to the tool bench, where he grabbed a rag and some heavy duty hand cleaner. As he was wiping motor oil off his hands, his phone beeped. Earlier today he'd sent Carolyn a photo he'd taken from his last flightseeing trip along the coastline. It was an especially beautiful shot of the sun reflecting off the observatory and the Seaview Inn, which sat on the next hill over. Behind those two hills spread an ocean of green, the Sierras unfolding in endless pine-studded waves.

Not quite Renaissance art, but not too shabby, he'd written. For some reason, every beautiful sight he saw, he wanted to share with her. But he didn't tell her that. Too freaking sappy. And they didn't have that kind of relationship, after all. They'd been texting casually, exchanging fun notes about things happening in their lives—Dragon's new chew toy, Jupiter Point's new Thanksgiving parade, that sort of thing.

Also, she gave him reports about Aiden, for which he was eternally grateful. Things like, *Spotted Aiden with a cute soccer player at the Caf. He seems happy.* And, *Aiden actually raised his hand in class today. That's a first.*

Now she'd texted again, probably about the photo he'd sent. He was so anxious to see her response that he tried to open the text with the heel of his hand, since his fingers were still slick from the cleaning compound. The phone went flying off the tool bench and skittered across the concrete floor, coming to a stop at Ben's feet.

Ben bent to pick it up, and Tobias panicked. What if he saw Carolyn's text? What if he put it together that she was the mystery woman from Evergreen? "I got it," he barked, hurrying after his phone.

Too late. Ben had already snagged it off the floor. He laughed at Tobias's frustrated growl and held his phone behind his back. "You look the way you used to when Dad caught you reading comics instead of studying. Whazzup, dude?"

"Hand it over."

"Are you blushing?" Ben peered at him, a wild light in his blue eyes.

"I'll kick your ass."

"Bring it, big guy. It's worth it, just to see what you've got going on."

"Nothing's going on, jackass." Time to get down and dirty. "Hand the phone back or I won't tell you who I saw at the Quickie Mart this morning."

Ben narrowed his eyes at him. "Is this something I want to know?"

"Oh yes." His brother gave in and handed back his phone. "I'm not giving in to your blatant extortion, by the way. I just realized that I'm not twelve anymore."

"Are you sure?" Tobias muttered as he stuffed the phone back in his pocket.

"Pay up, big guy. Who'd you see at the Quickie Mart?"

"Julie."

Ben froze for a fraction of a second, then continued on as if that fact meant nothing to him. But anyone who knew Ben knew that couldn't possibly be true. Ben had been so deeply in love with Julie that when she'd dumped him, right before the murder, he'd joined the Air Force almost immediately. His brothers had wondered if he had some kind of death wish.

Since the military didn't want people with death wishes, they'd quickly gotten his head straight for him. The next time Ben had come back to Jupiter Point, he'd been a different man. He'd developed an outer shell that let everything bounce right off him. Nothing upset him anymore, almost as if he'd been so deeply wounded that other painful events didn't register.

But Tobias knew him well enough to know that wasn't true. Ben had a huge heart, and he'd given it to Julie one hundred percent. How would he handle her reappearance?

"Interesting," Ben said, in a brittle voice. "I thought she was down south somewhere."

"She just moved back. She asked about you. I told her about Knight and Day, so she might drop by."

Ben's mouth twisted for a moment, then he shrugged lightly. "Great. I'll show her around. Maybe take her up in the chopper."

"And push her out?" Tobias asked wryly.

"Probably not," Ben said. "But you never know."

Tobias made a note to tell Julie to avoid Ben at all costs. Until now, he hadn't realized there might still be bad blood between them. What the hell. He couldn't fix all his brothers' love lives. Not when his own was in such a frustrating state.

13

HE WAS FINALLY ABLE TO CHECK THE TEXT FROM CAROLYN IN THE truck as they headed to their old house. While Will drove, Tobias scanned through his messages.

You have a real eye, she wrote. *I could teach this in a class. Master Tobias of the Jupiter Point school. By the way, I thought of you today when I discussed the Mannerist movement. Look at this portrait. Remind you of anyone?*

She'd attached a photo of a moody-looking prince staring into the distance. He wore a floppy gold hat and a velvet doublet and yet somehow managed to look like a badass. A badass in a very bad mood.

He looks like he ate a bad burrito, Tobias answered. *Did they eat those in the Renaissance?*

Interesting perspective. She added an eye roll emoji. *Remind me not to invite you to be a guest lecturer.*

Done. Tho now I have my next Halloween costume. Halloween had already passed. He and Ben had dressed up as scary carrots. No one got it, until they'd explained to the trick or treaters that nothing was more terrifying than having to eat your vegetables.

That had gotten some laughs from the kids.

I'd give you ALL the candy if you dressed as my favorite portrait.
Okay then. That sounded flirtatious to him. *Tell me more.
What kind of candy are you handing out?*

"Tobias!" He jerked his head up. Will was frowning at him
from the driver's seat. "Jesus, I've been saying your name for the
last two minutes."

"Sorry, man." With a last regretful peek, he tucked his phone
away. His text flirtation would have to wait.

Will was still giving him odd sideways looks in between navi-
gating the curves on the road that led to the unincorporated area
past Jupiter Point. "Who were you talking to?"

"No one. It's nothing important. Just a...someone. Someone I
met recently."

"Yeah? Well, you look pretty into her, based on that smile you
can't keep off your face. Are you going to see her again?"

"Doubtful." The chances that he and Carolyn could find a way
past Aiden's former crush seemed remote. Even if Aiden wasn't
obsessed with her anymore, he might feel foolish if Tobias got
involved with her. In fact, out of all the single women in the
world, Carolyn was probably the one Tobias most needed
to avoid.

"Huh. Well, if you want to talk about it, you know where
to go."

"You giving out romantic advice now?"

"I didn't say me. Merry's great at giving advice. Ask any of her
friends. Brianna, Suzanne, Lisa."

Carolyn, he wanted to say. *Carolyn's one of her best friends, and
she's a knockout and what am I going to do when she comes back to
Jupiter Point and I run into her at a barbecue or something?*

One worry at a time.

"Uh, that's okay. I got this."

"You'd better. We can't have all the Knight brothers falling in
love at once."

"In love?" Tobias snorted. "You can cross that off your list. Ain't happening, bro. You got that end of things covered. I'll stick with meaningless hookups."

Truth to tell, he hadn't had one of those in quite some time. Definitely not since he'd met Carolyn.

"Any luck locating the girl from the sheriff's office?" he asked Will. "The one letting suspects go?"

"Cindy Tran? I have some leads, but not yet. I'm worried about her. I hope she's safe. She's smart, but she's up against a ring of drug smugglers."

Will pulled into the driveway of their old house, and Tobias forgot all about their conversation. His gut knotted into a tight ball. This was almost exactly where he'd argued with his father that last night. The basketball hoop was still there, but the garage door had been repainted. The big eucalyptus tree was even taller, and someone had planted brilliant dahlias by the front walkway.

He let Will do the greeting and the talking until they reached the spacious old kitchen, with the farmhouse sink and windows that looked out on the vegetable garden and barn. The new owners let them be, requesting only that they put everything back as they found it. With the door closed, they stood in silence, gazing at the spot where Robert Knight had been discovered with his throat cut, a pool of blood congealing around him.

Where *Tobias* had discovered him.

Will cleared his throat. "Looks like they've done some renovating in here."

Tobias recognized an attempt to make this seem normal. "Yeah, I like what they've done with it. The fewer murder victims, the better."

Will snorted and strolled over to the drainboard next to the sink. Tobias flashed on the last time he'd been hanging out in a kitchen, with Carolyn tending to his scratched arms. Even though he'd been in more physical pain at that point, he'd choose that moment over this one.

"Want to take me through it?" Will asked.

"Sure. I..." He ran a hand over the back of his neck. This was hard. Even harder than he'd expected. "I hadn't slept much the night before. Don't know if you knew, but Dad bailed me out of jail that night."

"Jail, huh? They actually arrested you?"

Tobias gave a one-sided smile. "They usually didn't out of respect for Dad. But I got into a fight and I guess they'd had enough of my shit. So they tossed me in. Dad was furious, obviously. We got into a huge blowout that night. Even worse than usual. Anyway, I was tossing all night. Remember how I was staying in the barn then?"

Will nodded.

"They sometimes kept the kitchen door unlocked for me because all I had was a like, a rice cooker I'd picked up at a garage sale..." He realized he was rambling, and dragged himself back to the point. "Anyway, I think Dad probably left the latch off because he knew I'd get hungry. But I refused to go in, I was so pissed. I lay there making all kinds of plans to leave Jupiter Point. If only I hadn't been so fucking childish..." He broke off.

Will squeezed his shoulder. "Hey, don't do that to yourself. The only person responsible for Dad's death is the one who murdered him. Anything else is just noise."

Tobias nodded, though the words felt so empty compared to the crushing weight of his guilt. "I could have scared the guy off, or interrupted him, or got Dad help in time."

"A million things could have happened. We don't know. All we know is someone came in and killed him. Probably someone he knew. Dad was a soldier. He would have fought back against a stranger. Did it look as though he'd fought?"

"Not really. He looked like..." Tobias swallowed hard. "It looked like he was smiling, a big dark-red grin right across his neck. Like he was laughing with his throat. I couldn't even understand it at first. As if he'd slipped in a puddle of something on the kitchen floor and was laughing about it. And I—"

"What?" Will prompted gently.

"I laughed back. I kind of snorted, the way I always did when he tried to make one of his 'dad' jokes that never came out right. I laughed, Will. He was lying there in his own blood and I laughed." The horror rushed through him, same as it had the moment he realized what he was actually seeing. He turned away and passed a hand over his face, blocking it from view.

Will put a steadying hand on his shoulder, waiting while Tobias struggled to get a grip on himself.

"I'm okay. I just need a second." He waved his brother off. If he let himself go down the emotional rabbit hole, he'd never get through this. He whooshed out a breath, then another one. When he was finally back on solid ground, he continued.

"After I figured out that he was...that his throat had been cut, I went down next to him and listened for breathing. I tried his pulse, but it was pretty clear he was gone. I called nine-one-one. And then I went up to wake Mom. I didn't want the police to show up and freak her out. But of course there was no avoiding a meltdown."

Will shot him a look of purest sympathy. "I'm really sorry I wasn't there to take some of the burden off you. It all fell on you. Not fair."

"Ben took care of Aiden. If he hadn't been here, it would have been a thousand times worse. And you came as soon as you could. Like you say, there's no sense in any of us beating ourselves up."

"I won't if you won't." Will walked to the spot on the floor where Tobias had found Dad. He traced the perimeter of an imaginary chalk line. "So he was sprawled like this, legs toward the door. Which way was his head facing?"

Tobias called up the gruesome memory. "Toward the hutch. Remember that old pistachio-green thing that sat in the corner? He was looking that way."

"Huh." Frowning, Will flipped through his pocket notebook.

"But his body was oriented more the other direction, toward the sink. Kind of an awkward position."

"Well, I guess. Aren't most positions awkward when your throat's been cut? Maybe he was looking for help, or maybe his head just angled that way when he fell."

"Maybe."

"Did the police think there was something funny about his body's positioning?"

"No." Will shrugged. "But then again, the police haven't solved this. So they missed something. Just gaming it out here, if Dad was looking at the hutch for a reason, what could it be? What was in that thing besides Grandma's wedding china and our collection of birds' nests?"

Tobias wrinkled his forehead, trying to summon some shred of memory about a piece of furniture he hadn't seen in over a decade, and didn't pay attention to then. "You might have to locate Mom for the answer to that. Or Cassie."

"Nah, we can do this. We all carried our share of chores, including dishes and setting the table. I remember the fancy dishes stayed in the hutch, and..."

"Dad's medals," Tobias said suddenly. "He kept them on the bottom shelf. Remember, he didn't like to display them? He felt funny about it, because they reminded him of his fellow soldiers who had died."

"Hot damn. You're right." They stared at each other. "I bet he was looking at his medals."

"But why? He wasn't sentimental about them at all. That's why he kept them in the damn hutch instead of on display somewhere."

Tobias scrubbed a hand through his hair. "A clue? Maybe he was trying to tell us something?"

"Maybe he was. Okay, Tobias. That's it. We have to find those medals."

14

As November wore on with no more strange incidents, Carolyn almost forgot the crazy drama around the letters and the vandalism. She plunged into preparing her final exams, and spent hours helping the lagging students get their grades up. The semester passed in a blur of swirling autumn leaves and red pencil marks on papers. She spent Thanksgiving with her office neighbor Amanda and her family. She occasionally spotted Aiden with various girls around campus, which was normal behavior for a freshman. He would wave at her but show no signs of wanting to talk to her.

Perhaps he was afraid of another secondhand smoke incident.

The FBI called and told her that they'd gotten word that Joseph Brown had returned to the Light Keepers. They refused to comment on whether something unusual was going on at the compound, but they asked her to keep her eyes and ears open in case anything else happened.

Wonderful. That definitely made her feel safer.

Carolyn located a nearby firing range and put in some hours at target practice. She didn't own a gun, but refreshing her skills made her feel more prepared. It also turned out that the athletic department had a great martial arts teacher, a former refugee from Cambodia. She hired him to spar with her a few times a week. No harm in keeping all her self-defense skills on point.

When she walked Dragon, she got in the habit of keeping him close to her side. Even though he was huge, she'd realized that he wasn't the best at defending himself. He was too lumbering and affectionate. Keeping him safe was her job, so the poor dog never got to wander by himself anymore.

"It's okay," she kept telling him. "Your real owner will be back by Christmas. Your lockdown will be over."

It was such a sad thought, she could hardly face it. Dragon had become such a big part of her life.

"If I could keep you, I would," she liked to tell him, whether he understood her or not. "You're better than most boyfriends, if I don't count your unfortunate liking for tennis balls and fear of vacuum cleaners. Not that I've had a lot of boyfriends. Just enough to know better."

Since meeting Tobias, her romantic history seemed like something from another lifetime. Her previous boyfriends paled compared to him—and she and Tobias hadn't even kissed. Didn't say much for her exes, quite honestly.

Each of the men she'd been involved with since leaving the Light Keepers—a math tutor, the owner of a dry cleaning business, and a wine salesman—had one thing in common. They were completely unthreatening and let Carolyn call all the shots.

At the compound, no one had talked about sex. Starting around the age of twelve, she'd been consumed with curiosity, but also ashamed of her interest. With Chip, Brad and Keith, she'd taken each step toward intimacy with extreme caution, like venturing onto a pond with thin ice.

With Tobias, she kept telling herself to be cautious, but it didn't work. When texting with Tobias was more interesting than actually dating Chip, Brad or Keith, she was in big trouble.

As November faded into December, and the air grew crisper, her favorite nights were those she spent snuggled on her couch talking to Tobias on the phone. Oddly enough, they were able to talk even more intimately that way than in person.

Tobias told her about the morning he'd found his father dead, and how he and Will had gone back to the scene in order to relive it. After Merry had told her about the murder, and her article, Carolyn had looked it up online. She'd read all the heart-wrenching details, but hearing Tobias talk about it was different. It revealed a different side of him. A vulnerable, aching side.

And now Will was chasing down the lead about Robert Knight's medals.

"One of his medals came from an incident in Vietnam right before he left the Army. He never talked about it. Will thinks there might be a connection, so he's working on locating the other soldiers who were there."

"I hope he finds something. Is it hard not knowing who was responsible?"

"The strange thing is, I haven't thought about it like that. I thought more about all the things I could have done to prevent it."

His deep voice did something to her on a primal level, even when they were talking about such serious matters.

"You carry the weight of the world, is that it?"

"No. Do I?"

"It's hard to slash someone's throat. Whoever did it was strong and determined, and stealthy. How were you supposed to single-handedly stop him? You were what, twenty or so?"

"Twenty, yes. But I was strong too. I was building rock walls for a landscaper. I could have done some damage. If I had the skills then that I have now..." He trailed off.

"Is that why you joined the Army? So you could keep something like that from ever happening again? Or maybe go back in time and fix it?"

He gave a low, slightly pained laugh. "You go right for the jugular, don't you?"

"I'm sorry, I didn't mean it that way. I'm sure you had many reasons for joining up and I respect you for all of them. I didn't mean to cast any doubt on your motivation. It's just..."

She paused to adjust her Bluetooth. With all the time she spent on the phone with Tobias, she sometimes did things like yoga while she chatted. Right now she was stretched in a downward dog position on her yoga mat.

"Go ahead. Speak your mind. This is new for me, you know. I don't talk about this stuff to anyone. My brothers haven't either, until just recently. Really. I want to hear what you think, because so far, you've never let me down. You go right to the heart of things."

"Is that a good thing?" She stretched forward to grasp her toes.

"It is in my book."

"Okay, what I wanted to say was that the hardest thing for me when I left the Light Keepers was accepting that I could never go back. So many times, after I left, I fantasized about going home and being welcomed by my father and stepmother, except everything was different and better. They loved me as I was. They embraced me instead of scorning me. That sort of thing. I'd start to weaken, and think I should go home. Maybe I could change my parents. Maybe they'd listen to me. It was such a dangerous fantasy because I wanted it so *badly*. One time I gave in and called the compound. I pretended I was calling from the feed store and asked to speak to Levi Moore. When he came on the line and realized it was me, he told me liars were the devil and I should never call again."

Her heart was pounding all over again at the memory. She eased herself into a forward fold.

"That's...pretty brutal," Tobias said softly.

"Yeah. It was. It took me a while to recover from that phone call. I learned to be very real with myself and not give in to the fantasy that I could get my family back."

The downside of talking on the phone was that she couldn't see Tobias's reaction. Was he with her? Or did he think she'd veered off onto a tangent?

"You think I'm living in a fantasy?"

"I suppose, in a way. You're living in the fantasy that you could have stopped it. That you were responsible."

"A *guilt* fantasy? What kind of crap fantasy is that?"

She snorted softly. Tobias had a blunt way of putting things that she appreciated. "Good question."

When more silence followed, she twisted her face in regret. Back to her old tricks, finding ways to drive away this attractive, fascinating man. Her light conversational skills needed some serious work.

"On another topic, what do you think of the new Kardashian app? Seen any good movies lately?" she asked lightly.

"Hey, don't confuse me. I'm busy trying to translate everything you just said into man-language."

"Man-language?"

"Yes, that's my native tongue. I might need some remedial lessons in all this other shit. Maybe I can get Aiden to translate. I think the younger generation might have a leg up when it comes to the emotional stuff."

She laughed as relief spread through her that he wasn't fleeing for the exit. "You underestimate yourself. And possibly your entire gender. There's no reason why men can't talk about their history and their motivations and so forth."

"Why talk when you can punch something?"

"Well, because not everything can be punched."

"You mean like the fact that my last word to him was an insult."

She moved into her favorite yoga pose, resting on her back at the end. "Maybe it was just a random mention of a body part, ever think about that?"

"Now that's pure genius. How am I supposed to keep up with you?"

"You're not. You're supposed to bow down before the golden goddess."

"Ooh, you went there, didn't you?"

She grinned widely as she pulled a throw over her. "First rule of guerrilla combat, use whatever weapons you can put your hands on."

"I have some weapons you can put your hands on." His teasing voice rumbled through her, setting off vibrations in places she didn't usually think about during yoga.

"Sorry, I gave up guns when I left the compound."

"Guns are the least of it. I'm most effective with the weapons I was born with."

A flush of heat burned in her cheeks. Maybe she should open a window or something. All that yoga sure made it hot in here. "Are you flirting with me, Night Stalker?"

"Oh ho. You know my regiment."

"Research." Her face got even hotter. "I like to know exactly who I'm texting with. You flew Chinooks for the 160th Airborne."

"Bingo. At this rate, you might know me better than anyone. You've actually looked under the hood of this old wreck. Don't be surprised if I blush like a baby the next time I see you."

Next time...she really liked the definitive way he put that.

"Speaking of which, I have a delicate question for you. Merry called me. She and Will are planning a Christmas Eve dinner at their house. It's also a housewarming, sort of, because she's moving in with him."

"Yes, I'm aware of all that. Ben and I are looking for our own place to give them some space. So what's the delicate part?"

"Well, she invited me. I'm driving back to Jupiter Point on Christmas Eve, because I need to stay with Dragon until his owner gets back. So I have a built-in excuse if you prefer that I say no."

"Why would I want that?" He sounded genuinely confused.

She rolled her eyes. *Men.* They never thought about the subtleties.

"Aiden might feel awkward. I would hate to make his Christmas Eve uncomfortable. I mentioned that to Merry."

"What did she say?"

"She said that's silly, and there's no reason to avoid Aiden for the rest of my life. She said it was a harmless crush and he's young and I'm her friend and she really wants me there. Then she said I should talk to you about it before I made a final decision."

"Does she know we're...?"

"What? Talking, texting? Flirting?"

"Right. Something in that territory."

"Maybe. She's pretty perceptive. She may have picked up on something." She tried so hard to sound neutral whenever Tobias's name came up, but it was nearly impossible. Her fascination with him was so intense, it filtered into her voice despite herself.

"What would you do for Christmas Eve if you don't come to Merry's dinner?"

"Move back into my house. Unpack boxes. I don't usually do much for—" She was about to explain that Christmas, for her, was often the most miserable time of the year, the time she missed her family the most. But he interrupted.

"You should come," he said abruptly. "I'd like you to come. Please come."

Her breath caught in her throat. That was what she'd wanted him to say. But what about his brother?

"And Aiden?"

"We need to give Aiden a little credit. Sure, he had a crush. But he's nineteen years old with the world at his feet. I think he'll be fine."

"Should I mention this to him so he isn't surprised?"

"I will. It might seem odd coming from his teacher. I'm his brother, I'll find a way to casually let him know that Merry's good friend Carolyn is joining us for Christmas. Besides, he thinks you're a nicotine-stained old hag now. You don't have to worry."

"I'm not bringing cigarettes," she warned. "My fake-smoking days are over."

"So you quit. Good for you. That's all that needs to be said."

"And what if it turns out that my presence makes things awkward?"

Tobias didn't answer. She could imagine his thoughts, though. Aiden's wellbeing was the most important thing to him. How guilty would he feel if his little brother's Christmas was ruined?

"I can always make an excuse and leave," she said.

He didn't object to that.

Which made her wonder...did this thing between them, whatever it was, realistically have any chance, given how it had started?

Tobias always watched out for his brothers first. And she respected that. But where did it leave her? Or them?

Where did she *want* things to be with them?

If a real relationship wasn't possible because of Aiden, maybe they could go for something else. Something secret, forbidden, and hot as hell.

That worked for her.

15

Once he knew that he was going to see Carolyn on Christmas Eve, Tobias's whole world brightened. He even started smiling at the tourists he took on their flights along the coastline. Not even the honeymooners irritated him the way they used to. So what if they held hands the entire time and took selfies of each other kissing? They were in love. It made sense. Love finally made sense to him, because if he had Caro next to him, he wouldn't let her hand go, not for a second.

Unless she pulled some kind of karate move to get rid of him.

Aiden came home a few days before Christmas and slept for three solid days. Tobias looked for opportunities to tell him about Carolyn coming, but never found a chance. His ex-girlfriend, Daisy, came over on the first day he stumbled out of his bedroom.

She took one look at his groggy, sleep-puffy face and announced she was taking him to Stargazer Beach for a winter swim and then to the Milky Way for pancakes and no one better try to stop her.

They'd been joined at the hip ever since. The two of them were looking at each other the way they used to. They'd been best friends, then sweethearts, then back to friends when Aiden left for college. And now?

Who knew?

Tobias, Ben and Will made a pact to keep their mouths shut so they didn't scare Aiden off with their teasing. They all loved Daisy. She'd been in and out of their lives for years now, and it was good to have her back. At least for now.

Tobias was especially happy about it. With Daisy around, maybe Aiden would barely notice when Carolyn arrived for dinner on Christmas Eve.

When that moment came, Tobias forgot about Aiden, Daisy, and every other human being in the old farmhouse. He hadn't seen Carolyn for almost two months, and he'd forgotten how goddamn beautiful she was.

Even in the crowd of family and guests, she stood out like a living ray of sunlight. She wore a dress made from soft bronze wool that draped gracefully over her slender curves. She'd curled her hair so it fell in loose blond waves over her shoulders, held back with a pin adorned with bright holly. She carried a big pink cake box from everyone's favorite local bakery, Pie in the Sky.

Merry skipped forward to greet her. "You came! I'm so happy!"

She threw her arms around Carolyn and the two friends hugged. Tobias wondered if he could get away with the same kind of embrace. Probably not, since officially they barely knew each other.

Merry kept a hold of Carolyn's hand as she raised her voice over the chattering of the crowd. "Everyone, this is one of my besties, Carolyn. She just got done with a long drive, so be extra nice and pass the eggnog. Carolyn, just to keep it simple, this is the Knight family, some of the staff from the *News-Gazette*, various members of law enforcement, and most importantly, my mother, Gabriela Joao Warren."

Merry's mother, a gorgeous Brazilian woman with a wild afro and a magnetic smile, surrounded Carolyn in another embrace.

Merry barely managed to rescue the pink bakery box before it got smushed.

"*Meu amor*, I've heard so much about you. All friends of Merriweather are my friends."

Looking dazed, Carolyn smiled warmly back at Gabriela, then waved at the rest of the group.

"I'll take this cake into the kitchen," said Merry. "And by the way, watch out for the mistletoe over the kitchen door. It seems to be extra powerful, Will's already kissed me like, five times. I'm considering sending someone else in the next time I need something from the kitchen." With one of her infectious, dazzling smiles, she headed for the kitchen.

"That's my cue," said Will, heading after her in hot pursuit.

And Carolyn finally spotted Tobias. A shock of happiness passed through him as their eyes met. The reality of seeing her in the flesh after all those texts and phone calls nearly knocked him off his feet. She looked beyond beautiful to him, practically luminescent. Her blue-gray eyes held a soft glow, as if lit by candles.

He wasn't the only one who noticed.

Ben started to move toward her, but Tobias stepped in front of him and cut him off.

"Hi Carolyn. Nice to see you again. Happy Christmas Eve."

"Same to you." As they formally shook hands, Tobias felt something in his heart expand. Her presence, her golden glow, that secret light in her eyes just for him, made everything else fade away.

Ben shouldered past him. "Hi there. I'm Ben Knight, the handsome brother."

Carolyn's soft lips curved in a smile. He'd come so close to kissing her back in Evergreen. Why had he let anything stop him? He should have followed the invitation in her eyes and shoved her up against the counter and plundered her sweet mouth the way he'd wanted.

Where was that mistletoe again?

"Nice to meet you, Ben," Carolyn said politely. "Thanks for including me in your Christmas."

"You are welcome any time. Any holiday. New Year's Eve, Martin Luther King Day, what's after that? Groundhog Day? You're welcome to that one over and over again."

She laughed. Tobias ground his teeth together. Did fucking Ben have to be so damn charming? All the girls thought he was cute and funny, but they didn't know that his heart was walled off and couldn't be touched. He ought to have a "damaged goods" sticker plastered across his chest.

Funny that he had to contend with Ben, not his other brother. In fact, he couldn't even see Aiden in the crowd. Maybe he was off somewhere with Daisy.

That was what *he* wanted—to be off somewhere with Carolyn. Alone.

He elbowed Ben aside. "Would you like a tour of the house, Carolyn?"

"Why would she want a tour?" Ben scoffed. "She's here for dinner, not real estate."

"I'd love to see the house," Caro said quickly. "This area used to have so many of these old Victorian farmhouses, but most have been torn down."

"Are you a fan of local architecture?" Ben asked in surprise.

"She's a professor. They know things," Tobias growled as he took Caro's arm.

"Adjunct professor," she explained. "I don't have my PhD yet, let alone tenure—"

"Excuse us." God, was she going to tell Ben her whole life story? Tobias guided Carolyn toward a side door, away from his nosy and flirtatious brother. "How about if I show you the outside first? There's a classic old barn we use as a gym."

"Sure, sounds good. A gym. How interesting." She slid a sidelong glance along his chest, her eyes brimming with mirth.

He couldn't help it—he touched her shoulder. Her feather

soft hair brushed against the back of his hand. He ached to slide his hand along the satin curve of her cheek. The light floral fragrance she wore drifted into his nostrils, so intoxicating he felt drunk from the sweet combination of nutmeg and cinnamon and flowers.

He leaned his head closer, forgetting where he was and who might be watching. She tilted her head up and he saw that her eyes had gone a deep storm-blue, her pupils widening with the same adrenalized desire that ran through his veins.

Oh man. This was freaking combustible. How was he going to get through an entire party without giving away how much he wanted her?

"Tobias," came a young, angry voice. "Can I talk to you for a second?"

He snapped back to reality. *Aiden.* Sweet Jesus, he'd nearly forgotten about Aiden and the real reason he should have nothing to do with Carolyn.

Guilt flooded through him. "Uh, sure. Carolyn, if you'd like a drink, there's mulled wine and spiced apple cider over there, and I can join you in a minute."

She nodded, offering Aiden a tentative smile. "Hi Aiden. I'm glad to see you survived finals week."

Aiden's return smile looked more like a snarl. "Hi Professor Moore. I really need to talk to my brother for a second."

"Of course." With a narrow-eyed glance at Tobias, she headed in the direction of the bar Merry had set up on an old mahogany side table. He could guess what that look meant. *Why the hell didn't you tell Aiden I was going to be here? If he's upset, I'm leaving.*

Damn it.

He followed Aiden into the first floor guest bedroom, which was being used as a coatroom, the bed piled with winter coats and scarves. "Listen, Aiden, I'm really sorry I didn't—"

"What's going on between you and Professor Moore?" Aiden folded his arms across his chest and glared at Tobias.

"I wasn't...there isn't...it's not what you think..." Good lord, was he stammering? He sounded like a kid busted for breaking curfew.

"Don't bother to defend yourself," Aiden continued in that severe voice. "I get it. She's attractive. She's beautiful. She's smart." *Oh hell.* Did Aiden still have a crush on her after all? "I know she is. And I'm sorry I didn't warn you she was com—"

"But don't be fooled, T. She's not how she seems."

Tobias snapped his mouth shut. That didn't sound like a boy with a crush.

"She *smokes*," Aiden said, horror in his voice. "And she has a *tattoo.* Like a really tacky one, not a cool one. At first I thought she was amazing, really kind and intelligent. But that is completely *not* how she is. You should stay far away from her."

"Well." Tobias cleared his throat. "Thanks for the warning. Maybe I can convince her to quit smoking."

"That would be a start. But she still wouldn't deserve you. She *doesn't like dogs.* What kind of person doesn't like dogs? No one you can trust, that's for sure."

"Maybe she's more of a cat person," Tobias ventured.

"A *cat person*? Like that would be better? You're making excuses for her. Seriously, learn from my experience, Tobias."

"I'm more than ten years older than you," he pointed out. "I've been to war."

"Yes, but love is a lot harder than war."

Now wasn't that the damn truth. "That's...uh...thanks for the warning, Aiden. Got it."

But Aiden wasn't through yet. "Do you promise to stay away from her?" he demanded.

"What?" Tobias scowled at his little brother. "That's taking it too far, bro."

"Is it? Really? Why?"

"Because I can handle my own life. You don't have to get in the middle of it."

Suddenly all the hostility vanished from Aiden's face, replaced by a big grin. He formed the shape of a gun with his fingers and pointed at Tobias. "*Exactly.*" He pretended to blow the smoke from the gun. "Gotcha."

Tobias shook his head, bewildered by his sudden switch in attitude. "What are you talking about, gotcha?"

"You came to Evergreen to interfere with *my* love life, and now you know how it feels. It sucks."

"That's different." Frustrated, Tobias ran a hand across his scalp, feeling the thick new growth of hair. "You're young, you lost your head over an older woman. I didn't want anyone to take advantage of you. I was trying to keep you from screwing up your life."

"Which is the *only* reason why I'm still speaking to you."

Tobias closed his eyes, inwardly cursing himself. Yeah, maybe he'd been a little overbearing. A little too 'brother knows best.' "Sorry, dude. Point taken. No more interfering. Daisy's awesome, by the way. But you know that."

"Yeah, I know." Aiden adjusted the cuffs of his cable-knit sweater. "By the way, there's something else you might want to know about Professor Moore."

Tobias's heart sank. If Aiden was this antagonistic to Carolyn, how could he justify getting involved with her? He couldn't. "What's that?"

"I never had a crush on her."

16

It took a moment for that to sink in. "What?"

Aiden grinned at Tobias's stunned expression. "It was Melanie, the girl in the front row of that art history class. The one with the long blond hair. Just thought you might want to know."

Tobias scrubbed a hand across his scalp. "So Carolyn wasn't the golden goddess?"

"She might be *your* golden goddess. But she's a little old for me." Aiden couldn't hold back his laughter anymore. It bubbled out in long snorting hoots.

"But—how—who—what—"

"I was crazy hung up on Melanie but she's a senior graduating early. I decided to transfer to JPCC so I could be with you guys. I wasn't going to waste my trust fund, I just wanted...well, her family's loaded. I wanted to impress her. It was dumb."

"So what changed?"

"When you came to Evergreen, it actually helped. It brought me back to reality, I guess. When we talked about Daisy, I remembered how she always had my back. I called Daisy and she freaked. She said if I left Evergreen she'd kill me. She told me to suck it up and if Melanie wasn't interested unless I had money, she didn't deserve me."

"Smart girl."

Aiden broke into another grin. "Also, it cracked me up that you thought it was Professor Moore. That angel was awesome. Fakest tattoo I ever saw."

Tobias gaped at him. "So you *knew?* About the fake tattoo and the rest?"

"I saw you two talking. At the Caf, after I stormed off in a huff, I felt stupid for doing that. I came back and saw her helping you pick up those cheese puffs. There was just something about the way you looked at each other, I thought, hmm. Then you were asking me about all my likes and dislikes, and I thought that was weird. I kind of put it together when she showed up for my teacher meeting with a pack of cigarettes. She didn't even know how to hold a cigarette right. It was pretty funny, so I decided to play along with it."

The kid looked so pleased with himself, Tobias couldn't even be mad that he and Carolyn had been completely played. He threw back his head and laughed, long and hard, until his stomach muscles hurt. "Shit. You've been five steps ahead of me this whole time, haven't you?"

"Pretty much." Aiden grinned. "I have to admit, revenge is sweet."

"All I can say is, you better watch your back. My revenge will be even sweeter."

"Dude. Forget revenge. Go after Carolyn. You like her, don't you? Ben's probably already snagged a date with her, knowing him."

Tobias's smile dropped. "Ben knows she's off-limits. I gave him the glare. He knows exactly what that means."

"Whatever. Feel free to take your chances." Aiden shrugged and headed for the door. Tobias followed this time. As he pushed open the door, the sounds of laughter and Christmas music flowed past them like a welcoming river of joy.

"One more thing." Tobias snagged the sleeve of Aiden's sweater before he could disappear into the crowd. "You're really okay with me and Carolyn uh...getting together?"

"Totally. She's cool. Like I said, I thought she was kind and intelligent until she got that tattoo." With a big grin, he slipped into the crowd of guests.

Tobias hung back, taking a moment to fill his lungs with the scent of Christmas cookies and the big Douglas fir Christmas tree in the corner. Best Christmas present ever—he wouldn't be crushing Aiden's heart if he spent time with Carolyn. The field was clear. It had always been clear. He could have kissed her weeks ago and it would have been fine with Aiden. How much damn time had he already wasted?

Scanning the guests, he caught sight of Carolyn chatting with a group that included Police Chief Benson, Gabriela and her husband, and of course his brother Ben.

Damn it. He caught Carolyn's eye and beckoned to her. He wanted to get her alone. Had to get her alone. If he joined her over there, in the thick of the party, they'd both be stuck making chitchat about Jupiter Point town gossip. The only thing he wanted to talk about was the fact that nothing stood in the way of them getting together.

Unless it was Ben, that weasel.

He glared at his brother, who caught a glimpse of his face and flinched with exaggerated alarm. There. That was the signal they both knew from all their nights at the local bars. That meant Carolyn was *his*.

Unless she didn't want him, of course. Ben had a way of winning women over in record time. Tobias had seen him work his magic and it was truly impressive. Tobias didn't have any particular claim on Carolyn. If she preferred Ben, there wasn't much Tobias could do about it, other than try to win her back.

Or win her for the first time, to be completely accurate.

She excused herself from the group and walked toward him. As she drew closer, his entire body went into a hyper-aware state in which everything moved slowly and his blood pounded through his ears. Her soft blue eyes clouded with concern as she reached him. "Are you okay? You look funny, like you just got some bad news."

He shook his head, then took her hand and drew her down the hallway and out the side door. The crisp air nipped at his face. Jupiter Point didn't get especially cold in the winter, and it rarely snowed. But as winter advanced, the night sky grew clearer and more sparkly, and the air tasted like chilled champagne.

"Are you cold?" he asked her, his voice gruff with the need to touch her.

"No, it feels good to get a breath of fresh ai—"

The rest of that sentence ended in a gasp as his mouth descended on hers. As their lips met, the shock of brilliant pleasure made his head spin. His arms went around her, his hands splayed across her middle back. She molded her body against his and raised herself onto her tiptoes. Her mouth opened under his, slick and sweet and warm and eager.

Better than the first taste of ripe peach on a summer day, better than diving into the creek behind their old house, better than whipped cream for breakfast or a cozy sleeping bag on a cold mountain night...their kiss blew every other sweet, lost moment out of his head. Kissing Carolyn instantly became the new best thing in the world; he felt drunk with it, wild with it.

He stroked the curve of her back, moving his hands upwards until he was cradling her head, that soft waterfall of hair tumbling over his fingers. He slanted his mouth over hers, greedy, desperate for more of that electric intoxication. He grew hard, his cock pounding with arousal against the warm cradle of her thighs. She shifted her legs apart a tiny bit to accommodate him; that one movement nearly killed him.

They could do this. She was willing. She wanted him, and God, how he wanted her.

A sound from inside—someone laughing and opening the refrigerator—bought him back to his senses. He drew away, expelling a harsh exhale of breath from his lungs. "Jesus."

She put a hand to her lips. Dazed, she blinked at him. "What...um...wow."

"You weren't the golden goddess."

She wrinkled her forehead as if he'd lost his mind. "What was that?"

"Aiden's golden goddess, the one he had a crush on. Turns out it wasn't you."

"Right, because I did the tattoo and the smoking and the—"

"No. It never was you. It was a girl in your class, some blonde girl."

She stared at him, then burst into laughter. "Melanie Blake? Melanie's the golden goddess? Okay, mister, you're in big trouble. You're telling me I dropped ash on my favorite jacket and hurt poor Dragon's feelings for nothing?"

He looped his arms around her shoulders. "I know, my reconnaissance skills are for shit. I'm sorry. I think I took one look at you and figured you had to be the one. Who would notice anyone else with you in the room?"

Her breath caught through her laughter. "Good save, but boy do I feel ridiculous. I hope Aiden never finds out that I thought he had a crush on me."

"Um..."

She swatted his forearm. "He already knows, doesn't he?"

Tobias winced, twisting his face into something that hopefully indicated apology. "He knew at the time. He says he played along because he thought it was pretty funny."

"Oh God. That's mortifying." She buried her face in her hands. "Please tell him *you're* the one who thought it was me. I never really believed it."

He rubbed her shoulder, both to comfort her and because he loved touching her. "It's okay, I swear. I'll take all the blame. He still thinks you're cool, in case that matters."

"*Cool*? I had a fake crying angel tattoo on my arm!"

"He said it was awesome." He pried her hands away from her face, which was still filled with both laughter and mortification. "Sweetheart, I think you're missing the main point here. I can kiss you now without worrying about hurting Aiden's feelings. There's nothing standing between us anymore. All those deep dark fantasies I've been having about luring you into my bed...I don't have to feel bad about those anymore."

She ran her tongue across her lips. The pink tip traced the seam, then disappeared as she folded her lips together. "You called me sweetheart."

"Yeah. Is that okay? It just came out. Sweetheart." The tenderness in his voice surprised him. He hadn't known that he had it in him. He couldn't stop looking at her mouth and remembered just how delicious she tasted—and wondering when he could taste more.

"What are we doing here, Tobias?" The sound of his name, spoken in her soft voice, felt like an audible caress.

"Whatever we want. I can tell you what I want." He moved his hands to her hips, spreading his fingers apart so he touched both her hipbones. What he wanted to do was tug her against the bulge that graphically proved how much he wanted her. But he waited, needing to make sure she was on the same page with this.

"Okay, so tell me." Her warm breath, scented with cinnamon and cloves from the cider, wafted across his face. "You've been confusing me for weeks now. At first I was the bad guy. Then Dragon and I were victims in need of saving. Then I was the hero because I got a fake tattoo. But then you promised not to try to kiss me. And then you *did* kiss me. I have a small case of whiplash going on here."

"It's pretty damn simple. I want you. Even back at Evergreen I wanted you. I also want you to be safe. And I also don't want to hurt Aiden. I'm here for this. One hundred percent. Ball's in your court, babe. You're a smart, beautiful, sweetheart of an art history professor. You might not want anything to do with someone like me. I didn't even go to college, just flight school and Green Platoon training, and the school of life. A roughneck like me and a refined, educated sort like you...I don't know. Maybe you're not feeling it."

With his thumbs, he traced light circles on her lower back. If she wasn't feeling it now, maybe he could *inspire* her to feel it. Her eyes half closed. "You signed up to defend our country instead of going to college. How could I hold that against you?"

"If it's any help, after I got back to Jupiter Point, I signed up for some online courses. I might even take a few at JPCC. I heard they have some hot teachers over there. I have a feeling a degree might be in my future."

Her eyes flew open and she scanned his face in surprise. He hadn't mentioned anything about this new direction—he hadn't even told his brothers. It was so new, and he wasn't sure it would work out. His school days seemed like an eon ago.

"A degree in what?" she asked.

"Don't laugh."

"I won't. I swear. Why would I laugh?"

"Doing something like this at my age..."

"What are you, thirty-something?"

He nodded, amused by her enthusiastic reaction. It figured a teacher would be in favor of degrees. But once she knew what he was interested in...well, that was where the laughter might come in.

"Tobias, I promise I won't laugh. I think older students are great. We have quite a few at JPCC. They bring so much experience with them. They're very focused and committed. Especially someone like you, who's been in the military and spent time in war zones. So what are you interested in studying?"

He cleared his throat. "Nonviolent communication."

Her eyebrows lifted, her mouth dropped; her whole face opened up into an expression of joyous laughter. "Are you kidding? The warrior Night Stalker Tobias Knight wants to learn how to communicate without violence?"

"It's a tool in the toolbox. Why not?" Feeling suddenly awkward, he started to draw his hands away from her hips, but she stopped him by clamping her hands on his forearms.

"I think it's great. Believe me. I thought you were sexy before, but you just shot up to the red zone of sexiness." She stepped farther into the circle of his embrace. The way she filled his arms, so warm and pliable and vibrant, made his heart sing.

"The red zone." He dipped his head to sniff the sweet fragrance of her hair. "What happens in the red zone?"

"All your deep dark fantasies come true," she whispered.

17

EVER SINCE SHE'D WALKED INTO THE KNIGHT FAMILY FARMHOUSE
and spotted Tobias in a sweater in the same midnight blue as his
eyes, Carolyn had been existing in a feverish fog of desire. God,
the way he looked at her, the way he moved across the room, all
long legs and coiled tension. It went right to her head, even faster
than the mulled wine. Here at home, surrounded by family and
friends, he looked more relaxed, smiled more easily. His hair had
grown out more since she'd seen him at Evergreen, and the extra
length brought out the strong molding of his cheekbones and the
dark sweep of his eyebrows.

He was no longer the Man in Black; now he was the man who
made her heart light up.

And then he'd swept her behind the house and mentioned
deep dark fantasies and her entire body was now melting into a
puddle of want. Every time he touched her, her desire ratcheted
up to another level. She wanted to lose herself in his dark, quiet
intensity, in that deep heart, that powerful spirit.

As soon she used that phrase, "deep dark fantasies," she felt
his body tense.

"Don't tease me," he warned, pulling away so he could see her face.

"Hm, who's teasing who here? You're the one who dragged me out here to show me your 'barn.'"

"So this is real? You want this too? Because I gotta tell you, Caro, you've been on my mind nonstop since I met you. And that's never happened to me before. This is something different for me. I don't know how to explain it. You do something to me, something crazy."

Another throb of lust struck, like someone plucking a cello string deep inside her. "Me too," she confessed.

"So we're doing this? You're with me? I keep wanting to touch you, to keep you close, but I want to make sure you're feeling the same sort of things."

She reached up and touched his cheek, wondering at the concern in his eyes. For such a big, powerful man, he showed a lot of sensitivity. "You don't need to worry so much. Haven't you noticed the way I can't keep my hands off you either? If you like, I can write you a ten-page report on all the dirty thoughts I've had about you over the past couple months."

His eyes darkened to deepest twilight. Inside the back door, someone did something that involved bottles and glass, creating a dissonant noisy chime.

He winced at the interruption. "There might be one problem," he murmured

"You have a houseful of people?"

"I'd kick them all out, but that's not exactly the Christmas spirit."

"Bad Grinch."

He nuzzled her hair again, sending sweet drugging waves of pleasure across her skin. "What's going on at your place?"

"No Christmas spirit whatsoever. I haven't even unpacked yet. I just drove back today."

"Is there floor space? Wall space? Either of those will do." His deep, dark growl made her weep with desire.

She stepped back and took both his hands in hers. She loved the way his big palms engulfed hers, the rough surface creating such delicious friction. "We can't just skip out on Merry's party. She might be hurt. She's worked so hard on it. She actually took a week off from the newspaper to make everything perfect, and you know what a workaholic she is."

He groaned, all exaggerated frustration. "Damn it. Why do everyone else's feelings keep getting in my way? First Aiden, now Merry. When is it my fucking turn?"

"A little Christmas spirit won't kill you. Come on. We'll stay at least for the baked brie and the apricot strudel. Also, I think Merry's mother is going to sing for us. Apparently in Brazil they eat Christmas Eve dinner precisely at ten, then at midnight they make a toast and exchange presents."

"*Midnight*?" He looked so appalled she had to laugh.

"We don't have to stay that long. Merry knows I just got back. A little longer, that's all. I don't want to look too obvious." She tugged his hand to guide him back inside.

"Fine, as long as you know that no matter what Christmas-related thing is going on, there's only one thing on my mind."

"Really?" She pushed open the door. The smell of melting cheese and bread nearly made her forget that there was an insanely sexy man right behind her, one who wanted her as badly as she wanted him. "What's that?"

"You, wearing nothing but that bit of holly in your hair," he murmured in her ear.

She giggled, her face turning pink as the guests in the kitchen turned to welcome them back. Merry, Ben, Will, Merry's mother. On every face she noted the same knowing expression.

Jeez, was it that obvious after all?

Merry winked at her and gave her a surreptitious thumbs-up.

Gabriela lifted a glass of champagne in their direction and executed a sexy, sly wiggle of her hips.

Will took one look at them and pointed toward the arched opening that led to the living room. "The mistletoe's that way," he said, smirking.

THE REST of the party passed in a hectic blur of laughter, a divine performance of "Silent Night" by Gabriela, chitchat with the other guests, and the intoxicating joy of secret touches from Tobias. A little finger linked around hers. The brush of his hip against her. A warm hand on her lower back.

With Tobias's air of restrained power, she wouldn't have pegged him as a physically demonstrative man, but he was. Maybe he was comfortable with anything physical. And didn't that thought make her want to swoon.

Finally, it was time to go. With a flurry of warm hugs and kisses, she said goodbye and raced home, taking the curves of the dark highway that led back to Jupiter Point much faster than she usually did. If she got enough of a head start, she could do at least a little cleanup at home before Tobias showed up. Maybe shove aside some boxes, possibly make the bed. At the very least, she could dig out her nicest lingerie from her suitcase. Where had she put it again?

But none of that mattered, because a few seconds after she'd flown through the door, tossed her purse on the couch, and stashed her plate of leftovers in the fridge, someone rang her doorbell.

"It's me," Tobias reassured her in a low voice.

She flung open the door. He filled her doorway, all broad shoulders and long legs and smoldering dark eyes. "How the heck did you get here, by jet pack?"

"Nope." He stepped inside and nudged the door shut. "I'm running on a special kind of fuel called, 'I want Carolyn and I want her now.' It's like a turbo boost." He swept her into his arms and lifted her off her feet. With the front of her body clasped tight against his, she experienced an intense and fiery rush of lust. She went weak in his arms, her heart fluttering madly. She wrapped her legs around his hips, her dress falling back to her thighs. She was still wearing her shoes, a pair of bronze high heels that made her legs look extra sexy.

"Here's what I want," he growled. "I want to strip this gorgeous dress off you. I want you in nothing but your underwear and those sexy-ass shoes."

She managed to squeak some kind of response, but it was nothing coherent. She felt the hard bulge of his erection pressing between her legs, and that sensation pretty much blotted out everything else. He took it for what it was—complete and total agreement—and marched toward her bedroom, carrying her with him as if she weighed nothing.

Her sweet little two-bedroom cottage had never seen anything like Tobias Knight. She'd bought this house because it was hidden from the street by a riot of rose bushes. Carolyn had imagined herself growing old here, a happy spinster tending her flowers and grading her papers. It was a serene haven, safe from the craziness of her past. That lonely but peaceful vision of the future had seemed inevitable.

She'd definitely never imagined being carried to the back bedroom by a six-foot-plus tower of power, a honed hunk of raw manhood.

And loving it. Every flex of his muscles against her, every heave of his lungs, the warmth of his breath against her cheek, the smell of wood smoke and pine needles caught in his sweater...it all swirled together in a cocktail of pure intoxication.

Inside the bedroom door, she slid out of his grasp. He helped her get her feet on the floor. "What's wrong?"

"The bed. I have sheets here somewhere." She looked around the room in a daze, all memory of her previous household arrangements gone. Her mattress was bare, she knew that much. But at the moment, she couldn't think how to fix that.

"Here." Tobias strode to a box in the corner, from which a sheet peeked. He ripped open the box and pulled out a pretty apricot cotton sheet that she'd taken to Evergreen and back again. He flung it on top of the bed. "Satisfied?"

She looked at it and burst out laughing. It was a bottom sheet, but he hadn't bothered to tuck its corners around the mattress. It just lay there, a bunched-up sheet on a mattress, and he couldn't care less, because he wanted *her*. It didn't matter where.

"Hang on." Making a tease out of it, she bent over to properly fit the sheet to her mattress. She felt his gaze on her, scalding hot. When she was done, she straightened up and crooked one finger at him.

He was on her in two strides. They tumbled onto the bed. She laughed with pure joy at the feeling of his rock-solid body against hers. He settled between her legs, and with a long, lingering motion, he dragged his groin against hers. They were both still completely clothed. Only their combined layers of clothing kept her from sliding right into a screaming orgasm. Judging from the tense strain on his face, he felt the same way.

It drove her wild, the sight of his dark head bending over her while he pushed her dress to the top of her legs. He inhaled deeply, as if he'd been craving the intimate scent of her. The scent of her arousal. God, it was so obvious how much she wanted him. She was drenched with it.

And with a man like Tobias, she'd never have to hide that. She'd never have to feel the kind of shame she'd felt at the compound. With Tobias, she could be free and wild and he'd love it.

"Sit up," he said in a voice that was all gravel and heat. That voice alone might do it to her, she thought as she raised herself into a sitting position. He reached behind her and unzipped her dress, the slow descent of the zipper bringing the prickle of air

Coming In Hot   139

against her skin. He tugged one sleeve off her arm, then the other. The two pieces fell forward, exposing her chest and the sheer ivory bra she wore underneath.

She wouldn't have chosen it as her sexiest lingerie, but now that she saw his expression, maybe she should rethink that.

With burning eyes, he scanned her breasts. Under his gaze, her nipples hardened to deep red points against the sheer fabric of her bra.

"Damn," he breathed. "You put all my fantasies to shame, Caro." He bent his head and put his mouth over one nipple, his hot breath steaming against the sensitive flesh. With his teeth, he dragged the sheer fabric against her nipple. She cried out and arched her back. "That's right. Show me how it feels." The words sent more hot air against the tender flesh, which puckered even more.

She moved to get her dress out of the way, but he stopped her by firmly pressing her arms against the mattress with both hands. A dark thrill rampaged through her. "For God's sake, Tobias."

"Stay still or I might lose it," he growled. "I'm hanging by a thread as it is."

So was she. She could barely stop from thrashing all over the place. The only thing that stopped her was knowing that she was in the hands of a master. Everything told her so—the power of his restraint, the slow control of his movement, his intense, dreamy focus.

He lavished her breasts with attention, as if he had all eternity to drive her mad. He feasted on her, savoring each stroke of his tongue and scrape of his teeth against her flesh. Her nerves sizzled, deep pulses of electricity leaping from the tips of her breasts to the core of her being. The bra disappeared, she barely knew how.

His mouth left her briefly so he could strip the rest of her clothes off her. While he was busy doing that, she existed in a pool of flame, her breasts craving the return of his touch. It was addictive, the sensation of that wet devilish tongue teasing her flesh. Her nipples felt enormous, practically obscene, swollen to wet peaks of throbbing desire.

When she was naked—except for her shoes, which he put back on her feet—he pulled her to the edge of the bed and tugged her into a standing position. "Now that's the fantasy I've been thinking about all night. Look at you." He shaped the curve of her waist, ran his hands across the bare slope of her ass. A little dizzy from the sensations pouring through her body, she balanced naked on her high heels.

Seeing the hot excitement on his face, she cocked her hip and arched her chest, making more of a pose out of it.

He growled deep in his broad chest. "Good lord, woman. You're trying to give me a stroke, aren't you?"

"Not a chance. Not until you make me come." She reached up and twisted her hand in the neck of his sweater.

Okay then. Tobias's raw sexuality was rubbing off on her, apparently. She didn't usually say that kind of thing. It felt...liberating.

"Not just come, but come hard," she added, feeling her cheeks turn pink as the raunchy words left her.

But he didn't blink an eye. A wicked grin spread across his face. "At your service." He kneeled on the floor and blew on the mound of curls at the juncture of her thighs. His hot breath scalded her already screaming nerve endings.

She gasped and grabbed onto his shoulders as he cupped her sex. His long fingers grazed across her curls, then brushed her clit lightly. No fumbling here, nothing tentative, no doubt about where her most sensitive spot might be. This man knew exactly where it was and what to do with it. His thumb slid across the tight knot of nerves, stroking the seam of her lips, tangling in her curls. He tugged lightly at her hair, pulling a gasp from her. Then he went back to her clit, slip-sliding through the thick moisture, drawing hot ribbons of pleasure in his wake.

Direct, full-on, Grade-A, pedal-to-the-metal fondling, by a master of the technique.

She started babbling mindlessly, letting him know how good that felt, how amazing his hands were, how much she wanted him.

Hot strokes, more pressure, more friction, rising and building and moaning and pushing and...oh my God. *Exploding.* In a white-hot burst, fierce waves overtook her, rushed through her body and emptied her mind. *So good.* So good. Sweet exultant joy turned her tongue thick, her brain hazy. She hung over him, letting him support her while she rode out every last twitch and spasm of her orgasm.

"Oh my God," she moaned finally, when words came back to her. "I don't even...I can't even..."

She needed more time to recover. She heaved in a long breath, her entire body tingling. Gradually things came back to her, like the fact that she was still draped over Tobias, and that she still wore her heels, and that with her legs this shaky, she might break her neck.

Shaking her head, almost laughing at the intensity of that orgasm, she straightened up. She toed off her shoes and kicked them away. He was still on his knees, watching her, breathing fast.

"Any chance you have a, um, Christmas Eve condom with you?" she asked, still a little breathless herself.

He stood up, towering over her now that she was barefoot and he still wore his boots. Like a genie answering a wish, he pulled a condom from his back pocket.

"Just so you know, I didn't have this at the party," he told her. "I wasn't planning all this. Ben stuffed it in my hand on my way out the door. He had it wrapped like a present."

She smiled slightly. "Just one?"

He cleared his throat and reached into his pocket again. A strip of condoms came rippling out, along with a piece of gold tinsel ribbon. "He's a jokester."

She laughed, joy fizzing through her system. She felt as if someone had replaced all her blood with laughing gas. "You Knight brothers. You're all crazy."

"We might be. Is that a problem?" He cupped his hand around her waist, heavy and warm, comforting in its solid weight.

"Nope. I like it. I don't have to be all nice and proper with you. I like the way you think, Tobias."

"Really? Wait'll you see the way I fuck."

Oh God. When he talked like that, flames ignited inside her. "You have a lot of clothes on," she said roughly. "And I've been wondering every day since you walked into my class what you might look like without them."

"Well damn. With an invitation like that..."

He put his hands to the hem of his sweater and yanked it over his head. He moved toward her, but she stopped him.

"Might as well take it all off." She gestured at the t-shirt he wore under the sweater, the dark jeans that didn't hide his erection. "Get comfortable."

He tugged off his t-shirt in one swift motion. She'd already seen him down to his undershirt, when she'd tended his scratches back in Evergreen. But taking in the complete spectacle, with no clothes at all, was something else entirely. It was like witnessing some kind of natural phenomenon. Ripples of muscles battled with ridges of sinew. A few scars broke the landscape of his skin, enhancing instead of marring it. A scattering of dark hair led the way down his chest, past the sleekly defined V of tendons near his pelvis.

Great God Almighty. "Michelangelo would have a field day with you," she murmured. "They ought to cast you in bronze. Preserve you for all eternity."

"No thanks. When it's time to go, I'll smile and say thanks for all the fish. I decided that a long time ago. Unless I say 'thanks for all the orgasms.'" He undid the top button of his jeans and unzipped himself. He wore black boxer briefs that barely contained his raging erection. He shucked his pants, then stood before her, the black-covered bulge between his legs drawing her fascinated attention.

She stepped forward and cupped her hand against the private bundle tucked into his briefs. He closed his eyes, tilted his head backwards, and released a long groan. A sense of power raced through her. This tough, battle-hardened man was completely at her mercy right now. His body was taut as a bow, rigid with desire. Electricity throbbed and sparkled between them.

Sliding her hand inside his briefs, she found hot skin and the eager thrust of his penis. He pushed his underwear down his legs, kicked it aside. Completely nude, he stood before her, a picture of pure male physicality, muscular, virile and fully, magnificently erect. His thick, hard organ protruded straight toward her, just as direct and raw as Tobias himself.

He ripped open the condom and slid it on. He came toward her and curved his hand against her mound. "I can't wait to get inside that sweet pussy."

A rush of liquid heat spiked through her lower belly. God, she could listen to his hot words all day and all night. They revved her up like nobody's business. They stood pressed together, his erection nudging the space between her legs, their bodies slick and quivering and right on the edge. Even though she'd come so hard just a few minutes ago, her body craved more. He put his hands on the globes of her ass and squeezed, rotating her hips against him.

She moaned loudly and parted her legs enough to allow his iron-hard flesh to tease her lower lips.

And then the whole room was flipped around and she was flat on her back on the bed. He braced over her, every tight muscle of his shoulders and chest standing out in sharp relief. A bead of sweat ran down his neck. His eyes smoldered with the heat of a thousand midnight suns.

"You ready?"

She appreciated the check-in, but it was so unnecessary it was almost laughable. The restless ache between her legs, the liquid weeping down her thighs, the flush on her chest—all pretty freaking obvious signs that she wanted him inside her.

"So ready," she told him. "So incredibly ready."

She closed her lips around the other words that wanted to come out. *Fuck me hard. Rip me apart. Break me into a million pieces. Shatter me, Tobias Knight. Shatter me hard.*

She might think them, but saying them aloud was still a little outside her comfort zone.

Then she forgot all about comfort zones as he felt between her legs for the place that begged for him. He stroked her again, firing up the embers of her lust with his rough, skillful fingers. Then he fisted his erection in one hand and spread her apart. Her heart fluttered in her throat, mad thoughts flying through her head as he moved inside her, claiming her inch by inch. Her inner channel opened for him, welcoming him in a tight grasp. She moaned at the sense of fullness, of surrender, of completion. So thick, so hard, so essential.

And then he stroked with deep, long thrusts in a rhythm that captured her senses and scattered her thoughts. She moved with him, emotion building in her heart, tears springing to her eyes. The tears weren't caused by any pain, but because it felt so excruciatingly magnificent. It made her feel, of all things, secure. It was the strangest belief, surfacing out of nowhere.

This powerful man was wrapped around her, deeply connected to her, and together they'd be safe.

Then even that thought disappeared as pure sensation took over. A sweet blast of ecstasy swept her into a whirlwind. Her body clenched around him, pulling him after her. He went rigid and cried out, and together they surfed the wave of pleasure to the edge of the universe and beyond.

18

"GOD DAMN," TOBIAS SWORE. THAT WAS HIS USUAL RESPONSE WHEN something spectacular happened, good or bad. Maybe it wasn't the most romantic trait, but right now he could barely form a word, let alone properly select one.

He rolled away from Carolyn, suddenly afraid he was going to squash her with his big bulk. She was so delicate and angelic-looking, even with her sweat-dampened hair clinging to her temples and her chest heaving.

Of course, he knew by now that appearances were deceiving. Carolyn was a lot tougher than she looked. And a lot wilder. That art-professor exterior hid a fiery passionate side. And he was damn grateful for that.

Her eyes were closed, her eyelashes fanned against the fragile skin underneath her eyes. A flush still burned on her cheeks.

"You okay?" he whispered, in case she'd dropped off to sleep.

"Mmmm," she mumbled. "'Okay' doesn't seem adequate. Delirious, maybe?"

"Delirious. Not bad. You saying I gave you a fever?" He stroked a finger down her soft cheek.

"Yes, you're like a virus. Really hard to get rid of."

He smiled and curled his finger around a long strand of her hair. "But why would you want to, when I'm making it my mission to make you feel good?"

"Mission accomplished," she purred, moving under his touch. "Thank you. I approve of your mission."

"I'm pretty fond of it myself. It has some nice side-benefits." He moved his finger to the breast closest to him and circled it gently. "Your breasts are a work of art. Look at this areola, it's such a pretty color, like a rose petal. And your skin is like ice cream. French vanilla."

She laughed. "Are you hungry?"

"I guess I am. I didn't eat much at the party, I was thinking about other things. Like your breasts." He grinned wickedly and touched his tongue to her nipple. The soft flesh pebbled immediately. "Can you make me a slide of this masterpiece? I want to drool over them any time I want." He took the peak of her breast into his mouth and sucked lightly.

She gave a soft gasp. "Don't get any crazy ideas. We're not doing this again until I recuperate. It's a good thing Merry gave me a plate of leftovers, because I don't have a thing in the house. Did you notice how she winked when she handed it over?"

"No. I didn't notice anything except your ass in that dress, with those heels." He slid his hand along the curves of her rib cage and waist, until her reached her rear. He lightly squeezed the smooth globes, then stroked small circles across the sensitive skin. "The first time I met you, your boots got me all hot and bothered. There's just something about your footwear, woman."

She sighed deeply. "Do you know that the first time I noticed your hands, when you were picking up cheese doodles off the pavers, I wondered what they'd feel like?"

"Really."

"Yes. It's silly, but you were so deft and gentle with those little orange puffs. It seemed crazy that hands like a bear's paws could be so precise. It made me wonder."

"So what do you think now?" He smoothed a path across her hipbone, into the valley leading to her pelvic mound. He tangled his fingers in the soft, sandy brown curls that covered her sex. So unlike his own darker skin and nearly black hair.

The contrast was arousing all on its own.

She shifted as he touched her. "Seriously," she sighed. "We should have a snack." But he noticed that she didn't move away, and made no effort to actually get off the bed. "And then we should come back and work it off."

"Now you're talking. We can finally have that rematch we keep talking about."

"Exactly." She rolled onto her side and tucked her hands under her face. "Tobias Knight."

He mimicked her seriousness. "Carolyn Moore."

"I've never had a one-night stand before."

He stilled. One-night stand? Is that what she thought this was? He'd had his share of one-nighters; it came with the territory of being at the military's beck and call. "Okay," he said warily. "That's good. They're not very satisfying."

Her eyelids flickered. "That sounds like the voice of experience."

"I've had a few. I wouldn't recommend it."

She brushed a strand of hair out of her eyes and scanned his face. "But do you know they're going to be one-night stands beforehand? Or do you decide afterwards? I've always wondered that."

He shot her a narrow-eyed look. He didn't like the direction of this conversation, not one bit. The thought of her walking away already—after one night, no, half a night—bothered him. "What are you getting at here? Do you see this as a one-night stand? Because I have something to say about that."

Her eyebrows lifted. "Like what?"

"Like, I haven't had nearly enough of you. Not even close.

Besides, this could never have been a one-night stand because the foreplay has lasted for weeks now."

"Excuse me? That was called 'getting to know each other,' not foreplay."

He shrugged. "Whatever. Back to the main point. This one-night stand concept. I'm opposed. I don't even know why you're bringing it up."

She smiled at him, and he noticed for the first time that she had the faintest trace of a dimple near her bottom lip. "Because this is different for me. I don't usually act like this. I'm a mild-mannered adjunct professor."

"Who can rock a pair of high heels like nobody's business." He ran his hand across the ridge of her hipbone. "Look, I don't know what you mean by 'act like this.' We had sex. Great sex. At least it was great for me. Is there a problem? Some reason why you never want it to happen again?"

"No. No reason." Her smile turned almost shy. "You think it was great sex?"

"Are you insane? Weren't you paying attention?" He swung himself on top of her and mimicked a shot in the heart. "It was bombs-away, fire- when-ready, nuclear-blast hot. You're a bomb-shell. If you don't know that, we have some serious work to do here."

She laughed delightedly at his little performance, and it occurred to him that growing up in that crazy compound must have done a number on her ideas about sexuality.

"Listen. I love sex, Caro. I'll never apologize for that. And you shouldn't either."

She struck an unbearably sexy pose, arms linked overhead, the tip of her tongue appearing between her lips. "So I can do stuff like this and you won't mind?"

"I'll just have to live with it."

LATER, they raided the fridge for the leftovers Merry had given Carolyn. He'd barely glanced at her living room when he'd first arrived. Now he saw that it was a small two-bedroom filled with books and framed art pieces on the walls. It had a vintage feel with its wide window sills, hardwood floors and cracked plaster walls. Cute, but it probably had plumbing problems. The place was a tumbled mess, with boxes and suitcases spilling open.

"Welcome back to Jupiter Point," he said dryly.

"Right? I guess you know what I'll be doing during this Christmas break." Wearing a robe printed with brightly colored parrots, she pulled a plate covered with tinfoil from the fridge. "I can heat this up really quickly."

"Nah, don't bother. In the military I learned to see food as fuel and I still haven't shaken it."

"Really? I'm obsessed with food. It feels like freedom to me. When I first left the Light Keepers, I was afraid of all the variety of food. Then I went crazy trying different cuisines. Greek, Ethiopian, Indian, whatever. I loved it all."

She peeled the foil off the plate to reveal a hunk of baked brie in soft layers of brioche, some pomegranate salad, cloverleaf rolls, sliced baked ham. His mouth watered at the sight.

"So this food was at the party and I didn't even notice it?" He laughed. "You really have my head spinning, woman. Normally I'd be all over a spread like this."

She laughed as she rinsed off a small plate, then filled it with a bit of everything. "I guess the magic has worn off, then. You're looking at that ham as if you want to marry it."

"Will you, piece of sliced ham, take this man, Tobias Knight, in holy matrimony, for better or worse, inside or outside the belly, in a sandwich or just rolled up and stuffed into the mouth..." He popped a slice into his mouth, enjoying her laughter at his goofiness.

"Looks like a match made in heaven. A happy life to you both," she said solemnly.

They grinned at each other as they dug into their food, sitting across from each other at the tiny cooking island that separated her living room from her kitchen. A comfortable silence settled over them. Often, after sex with a new lover, things felt awkward. But there was no sense of that with Carolyn. She knew so many things about him already—about his father, his feelings of guilt, his devotion to his brothers.

"There's something I've been wanting to talk to you about," he said, mock serious, after he'd taken the first edge off his hunger. "We need to discuss this dimple of yours?" He traced the little divot in her skin. "You must have been the cutest little kid in the world. Like a poster child for cute."

She flinched away from him, her smile disappearing off her face, along with the dimple. "Don't say that."

"Sorry. It was meant to be a compliment. You're not cute at all. You must have been a hideous child."

Finally she snorted, almost laughing, though she still wouldn't meet his eyes. "It's the term you used. Poster child. Hang on, I'll show you."

She went into the living room and crouched down next to one of the boxes. He watched the smooth line of her back and rear as she searched through the box. He loved the way she was built, so long and elegant.

Of course he also remembered what it felt like to be felled by one sweep of her right ankle. Elegant was only part of the story of Carolyn.

When she stood, she held a scrap of old newspaper slid into a laminated sheet. She handed him the newspaper clipping. It was an ad for a Light Keepers open house. Two young blond girls were hugging each other and smiling toward the camera. One of them flashed an adorable dimple. The ad read, "*Worried about your children's future? In a changing world, it's no wonder. Save your family, fight for your community. Visit us and learn how the Light Keepers can bring your family into the light.*"

"Is that you?" He squinted at the image.

"Yes. I was the poster child for the Light Keepers. The actual poster child. This photo was taken right after my dad moved us there. No one ever asked me if I wanted to be a recruitment tool. I was so embarrassed. People used to recognize me when I worked at the farm stand. It was horrible."

"Who's the other girl?"

"That was Tiffany. She was supposedly my friend. The kind of friend my dad and stepmother wanted me to have. Except I missed my *real* best friend. Her name was Mira Ahmed and she had gorgeous black wavy hair and an accent and she was hilarious. We used to laugh so hard together. She was the sister I never had and always wanted. Then my stepmother came along. She hated the fact that Mira and I were friends."

Tobias handed the photo back to her. "Just curious, why do you hang onto a photo with such bad memories?"

She tucked it back into the box. "I don't have any pictures of Mira. My dad got rid of them. But every time I look at this one, I remember her and how much I missed her. She was my *real* best friend."

"What happened to her?"

"My dad and Lilith got deeper into the Light Keepers, and all of a sudden they didn't want me to play with Mira anymore. I threw a fit, which made them decide I needed a more "wholesome" environment. So we moved into the compound." She walked back to the cooking island and slid onto her stool. "From then on, all my friends were white, just the way my stepmother wanted."

Tobias chewed on his ham sandwich. "What about Merry?"

"Now, it's different. I can choose my own friends. Of course, Merry doesn't know I was a poster child for blondness. I'm afraid to tell her."

"Knowing Merry, she'd probably laugh her ass off over it. She has a way of cutting through the bullshit."

Carolyn grinned and folded a piece of ham around a chunk of brie, then layered brioche around it. "And I love her for that. You know, when I'm hanging out with Merry, I see little things that drive me nuts. Store clerks accept my credit card without question, but she has to pull out her ID. She gets followed around in department stores, as if she's going to shoplift something. It's insulting. Merry shrugs it off, but I'm sure it hurts. It hurts *me*. I want to apologize for the whole world, for myself, for the Light Keepers. I have to bite my tongue because she probably doesn't want that. I wish I could apologize to Mira, too, for disappearing. I tried to find her after I left the Light Keepers. I never could."

"That's too bad. A good friend's like gold."

"Yes. Losing her, after my mother dying, it was really tough." She dragged a piece of brioche through a puddle of cranberry sauce. "I hope you know how lucky you are to have all those brothers."

"I can spare a couple. Want one? Not Ben, though. He might move in. Did he ask you out, by the way? At the party?"

She nearly choked on brioche she'd just popped into her mouth. "Ex*cuse* me? Of course not. I'm with—"

"With me. Exactly. Glad we cleared that up." He gave her a wolfish smile. "And that one night thing? Forget about it."

He loved watching that delicious pink color fill her face. "Who put you in charge?"

"I'm not in charge. I'm just hoping. Hoping the poster child of sexy goddesses gives me another shot."

She rolled her eyes, but the quirk at the corner of her lips gave her away. "You're ridiculous."

"I'm honest. I'd like a nice, big, life-size poster of you. Naked would be best."

She shook her head at him and swallowed her brioche. "In all my pale-skinned blondness? Ugh. Want to know something funny? After I left the Light Keepers, I got a job as a chambermaid at a hotel because they let me stay there in exchange for half my wages. I saved up and paid for a DNA test. I had all these weird feelings about being white, because they talked about it so much at the Light Keepers. I wanted to know exactly what was in my DNA. Turns out I have a certain percentage of African, another bit of Native American." She grinned widely. "It was such a relief. No more poster child for me."

"I guess you're just a mutt like the rest of us low-lifes."

"I like mutts. And dogs of all kinds." She pulled a teasing face at him. "Just don't tell Aiden."

"Have you thought about getting a dog in place of Dragon?"

"I can't, the poor thing would be stuck inside this tiny house all day while I teach. But of course I've thought about it," she admitted. "Having Dragon around was...I loved it. Closest thing I've had to a family in ten years. God, what's in this ham? Something's making me jabber on like an idiot."

"Maybe all that great sex loosened your tongue."

She stuck out her tongue at him. "I may never have sex again, in that case. It turned me into a blabbermouth."

"Now you're just being mean." He planted his forearms on the counter and leaned toward her, narrowing his eyes. "And unrealistic. It would take an asteroid hitting this house to stop us from having sex again."

He caught her quick shiver of reaction.

"Water?" she asked.

"Sure." Deflection. He was sure of it.

She pulled two glasses from a cupboard and filled them from the faucet, then handed one to him. Before he took a sip from it, he said, "There's something I've been wondering. How did you get into the field you're in? Art history?"

She drank half her glass, then set it down on the counter and climbed back onto her stool. "This might sound rather random. And seriously, are you sure you want me to keep talking? I've been going nonstop since we got out of bed."

"I love to hear you talk. Consider it more foreplay, because watching your mouth move, and all those interesting words come out of it, mm-mmmm. It's a turn-on, babe."

She tossed her hair over her shoulder and planted her elbow on the counter, pinning him with a provocative under-her-eyelashes look. "You know what's a real turn-on? You *listening* to me say all those words. Makes me want to lick up one side of you and down the other. Then I want to find that spot right in the middle where your gorgeous shaft is waiting for me. That big, thick, hot—"

"Okay, okay, you win." He shifted uncomfortably on his stool, because that big thick cock she mentioned was getting bigger and thicker with each word. "Let's just agree that you can get me turned on without hardly trying. Now back to the question."

She sighed and abandoned her flirty position. "Fine. I told you that we had our own school at the Light Keepers, right? We had math and English, stuff like that. No science or history, unless it was religious history. I don't know how it happened, but one of the books in our tiny school collection was about Italian art. It had an angel by Raphael on the cover, so somehow it slipped past the teachers. However, most of the photos in the book did not show paintings of angels."

"Let me guess. A bunch of old men in red velvet hats?"

"No." She lowered her voice, as if sharing a naughty secret. "They had naked people. Botticelli's Venus on her clamshell. A photo of Michelangelo's David, without a trace of a fig leaf. I saw his *penis*. You have no idea how revolutionary that was for me."

Tobias felt his own penis swelling in response to her story. Was that pathetic, that merely hearing her mention the word "penis" got him aroused?

"I found that book when I was thirteen or so. I was dying of curiosity about my own body, and no one would tell me anything. That book was like a lifeline to another world. In that book, bodies weren't secret or shameful somehow. I *memorized* that book. Every word, every photo. I can't even really explain what it meant to me, except it felt like home. Maybe I was Mona Lisa in a previous lifetime." She ended on a light note and dipped a finger in the mustard that had dripped onto her plate. She touched it to her tongue.

He wanted that tongue on his cock so badly, his eyes nearly crossed. He grabbed his glass of water and downed it. She smiled innocently at him. Most likely, she had no idea what a powerful effect she had on him.

"I have my master's degree," she continued, "which was enough to get hired at JPCC, but I've stalled out on my doctorate. I love the teaching part, looking at those beautiful paintings. You know back then, they were just coming out of the Dark Ages. Discovering science and rational thinking, moving away from superstition. I think I connected with that as well. But mostly, with that first book I saw, it was the naked people that got me interested."

She gave his bare chest a suggestive once-over. "And now I have one in my very own living room."

"Okay, last question. Are you done eating yet? Because I'm all fueled up and ready to go, and you're still picking at that plate of food like it has to last all year."

"It's good to eat slowly. You just shoveled yours right down your throat. That's not healthy."

"Eat fast, fuck slow, that's my motto."

A satisfying blush crept up her cheeks. "Do you always talk like that?"

"I can be refined if I have to." He put on a British accent he'd learned while stationed in England. Whenever he used it, he sounded like an old British grande dame, like Judi Dench or Maggie Smith. It used to make his fellow pilots roll on the floor with laughter. "Dah-ling, this ham and brie is absolutely divine. Now I do hope you're nearly finished, dah-ling, as my cock has swollen to the size of an overstuffed sausage and I would very much like to put it in you."

She burst out laughing. "Is that so?"

"Indeed it is, young miss. Jolly good, upsy-daisy now. Up with you and off with your clothes. You've been a naughty girl, young miss, and naughty girls belong in one place only. That would be my bed."

"I have not been a naughty girl," she pointed out. "And that bed is mine."

"Enough of this tiresome quibbling." He wrestled with the smile that wanted to take over his face. The accent cracked him up as much as it did anyone else. "Why must the common people make everything so difficult? Christmas Eve, and all I want is a jolly good fuck. Is that so much to ask?"

Still laughing helplessly, Carolyn grabbed her phone and held it up so he could see the time. "No more Christmas Eve sex for you. It's Christmas."

They both went still for a moment. Quiet settled around them. He pictured the little town of Jupiter Point, all tucked in for the night, the ring of foothills rising toward the towering mountain range to the east. Acres and miles of forests and wilderness, stretching to the far horizon. To the west, the cliffs, the waterfront, Pacific Ocean, a moonlit path across endless waves.

And right in the middle, him and Carolyn. Wrapped up together in silence.

"Oh holy night," he murmured.

A smile shimmered across her face. "Is it?"

"It is to me," he said firmly. He got to his feet, rounded the counter and drew her off her stool. "There's no place I'd rather be than right here. With you."

This time, when they came together in her bed, it felt different. Almost sacred, as if the newborn day cast a spell around them. Afterwards, falling asleep in her arms, a sense of quiet joy filtered through him, lightening the shadows in his heart.

19

CHRISTMAS WAS PROBABLY THE TOUGHEST DAY OF THE YEAR FOR Carolyn. When she was younger, she'd missed her mother terribly on Christmas. After she left the Light Keepers, the day became even lonelier. She'd gotten into the habit of volunteering somewhere on Christmas Day—a soup kitchen, a homeless shelter, wherever help was needed. This year, she'd offered to help Suzanne Marshall at the Star Bright Shelter for Teens, which offered a temporary home for runaways.

The Knight brothers were having their first Christmas together in years, now that both Tobias and Ben were out of the military. She had to admit that a sense of sharp envy filled her as he walked away, down her little walkway, past thorny winter rosebushes.

He was heading for his family, while she was alone. As always.

But she was completely wrong, as it turned out. Suzanne had recruited more friends and practically the entire crew of Jupiter Point hotshots.

Her husband, Josh, and their little daughter Faith, now a boisterous toddler, were helping out—in Faith's case, by sampling pie dough by the handful. Rollo Wareham and his fiancée Brianna Gallagher, and Lisa Peretti and her boyfriend Finn Abrams were peeling potatoes, chopping up vegetables, arguing about how long turkey should be cooked, tossing big bowls of winter greens. Evie and Sean Marcus, who were with Evie's parents, had sent a gigantic basket filled with oranges and figs and chocolates.

About twenty kids lived at the shelter; all had left home for dire reasons that Carolyn didn't know about. All she knew was that they were away from their families, and she knew exactly how that felt. She'd left because she wanted to, but being away from her father and stepmother left a big hole in her heart. Especially on Christmas.

But this Christmas, for the first time, she wasn't quite as sad. She could still feel Tobias's big warm body next to hers, his hand resting on her hip when they woke up that morning. His rumbling voice wishing her Merry Christmas, the sweet kisses he landed on her jaw to wake her up.

Shelter from the storm, that was Tobias. In his arms, she felt safe in a way she hadn't since she was a kid.

"What are you thinking about? You look like the cat who ate the cream," Suzanne said as she kept one eye on Faith, the other on the potatoes she was peeling.

"Oh, nothing. Just that it's nice to be here. I'm glad we're giving these kids a party today."

"Oh, pssssht. You can't fool me. You look different. This isn't about Christmas, it's about a man. Don't even try to deny it."

Brianna butted in from the opposite side of the long wooden table, where she was slicing up beets she'd brought from her own root cellar. Brianna was a landscaper and gardener. A green thumb and red hair—a Christmas package all on her own. "Don't drive her away with your nosiness, Suzanne. We need her or we'll never get all those potatoes peeled."

Carolyn laughed; Brianna was known for her bluntness, also known as tactlessness. But everyone knew she had a heart of gold. Especially Rollo, the banking billionaire turned firefighter who had fallen in love with her. Brianna liked to refer to Rollo and herself as the prince and the peasant girl.

If she and Tobias were in a fairy tale, which one would it be? Carolyn mulled that over. Maybe Hansel and Gretel, each cast out from their childhood homes, lost in their own wilderness.

She smiled at the silly thought. Fairy tales were just stories. They had nothing to do with reality.

"Okay, that smile. Something's going on with that smile." Suzanne tossed her long lemony hair over one shoulder. Maybe Suzanne was Rapunzel, with that long hair. Hadn't she been rescued from the roof of her house, when it burned down?

"Sorry, I was thinking about fairy tales," said Carolyn, shaking herself back to attention.

"Good ones, I hope," said Suzanne. "Some of them are terrifying. I got a collection from Fifth Book from the Sun that nearly scared my socks off. No way am I going to read them to Faith."

"You should," said Carolyn soberly. "Kids get it. They know about monsters. Fairy tales help them understand." She looked up to see the other women staring at her. "What?"

"You sound like there's a story there," said Lisa softly.

Carolyn looked away, embarrassed. She knew these women because they were friends of Merry's. But they didn't know her whole story; not even Merry did. They were all friendly and lovely, but she had no idea how they'd react to knowing she used to be the poster child of a fringe pseudo-religious militia.

Josh, Rollo and Finn came strolling over. They were all hotshots or former hotshots, which meant they fought wildfires during the summers. In the offseason they got some time to relax, in between helping out the local fire department and reconnecting with their families.

Josh, the playful one of the crew, picked up his wife Suzanne's hand and twirled her around in a dance move. "Big news, everyone," he called to the group. "Kids, gather 'round. I have a story to tell you about a little thing called a wicket."

The teenagers, a mix of girls and boys, black and white, Latino and Asian, crowded into the kitchen. "What's a wicket, Josh?" asked a boy balancing on crutches. A bruise purpled his cheek; it made Carolyn's heart ache.

"I'm so glad you asked. A wicket, my friends, is something you use in a game called croquet. The famous Knight brothers happen to own a set. Y'all know the Knight brothers, who run that flightseeing service with the little planes?"

Carolyn felt a full-body flush sweep through her at the mention of the brothers.

"They just called me and challenged us to a match. The winning team gets a free flight along the coast. What do you guys say? Do we accept the challenge?"

Everyone cheered, the kids jumping up and down and clapping. Everyone except Carolyn, who was frozen with joy. Tobias was going to be here after all?

She fanned her face, which had gone hot and pink, and just happened to catch Suzanne's eye. Her blond friend winked at her, as if she knew exactly what Carolyn was thinking.

So much for discretion.

Then again, did it really matter? Was there something wrong with her and Tobias engaging in a mature, adult, X-rated affair? No, not at all. Was there something wrong with people knowing about it?

Half an hour later, the Knight brothers arrived in Tobias's Land Rover, pulling into the driveway with an emphatic screech of brakes. Watching through the kitchen window, Carolyn felt her heartbeat spike as they jumped out of the vehicle. Never step when you can jump—that could have been a Knight family motto, from what she'd seen.

They were such a physical family. The combination of the four of them was like a neutron bomb of sexy. Will, the oldest, tall and gray-eyed, his every move like a slow drawl. Ben had the most carefree appeal, his lips already curved around a joke. Aiden, the baby of the family, the ultimate surfer kid with his blond bedhead.

And then there was Tobias. If you could distill the core appeal of the Knight brothers to one man, you would get Tobias. Independent thinker, rebellious, fierce, strong, protector of the vulnerable and champion of the misfit. That was Tobias.

The teenagers knew it, too. As the kids gathered around to meet the brothers, Carolyn kept sneaking glances in between potatoes. Their voices drifted into the kitchen, introductions, laughter. She noticed how they flocked to Tobias, even though he was the scariest looking of the bunch. His aura of "don't-give-a-fuck" power paired with a core of deep-down kindness—kids picked up on that kind of thing.

He was especially kind to the boy on crutches, the one with the bruise. He gave his cast a thumbs up and offered to team up with him on the croquet field. Her heart pulsed as she watched him. How could such a powerful-looking man be such a softy inside?

The men she'd known at the Light Keepers weren't like this. They liked to control things, they wanted wives who would do their bidding. They didn't consider a teenager worth listening to, especially a female teenager. Listening and kindness were considered women's work; men were supposed to be deferred to in all situations.

Fortunately, Tobias's similarities to the men from the compound were only on the surface. He relied on his physical strength, his power, as they did. He knew his weapons, just like the Brigade men, but that was because he was former military. But he was different in some fundamental ways. For example, he respected her. He treated her like an equal.

She turned back to her task and shook off all thoughts of the

Light Keepers. What she and Tobias shared had nothing to do with them. The past was over and gone.

A deep voice spoke in her ear. "I pick you for my team."

Tobias. She swung around, feeling a rush of delight at his nearness. He held a grocery bag and sported a freshly shaven face and a big grin. "I'm not playing. I've got potatoes to peel."

"We can help." Aiden stepped to Tobias's side, glancing from one to the other of them. He didn't seem worried about whatever was going on between his former teacher and his big brother.

"Hi Aiden. Merry Christmas."

He gave her an innocent smile. "Merry Christmas to you. May the angels smile upon you."

She laughed. "I have a feeling I'll never live that down."

"That's a good bet. Knight brothers never miss an opportunity for teasing."

"You be nice, or I'll start smoking again," Tobias told his little brother in a stern voice, a smile playing at the corner of his lips. Aiden made a disgusted face at him.

"Where's Merry? How's the family Christmas going?"

"Merry took her mother to the airport. She has a gig tomorrow," Tobias explained.

"And we decided that we wanted to share the Knight family love," added Aiden with a grin. "Merry got us this croquet set as a joke, but we plan to conquer the world with it. Starting here."

Tobias put the grocery bag on the long table. "We brought some leftovers from last night's party. Aiden practically cried when we voted to give up the chocolate torte."

"I did not." Aiden scowled at him. "I simply made the point that some people are allergic to chocolate and it would make more sense to bring the fruitcake Aunt Mary sent us."

Tobias made a secret face of disgust for Carolyn's benefit. "Some of the candied fruit literally looks like bioluminescent mold. We didn't want to scare anyone."

"So." Aiden's smile dropped and he fixed Carolyn with a challenging glance. "You and my brother."

She folded her arms across her chest, trying to hide her panic. "Mmm, hmm?"

"You probably know by now that our father is dead. So we like to watch out for each other."

Tobias shot Aiden a warning look. "Where are you going with this?"

"You hauled your nosy ass to Evergreen, now it's my turn."

"That was different," Tobias growled.

"I don't see how." Aiden pushed back the sleeves of his sweater, looking unnervingly businesslike. "First of all, let me say that I already know my grade, or I would not be daring to have this conversation."

"Very wise," she said gravely.

"So ... what are your intentions toward my brother? Do you realize that those muscles are just the tip of the Tobias iceberg? And that he's not an iceberg at all, even though he can look a little intense?"

"I have figured that out, yes. It's true that I nearly called security on him when he first turned up in class. But I have since discovered a different side of him."

"This is completely unnecessary," said Tobias, turning a little red in the face. "Carolyn, ignore him. I swear to God, a kid goes to college and all of a sudden he thinks he rules the world."

"Wait, I'm not done," Aiden said stubbornly. "Professor Moore, did you know that Tobias personally saved an entire village in Afghanistan? He got them to evacuate just before a bomb hit a dam nearby. He got a Silver Star for that. The only reason he hasn't gotten a Purple Heart is that—"

Tobias clamped a hand on his brother's shoulder and marched him away, sending Carolyn an apologetic glance over his shoulder. She bit her lip to keep from laughing. Honestly,

Aiden had no need to fluff Tobias up to impress her. But it was pretty cute that he wanted to.

Carolyn took a break from her potato peeling and stepped outside for a breath of air, and to watch the chaos of twenty teenagers and a bunch of adults ready a course for croquet. Josh, deep into an intense discussion with Will, held a handful of wickets, which he kept waving around. Tobias and Aiden joined them, and the wickets got doled out for installation.

Tobias walked with Josh toward the first wicket location. Josh was carrying little Faith on his shoulders; she shrieked with laughter and her hands dug into his hair. At one point, when it looked like she might slip off Josh's back, Tobias put a hand on the little girl's back to steady her. She grinned at him like a gap-toothed little imp, and Carolyn's heart nearly melted.

Tobias, she realized in a flash, would be a jewel of a father.

No. No. *Don't go there, Caro.* Christmas was doing its usual thing—making her long for everything having to do with families. Stick to reality. *This is hot sex with a hot guy. Enjoy it for what it is. Live for the moment.*

20

CAROLYN WATCHED TOBIAS FOR ANOTHER LITTLE WHILE, LETTING the hot images from last night chase away her Christmas blues.

Then she sighed and walked back into the kitchen.

There she found Ben in a tense-looking conversation with Suzanne. His wide shoulders were hunched, his usually light-hearted expression replaced by a scowl. He was shaking his head at whatever Suzanne was saying. All Carolyn caught was the phrase, "her side of the story," before Suzanne caught sight of her and stopped talking.

"Hi Carolyn," she said, awkwardly. "Sorry, we were catching up on old times. I'd better go check on Faith."

"Faith is fine, Josh has her helping set up for croquet."

Suzanne looked alarmed. "He isn't letting her use a mallet, is he?"

"Of course not, they're taller than she is."

"Yeah, but that man would let her drive the car if she just batted her eyelashes at him enough. She loves fire trucks, did you know that? He took her on a tour of the Jupiter Point department and the firemen made such a fuss over her, she had a tantrum when they left. Now Josh is looking online for child-size fire-fighting tools for her. She barely just learned how to walk!"

Ben, who still looked preoccupied by whatever Suzanne had been telling him, gave a halfhearted smile. "I'll go check on them."

"Thanks, Ben," said Suzanne gratefully. She waved one flour-covered hand as he left, then went back to cutting strips of pie crust dough.

"I'm sorry I interrupted your conversation." Carolyn grabbed the potato peeler and got back to work. The oven was already producing the tantalizing scent of roast turkey and sage-apple dressing.

"No no, it's fine. Poor Ben. His ex-girlfriend is back in town and he can't handle it."

"Really? Ben must have a hundred of those. Tobias says he's the king of easy-come, easy-go. Never takes anything too seriously."

"That's now. Back then it was a different story. He and Julie were the ultimate happy couple. Like, blissfully happy. I assumed they'd get married as soon as it was legal. Then she just up and disappeared, right before their dad was murdered. It was the worst timing ever. Ben was so crushed, and then he joined the Air Force, and when he came back, he was a different person. He's still a great guy, of course. Super-cute, obviously. Lots of fun. But you should have known him before. He was such a love. He wore his heart on his sleeve, it was completely adorable."

Carolyn dropped a potato into the bowl of water keeping them fresh. "Like Aiden?"

"I guess so. Yeah, he was the most like Aiden. They both take after their mother, except she was...kind of a mess. An emotional mess. You know she left too, right? She had a breakdown after the murder. So poor Ben lost his dad, his mom, his sister and his girl-friend in the span of a month. Poor guy."

"I didn't know any of this. Not that I would, I mean, I only just met them. Well, recently. There's no reason they'd be sharing all their family secrets."

Suzanne shot her a sardonic look. "I get the feeling that you've been sharing a lot more than family secrets with a certain Knight brother."

"Well..."

"That's great. Just...be careful."

Carolyn looked up sharply. This was the first time she'd heard Suzanne be anything but positive about the Knight brothers. "What do you mean?"

"I'm only telling you this because you're a friend, and please take it with a grain of salt because people do change. A friend of mine was dating Tobias when Robert Knight was killed. She told me he was destroyed, that it was like a piece of him died. He broke up with her right after that. He said he had nothing to give and never would. She was crushed. Granted, he was only twenty, so like I said, grain of salt."

Suzanne's warning hit her right in the solar plexus, because it fit with a few things she herself had observed about Tobias. He'd said the same thing—that he was still haunted by his father's murder.

On the other hand, he didn't act as if he were dead inside, or as if he had nothing to give. Maybe he had changed since the trauma of the murder.

Still, being careful was never a bad idea. If her father had been more careful when he met Lilith, maybe they'd never have gotten sucked into the Light Keepers. She should take Suzanne's advice seriously.

Carolyn gave her friend a curious sideways glance. "You sound like you know a lot about the Knight brothers."

"Julie, Ben's girlfriend, was one of my best friends. I used to hang out with her and Ben and whoever I was dating. I always envied them because they were so in love with each other. I couldn't really imagine feeling that way about someone."

"And now you do."

"And now I do," she said softly, her eyes lighting up. "And it's the best feeling in the world, right up there with having Faith. But Ben and Julie, I don't know, it was something really special. Having that close a connection when you're so young and everything's so intense...their relationship was truly epic."

Really, the whole family was epic, if you asked Carolyn. Maybe it was the aura of tragedy that clung to them, but they all seemed bigger than life, somehow. Or maybe that was her Tobias crush talking.

"It's funny, I still don't know why she left. She's back, but we haven't talked much. I considered asking her here for Christmas, but I'm glad I didn't, judging by Ben's reaction."

Just then a horde of teenagers came trooping in. "Croquet's starting! Ben sent us in to get you." They spread throughout the kitchen to steal tastes of apple filling, spinach dip, cranberry dressing. The sudden blast of young exuberance felt like a wind sweeping through the kitchen.

Carolyn and Suzanne exchanged a glance. A pile of potatoes still remained to be peeled. A mound of pie crust hadn't been rolled out yet.

"I don't know, we're supposed to be the adults," Suzanne said dubiously. "We should probably stay here and keep working on this meal."

"Why should the kids get all the fun?" Carolyn winked at the teenagers. "You'll help us finish this up, right?"

"Of course!" the teens chorused.

"Okay then!" Suzanne whipped off her apron and tossed it aside. "Bring on the mallets!"

The kids cheered. One of them grabbed Carolyn's arm and she found herself being swept out of the kitchen. She caught Suzanne's glance again and laughed, feeling light and carefree in a way she never did.

Outside, the winter sun sparkled through the birch trees, and the sounds of kids laughing mingled with the deeper voices of the adults discussing the rules of the tournament. Brianna was running around making sure that none of her favorite plantings were in the line of fire from a croquet ball. Lisa knelt on the grass next to a girl who must have hurt her ankle; Lisa was gingerly rotating it to assess the injury.

And Tobias? He now carried Faith, who was using his ears like a joystick and shrieking with delight as he zigzagged across the lawn.

Josh came over and swept Suzanne into his arms. "Look, I found us a babysitter. Want to sneak off somewhere with your lawfully wedded husband? Faith just told me she wants a brother for Christmas. We'd better get on that."

Suzanne gave him a little shove. "Keep dreaming, hotshot. How would you manage to keep spoiling her rotten if there was another baby around?"

"See? Another great argument for number two."

Suzanne rolled her eyes at Carolyn. "Easy for him to say, right? As soon as they invent a way for the man to spend nine months puking their guts out, we can talk again."

Josh snorted. "For the record," he told Carolyn, "she's just as baby crazy as I am. She just hides it a lot better."

"It's true," Suzanne admitted cheerfully. "But I do enjoy torturing him. Now hand me a mallet so I can kick your ass at croquet."

They went off arm in arm to join their team. Carolyn took a deep breath, soaking in the joy all around her, and the crisp December sunshine. This would go down in her personal history as one of the best Christmases ever.

As for Suzanne's warning? *Be careful.* She could do that. Absolutely. She was going into this with her eyes wide open, with no illusions about forever. She'd lost those long ago anyway.

But that didn't mean she couldn't enjoy the hot sex.

21

TOBIAS HAD NEVER IMAGINED THAT A CHRISTMAS DINNER AND THE most rambunctious croquet match ever known to mankind would be such a turn-on. But he loved watching Carolyn lose all her inhibitions as she whacked his croquet ball into the weeds. He loved hearing her laugh with the teenagers.

After the match, and after the feast, she sat with a few of the more artistically inclined teenagers as they showed off their drawing and other artwork. She talked with them earnestly about art, and what classes were available at the community college.

He wouldn't be surprised if JPCC saw a sudden spike in enrollment thanks to her. Who wouldn't want to take a class with a kind, beautiful, patient teacher like Carolyn?

He and his brothers decided to gift every one of the shelter teens a ride in one of their planes. Of course, that made them instantly the most popular people in the room, but it was the expression on Carolyn's face that meant the most to him. He realized he'd do almost anything to see that soft light in her eyes.

And then there was the hot look that came later.

He peeled off from his brothers and drove back to Caro's place with her. Somehow, their relationship had become fact—it surprised no one when he looped his arm around her waist and kissed the top of her head as his brothers waved goodbye.

Okay, maybe it surprised him. He'd never been the public type when it came to demonstrating affection. He'd never felt inspired to let the world know his feelings. But everything was different with Carolyn. He wanted all of Jupiter Point to know they were together.

"That was the best Christmas I've had in a very long time," she told him as they drove to her place. "That was great, what you guys did. Those kids are going to love it."

"*You'll* love it too. I want to take you up there. Show you the world. *My* world."

"*Your* world?" she teased. "All that sky up there, it's yours?"

"When I'm up there, I sure feel like it is. Maybe it's a Jupiter Point thing. Growing up here, it's all about the sky. Constellations, planets, alignments. My dad was really into stargazing. We had a big telescope set up in the attic. He took us to the observatory every year. The first time I went up in a Chinook, I swear I felt my dad's presence."

He stopped, embarrassed that he'd veered into that direction. But she reached over and took his hand in hers. "Is Christmas tough for you too?"

"Not usually. I've been overseas for most Christmases. Once I met Will and Aiden in Mexico for Christmas. Being back here...I guess it's a little tougher. Brings back some memories. It's okay. I intend to make some new ones in about fifteen minutes."

"Why fifteen minutes?"

"That's how long it's going to take to get home, get your clothes off, and feast myself on your naked body."

Her hands jerked on the steering wheel, causing her to veer over the yellow dotted line. "Do you have to say things like that when I'm driving?"

"Things like what? Statements of fact about how I intend to lick you until you scream for mercy?" he teased. He put his hand on her thigh, spreading his fingers wide, his little finger edging oh-so-close to her sweet pussy.

She shifted her hips in the seat. "Stop that," she said weakly. "I'm driving."

But he couldn't help noticing that she'd actually managed to get her mound even closer to his finger. "I'm helping." He squeezed her thigh lightly. Her muscles tightened under his touch.

"*How* is that helping?" she gasped.

"Inspiration. Motivation. The quicker we get home, the quicker I can blow your mind."

"You're impossible." But her lips curved in the dim light of her dashboard.

"And you're impossibly sexy and sensual and gorgeous. Is there any way you could drive faster? You can always let me have the wheel. Army trained. I can make this thing rocket back to your house."

"Nope," she said firmly. "I like to drive. I wasn't allowed to at the compound, and now I love it. But maybe going faster isn't the worst idea." She pressed on the accelerator and zoomed through the streets of Jupiter Point, its quaint storefronts adorned with twinkle lights for the holidays. He held on, hoping the local law enforcement had better things to worry about on Christmas night than two people so hungry for each other they practically broke the sound barrier getting home.

When they finally burst through her door, he noticed with one part of his brain that she'd unpacked some of her boxes and tidied up. But most of him focused on getting naked. He spun her into a kiss as soon as the door closed behind them. As their mouths melded together, hot and slick, he ran his hands down her body, peeling away her clothes. He had to pull away briefly to tug her silky top over her head. Her bra took only a touch to undo. He slid off the shoulder straps as he dove back into that deep, urgent kiss.

Skirt, unzipped. Sleek flesh, unveiled. When she finally stood naked before him, he tore himself away from their kiss and gazed at her body, the creamy curves scalding his vision. He could look at her like this all day and all night.

"Know what I want for Christmas?" he said.

"What?"

"Stay like this for the rest of the night. Not a single stitch of clothing for you."

"Or you."

"I have no problem with that." To prove it, he shrugged out of his shirt and stepped out of his pants. He was already rock-hard from the sight of her naked body. He got rid of his briefs, freeing his raging erection. Her gaze dropped to it, and he saw her tongue do that delicious thing it did, that discreet little swipe across her lips.

That made him even harder.

He dropped to his knees and cradled her ass in his hands. The two globes settled into the palms of his hands so perfectly. He blew on her soft curls, spotting moisture hiding there in the lovely nest of blond hair. She drew in a long ragged breath and gripped his shoulders.

"You know, there's a bed in there," she murmured.

"I know." He blew another hot rush of air against her sex. "I intend to make good use of it. But I'm a little busy now. Can't you tell?"

He drew his tongue along the upper seam of her sex, where her clit pouted for attention. It swelled under the pressure, like a bud about to unfurl. Her taste drove him mad with need. He put one hand on his own cock, fisting himself as he worked his mouth deep into her folds. Her fingers dug into his shoulders; he'd probably have marks after this. He didn't care a bit. Bring it on.

He wanted her to come in his mouth. He wanted it so badly he couldn't see straight. Her hips quivered against his grip, her inner thighs trembled. He used the flat of his tongue to add more friction, lashed her with the tip, probing deep, finding the spot that made her cry out. Losing himself in her heat and wetness, in the flexing of her hips, her whimpers, her murmurs, he had no idea how much time passed.

All he knew was that suddenly she was arching against him and all he could do was hang on, mouth latched to her sex, while she rode out the fierce spasms of her climax.

When she finished, limp and sated and damp, her long body gleaming with sweat, he couldn't wait another moment to get inside her. He rose to his feet, his erection so hard, so swollen, he thought it might burst at the slightest touch.

"Bend over the couch," he told her, his voice about two octaves lower than usual. "Hold on to the back. Hold on tight."

Her eyes flared with sleepy heat. With her breath still coming quickly, she turned her back to him and bent over to place her hands where he'd asked.

Oh God. He was going to die, right here and now, at the sight of her pale curves spread out before him. The cleft between her legs gleamed from her orgasm. The soft opening called to him like a siren, the shadows promising hot release to his aching member. He didn't want to rush it, because the sight of her was just too tempting. He took a long moment to caress the curves of her ass, skim his fingers along the sides of her hips, to the tender flesh of her inner thighs.

Her skin twitched and jumped. She turned to look at him, her hair a wild tangle across her back, her eyes a deep, mysterious blue. And he couldn't wait another moment. He took his cock into his fist and rolled on a condom, then nudged her opening with the tip. The soft heat made his eyes close in pleasure. He groaned, a deep bomb of a sound that seemed to rip from his chest.

Her flesh gave way easily, so slick and lubricated from her climax. Her channel still fluttered from the aftereffects, or maybe a new orgasm was coming. She was panting again, pushing against him, urging him onwards.

"Nice and slow," he said in a tight voice, almost as much to himself as to her. "Nice and easy. God, you feel good. Do you have any idea how fucking sexy you are, bent over like that? I want to fuck you so hard."

"Do it. Fuck me hard. Don't hold back."

Was that really his civilized art history teacher talking? She didn't know what she was saying. He had to hold back. If he unleashed all the emotion and heat inside him, this whole room would be obliterated.

"Nice and easy," he repeated, almost like a mantra, as he slid farther in, parting her sweet inner flesh like butter.

"Harder," she urged. "I want it harder."

"You don't really mean that."

"I do. I mean it, Tobias. Let off the brakes. Go wild. Wild and dirty and--" She broke off with a gasp as he flexed his hips and buried himself deep. The satisfaction of that one stroke sent shudders up his spine. "Oh Caro. Fuck, that feels good."

She gave a strangled moan of agreement. He checked to see if she was still okay. Judging by the rapturous expression on her face, she absolutely was. So he let his primitive need for her take over. He stroked deep, his pace dominated by the frantic desire chasing through his being. He was barely aware of the speed and friction generated by his thrusts. It all fused into a blur of sensation. He kept an eye on Caro, watching closely for any sign that he was going too hard, too intense.

But the only sounds he heard from her were whimpers and moans and the occasional, *Oh my God, Tobias. So good, Tobias.* So he let his last bit of restraint disappear. He roared as he claimed her body with a fierce, incinerating passion. And once again, time disappeared. Only the glorious now existed, the smell of sex, the slap of flesh, the breathtaking arch of her spine, the fall of her hair, the sensation of velvet heat sliding against his cock, the tight grip of her inner muscles. He used his hands on her hips to bring her tighter, harder against him. *So good, so good.*

He felt the exact moment when she went rigid and clenched around his erection. Adrenaline shot up his spine, sheer blinding excitement turning the world fuzzy around the edges. His balls tightened. He took one more deep stroke into her fluttering channel and exploded into an orgasm that nearly stopped his heart. He rode it like the downward plunge of a rollercoaster, with an inward howl of elation.

He closed his eyes and saw stars expanding all around him, bright points of light in every direction. He became free-floating, weightless the way he sometimes felt in a chopper or the Cessna. A feeling of peace saturated him, body and soul. Nothing could harm him. Everything was as it should be.

He drifted, mindless and complete.

And in the timeless space that followed, he heard a whisper he hadn't heard in years.

Tobias, the voice said. *You're going to be all right, son. Just a fall. Anyone can fall. The true test is when you get back up.*

The memory came back to him in pieces. He'd fallen out of a tree; he was always falling. Because he loved to climb things, that was why. He climbed and he fell, that was the story of his childhood. He tested limits no one else wanted to touch. And for good reason, because he always ended up on his ass.

That time, he'd dropped like a stone from the old oak tree behind their house, near the creek. Ben had fled to tell Dad, who'd dropped his woodcarving project and come running.

Reminds me of my last mission, he'd told Tobias as he gently checked his leg. *The time I fell out of my hidey-hole and broke my leg. The guys had to haul me out on some tree branches tied together. They trekked two miles like that, under enemy fire. Hurt like the devil, but I couldn't cry about it, could I? Okay, son, want to try standing up?*

Of course he couldn't let on how much it hurt after *that* story. So he'd gritted his teeth and stood up. He'd allowed his father to help him back to the house, declining Ben's enthusiastic offer to make him a gurney out of his drumsticks. He'd limped home and insisted everything was fine. He'd ignored the nagging pain for weeks, until he'd fallen off a dirt bike and *really* broken his leg. Turned out he'd been suffering from a fracture the entire time.

You're going to be all right, son. The true test is when you get back up.

"HEY. TOBIAS. ARE YOU OKAY?"

He blinked his eyes open and looked at his surroundings with utter confusion. He must have fallen asleep and dreamed about that long-ago incident. It had felt so real, as if he were there. But now he was lying on Caro's couch, her soft body nestled against his.

"Hi." He struggled to wake up, but she put a gentle hand on his chest to prevent him.

"You conked out. You must be exhausted. All that croquet, you know. It's such good exercise."

Croquet. Christmas. Carolyn. *Right.* He settled his hand on her hip, the feel of her skin grounding him.

"And by croquet, I actually mean hot sex on my couch."

Hot sex. Yeah, it was. No argument there. But somehow he didn't like the way she put it. As if it didn't mean anything *beyond* that. He'd just experienced something out of this world—almost like traveling back in time—and she was talking about "hot sex" in that lighthearted tone.

He rubbed the heel of his hand across his eyes, trying to clear his thoughts. "I remembered something, some random moment with my father after I'd fallen out of a tree."

She lifted her head, eyebrows raised. "*That's* what you were dreaming about? You really are a romantic."

"Sorry," he said with a grimace. "I guess my unconscious is a callous unromantic bastard. I'll have a talk with it."

She tangled one finger in the dark swirl of hair on his chest. "I'm just teasing. That memory must be important to you. Maybe you remembered it for a reason."

The pieces fell into place, like the tumblers of a lock. "Shit. You're right. My dad was talking about one of his missions. He was a sniper, that was his expertise. He fell out of a blind and broke his leg, he had to get carried two miles to safety. And you know what? I think one of those guys might have gotten killed during the trek. I vaguely remember something about that. Damn. I have to call Will."

Again he tried to get up, and again she stopped him. "It's four in the morning. I think it can wait."

Reluctantly, he lay back down. Impatience burned through him. Now that Caro had pointed it out, he had no doubt that he'd remembered that moment for a reason. It was a clue, especially when considered along with the way his dad's head had possibly been pointing toward his medals.

"You know," he said softly. "It's damn handy having a professor around. Good thinking there."

"Hey, any time. Even though my specialty is art history, I'm more than happy to lend a hand with murder investigations." With a light touch, she smoothed her palm across his chest.

"I really want to find the bastard who did it." Strangely, that thought came almost as a surprise.

"Of course you do."

"No, it's...what I mean is that sometimes I forget that someone actually physically killed him. I get so caught up in my own guilt about the fight we had, and how I always pushed him, always challenged him. I was such a nightmare of a son. I think about that, and how I could have made life so much easier for him, that I forget someone *actually killed him*."

His chest tightened as if an iron vise had come around it. He couldn't breathe for a minute. Emotion hammered at his throat, as if clawing to get out.

But he wouldn't let it. That wasn't what Tobias Knight was about. Not Robert Knight's son. *Hurt like the devil, but I couldn't cry about it, could I?*

His blood pounded in his ears. He fixed his gaze on the ceiling, noting a discoloration in the plaster. He should repair that for Carolyn. It could mean a leak. He'd go up on her roof and make sure the tiles were solid, maybe a replace a few if they needed it.

Eventually he became aware of Carolyn's soft hand stroking his chest, soothing him back to the present. "Sorry," he muttered. "I don't know what's wrong with me. Must be all the tryptophans in that turkey. That stuff ought to be regulated."

"Maybe, or maybe it's the healing power of sex with the golden goddess." She tickled his ribs, somehow homing in on one of his most sensitive spots. He produced a sound somewhere between a giggle and a shriek.

"Oh my God." She sat bolt upright. "What was that?"

"That's what happens when people tickle me."

"That was the *most* unmanly sound I've ever heard."

He grinned at her. "Is that supposed to be an insult? I'm pretty confident in my manliness, no matter what sounds I make."

"So you knew about this?"

"You've met my brothers. Do you think I could have grown to adulthood without getting tickled? Actually, my sister Cassie was the champion tickler. She could make me cry real tears. It was pathetic."

"Can I do it again?"

"Have at it." He lifted his arm to give her access to his ribs. She tickled him again, and once again he let out that unearthly sound. But this time, he also clamped her hand against his side and rolled over so he was braced on top of her.

"By the way, I also learned a few anti-tickling tricks, just to survive." He dropped a kiss on her lips. "I never knew they'd come in so handy."

She nipped at his bottom lip in revenge for being pinned. "You know I could figure out a way to kill you if I had to. Or at least maim you."

"I know, you're a badass peace warrior. But why would you want to maim the man who's going to give you your next thousand orgasms?"

"A thousand?" she said faintly. "Tonight?"

"I'm thinking we should spread them out. Maybe five tonight, then we'll go from there."

"*Five*? That's a little overconfident, don't you think? Quite honestly, I'm thrilled if a man gives me one orgasm. I knew I got involved with you for a reason."

He paused for a microsecond, that discordant note striking again. But then her laughing eyes and sheer naked loveliness blotted out everything else. *Just enjoy this, Tobias. Why not?* "I've mentioned how I like to test limits, right? Brace yourself, professor."

22

CAROLYN KNEW PERFECTLY WELL THAT SHE'D BEEN BORN WITH A willful streak. The Light Keepers had tried their best to conquer it, but the rebellious side of her, that part that insisted on making her own decisions, refused to give in. Even when she was a kid, she was notoriously curious. There was the incident with Pete Broussard, when they'd snuck into the barn and shown each other their secret parts. The Broussards had left the compound shortly after that, and she'd always felt guilty since it had been *her* idea, not his.

Until the age of about twenty, she'd assumed that her curiosity was a grave mark against her character. It led her to do naughty things like look at Pete's male parts, and even touch her own self late at night. Only once she'd left the compound did she learn that her desire for sexual exploration made her normal, not a freak. One stolen moment in a barn and a few exploratory touches didn't exactly add up to depravity.

On the other hand, this thing with Tobias...hoo-boy. If the compound had any clue what she and Tobias were up to, they'd say she was going straight to hell for ten eternities.

The heat the two of them generated practically set her house on fire. He only had to look at her in that certain way, with that slow-burning smolder, that promise of mind-melting ecstasy, for the spark to flare deep in her belly. She threw herself into this "hot sex" thing, no holds barred.

The time they spent apart—while he flew shifts at Knight and Day and she settled back into her house and prepared for the spring semester—dragged at a glacial pace.

New Year's Eve came and went. They never made it to the big champagne party at the observatory everyone else attended. Instead, they spent the night in bed. Soon the spring semester would start and she'd be too busy to spend so much time with Tobias. But for now, she reveled in it.

Something about his bad-boy exterior paired with his rock-solid heart made all her inhibitions fall away. She felt free to do absolutely anything with him, because his acceptance was absolute. He didn't judge her at all, the opposite, in fact. His only desire was for her to enjoy herself. He was constantly monitoring her to make sure she was, to make sure he wasn't pushing her too far. That made her feel utterly safe and let loose all kinds of secret fantasies she hadn't known she had.

Like melted chocolate.

Who knew melted chocolate could give her the best orgasm of her life? It started with a blindfold, then the slow removal of all her clothes. When she was completely naked, he led her by the hand through her house to the kitchen. Even walking naked like that had a wild effect on her. She felt both vulnerable and powerful, because he kept whispering in her ear how sexy she was.

In the kitchen, the smell of melted chocolate made saliva spring to her mouth. She licked her lips, a gesture she knew turned him on. He growled in response and squeezed her ass. Her arousal ticked up another notch.

He turned her so she felt something against her back. The kitchen counter.

"I've had this obsession with countertops ever since Evergreen," he growled. "Lean your elbows back on the counter, please."

The 'please' always felt pro forma, as if both of them knew she'd do it with or without the please. Still, she appreciated it.

"Anything for you, lover," she purred. He also loved it when she acted bold and demanding, which worked out well because she did too. She leaned back provocatively, pushing her breasts out. He circled each breast with his finger, the calloused surface skimming across her tender skin. With slow, torturous movements he closed the circle, homing in on her nipples, which ached to be touched.

Even though she was blindfolded, she felt his gaze on her. She always knew when he was looking at her because her body came alive under his scrutiny. She could even narrow it down to specific body parts—he's looking at my ass, now my breasts. *He wants me. He thinks I'm beautiful.*

The anticipation generated by his slow survey made her bite her lip. What was he going to do next? When?

Then something warm and thick dribbled across her nipples. She cried out from the surprise sensation. The pinch of heat made them tighten instantly, even before his tongue swept across them to catch the sticky droplets. Thoroughly, meticulously, he licked her clean. She clenched her teeth against the sounds clamoring to come out of her mouth. If she released them, she wouldn't be able to focus on the physical sensation she was experiencing, and she wanted to savor every moment.

The way Tobias was savoring her chocolate-covered nipples, like a cat voraciously attacking a bowl of cream.

He feasted for what seemed like an eternity, finding chocolate in every sensitive crevice of her nipples. Then he brought his mouth, all warm and lush with chocolate, to hers. He ran his deliciously sweetened tongue across the roof of her mouth, the inside of her lower lip, generating wild tingles wherever he touched.

When she was sticky and wild for release, Tobias still made

her wait. He brought her into the bathroom, where the steamy warmth made her sigh with pleasure. He'd already drawn a bath and filled it with piles of foamy bubbles. He took off her blindfold before he helped her into the tub.

"I got this, sweetheart. You don't need to do a thing. Just lay back and let me take care of you," he murmured. That was another voice of his that revved her up. The tender, gentle one, the voice that said *I'd do anything for you, stand between you and any bullet you can name.*

Of course she would follow that voice to the ends of the earth. She lay back with a sigh in the old-fashioned claw-foot tub. She'd always loved this tub, but it had never been put to this kind of use before.

He wrapped her hands around the still-warm pipes that ran up to the ceiling. "Don't move," he murmured. "Stay just like that. I swear, I could look at you forever like this, all pink and steamy. You're like cotton candy and strawberry pie all rolled into one."

"I had no idea you had such a sweet tooth." She quivered as he wrung warm water from her big soft sponge over her breasts. Then he took her washcloth over the peaked mounds of her breasts, teasing her nipples with the rough, nubby fabric.

"No squirming," he warned. He moved to the other end of the tub. Lifting each foot in turn, he used the washcloth to stroke between her toes, until she was rosy and panting. The movement of the water sent soap bubbles foaming around her nipples with fluffy, maddening touches, like air kisses. She stretched like a cat, arching her spine so the water streamed off her in warm rivers.

"You're going to make a mess," he warned. "No splashing. Keep perfectly still."

"I can't." She squirmed deliciously.

"Try harder."

She bit her lip and stilled her body. When he put that extra bit of gravel into his voice it drove her wild. She loved following that dark voice wherever it might lead her, because a screaming orgasm was the inevitable end.

"Prop one foot on the edge of the tub," he commanded. "I need to clean you everywhere."

Oh God. She did as he said, which meant she was splayed open under the foaming bubbles. He worked the washcloth delicately against her folds, the warm friction sending her into a trancelike state. Then he found her clit with the wet cloth, rubbing until she throbbed and yearned for the magical shimmering joy hovering at the edge of possibility.

"Tobias Knight, you'd better do something quick, or I'm going to melt down right here in the bubbles."

"I don't do things quick. I do them slow." He grinned at her. At some point he'd shucked his clothes. His broad chest and rippling muscles flexed with each gentle movement of his hands. It blew her away, every time, that he could be in such complete control of those muscles, that he could be so explosive and so gentle in the next moment.

"I noticed," she said with gritted teeth. Her eyes drifted half closed as she pushed subtly against his hand. Would that count as moving? What bad thing would happen if she moved? Or would it be the best thing ever? "There's slow and then there's molasses."

"Hmm, molasses. How did you know I love molasses?" He drove a finger inside her as he brushed his broad thumb against her clit.

"Such. A. Sweet tooth," she managed. She pressed frantically against his thumb, needing more friction, more pressure, the hot, wet, slippery soap bubbles making everything so much more intense.

"I do love sweets, you're right." His growl sizzled across her nerve endings. She knew she was close. So close. She could only take so much.

"I'm going to come," she warned him breathlessly. "And there's going to be splashing."

He laughed softly. "Babe, if there isn't I'd be disappointed. Nothing makes me happier than to watch you thrash around while you orgasm."

She tried to make a face at him, but she felt too good and her face refused to do anything but grimace in ecstasy. And when she came in long rolling waves, ocean swells of sensation sweeping through her, she held on to those pipes as if they were the only things anchoring her to Earth. Other than Tobias's growls of encouragement and hot hand anchored to her pussy.

Afterwards, he helped her out of the tub and dried her off with her favorite fluffy towel. Every bit of her tingled under his gentle patting.

"Why did I never realize how fun something like this would be?"

He looked down at her, a puzzled frown denting his forehead. "This?"

"This...you know." She waved her hand vaguely. "This thing we're doing. This crazy, wild, live-for-the-moment thing."

His eyebrows lifted, almost as if she'd surprised him. "Is that what it is?"

"Sure, I mean, there's nothing wrong with it, right?" She put her hand on his cock and discovered it was hot and hard and eager. "By the way, you have a sparkling clean naked woman standing before you, ready for the next deep dark fantasy. What'll it be?"

He hesitated. "Live for the moment, huh?"

"Yes." Waiting for him to continue, her heart raced. Her nipples rose all on their own.

He put one big hand on her head and pushed her gently down. She kissed him as she went, pressing her lips to each chiseled muscle, passing a scar that slashed across his lower belly, following the dark trail of hair. On her knees on the bath mat, she touched her lips to the head of his erection.

His penis stood out like an exclamation point from its nest of dark hair. Its hot velvety skin brushed against her cheek. Its heft and weight felt nearly overwhelming. It was going to come into her mouth, that hard spear of flesh. It wanted her. And it would ravage her until it was satisfied. And she would love every minute.

As soon as she took him into her mouth, she felt the intensity of his arousal. The little twitches and jumps she'd come to know meant he was already wildly turned on. She'd gotten to know the feel of his skin better than her own. She knew every inch of his muscular frame, knew which spots made him growl with pleasure, which parts needed only a touch to make his cock spring into action. The sound of his breath, the deep sounds he made when he was close to coming, the pressure of his penis against her tongue—it all felt like home. It felt essential, like oxygen.

She surrounded him with her lips and mouth, wrapped her hand around the base of his penis. She tasted a hint of salt, maybe even some soap from the bubble bath. But mostly, she tasted passion. Not just his passion, as he moved in her mouth, taking up the rhythm she set. Also hers, as she gave him every bit of her attention. Giving him her mouth, her tongue, her lips.

Giving him her love.

The thought slipped in like a thief, stealing her pleasure. No, this wasn't *love*. This was thrills and chills, release and freedom and wild adventure. *It's live-for-the-moment, not love, you idiot. Get a grip.*

But try as she might, for the rest of that night with Tobias, she couldn't get her groove back.

23

Even through his orgasm, Tobias noticed that something had shifted with Carolyn. He waited for her to explain, but she fell asleep as soon as they crawled into her bed. He knew he wouldn't be able to focus on conversation while she was naked next to him, so the next morning he took her to the Milky Way for breakfast.

The Milky Way Ice Cream Parlor was not only famous for the "galaxy's best ice cream sundae," but for their banana walnut pancakes. It was a sunny place with a wall-size mural of cheerful cows wandering through a cartoonish galaxy. With its daffodil-yellow curtains and bright cutouts of animated ice cream cones and talking pancakes, Tobias felt as if he was sitting in a children's book.

"Have you ever noticed that pancakes solve most problems?" he asked as they scanned the menu.

"It is a universally accepted truth. I'll have the strawberry short stack," she told the waitress.

He ordered a full plate of buttermilk pecan pancakes with a double order of bacon. "And two coffees, as soon as you can."

"Any word from Will about the piece you remembered, about your dad's last mission?" Carolyn asked after the waitress had left.

"Yeah, he's working on locating the other soldiers who were there that day. Especially the one who got killed. There's a possibility that an angry family member blamed him and wanted revenge."

"That's a workable theory." The coffee arrived, steaming hot. She clinked her mug against his. "To the morning after."

"And the night after that."

They both smiled, and sipped from their mugs. Everything seemed fine on the surface, but he knew something was off. He felt it, and he always relied on his gut instincts, at least in war. And as Aiden had said, love was even harder than war.

So much harder that he didn't even know what to say.

Instead, he asked about something else that he'd been wondering about. "That little crescent scar on your cheek. Where did that come from?"

"Oh." Her gaze slid away from his. "That was a long time ago."

"From the compound?"

She nodded with a rueful expression. She'd twisted her ash-blond hair into a low knot and stuck a pencil through it. In her scoop-necked pink t-shirt, face freshly washed, she looked much younger than her age. She didn't look like either a professor or an expert in martial arts. She looked vulnerable and fragile. He had to consciously tell himself that wasn't the case. Carolyn was so much tougher than she appeared. "You don't go through militia training, even the kid version, without a few scars."

"There's one on your hip, too."

"Yes. Sharp eyes."

"What else?"

"Oh, just a few psychic scars, nothing too serious," she said lightly. "Nothing that prevents me from screwing your brains out on a nightly basis."

"Yeah, I've...uh...noticed. And I appreciate that." Even though he maintained their light tone, his gut grew a knot. Something was definitely wrong here.

Their pancakes arrived. He watched her pour syrup over hers, trying to pin down his uneasiness into an actual question.

Before he could, she spoke. "It's such a relief to know that we're on the same page with this thing. The non-marriage page."

"What page now?" The shift in topic disoriented him. Why were they talking about marriage? Or non-marriage?

"My independence is very important to me." She passed him the syrup. He focused on saturating his pancakes until Carolyn's eyes widened.

"Sweet tooth, remember?"

"I'm impressed. And horrified."

He grinned, then took a syrupy bite, which gave him time to figure out how to respond to her comments about marriage. Keep it light, he decided. The way she was.

"Have to admit, I never pictured my name on a marriage license either."

She didn't look very surprised by that. "What a shocker. Why not?"

He wasn't sure what to make of that comment. "I always figured I'd be the cool uncle. Will's the oldest, and he did a kick-ass job raising Aiden. He already has the drill down, whenever he and Merry decide it's time. Ben was all ready to have a baby with Julie, way back in the day. As soon as he gets over this party phase, he'll make a great dad. Aiden's a lot like Ben. That's why we were so worried about 'the golden goddess.' Aiden is the kind who would turn his life upside down for a woman."

"And you're not, clearly?" Her blue eyes caught his briefly over the edge of her mug, then looked away.

He dug into his crispy bacon. He'd never considered himself to be the type who would be turned inside out by a woman. But maybe things were changing. "I've been told by several women that I'm not marriage material. I didn't disagree."

A funny smile spread across her delicate features. She ripped open a sugar packet and poured it into the puddle of maple syrup. Using the tines of her fork, she pushed the sugar crystals this way and that, as if they were tea leaves.

"Maybe that's a good thing," she said.

"How do you figure?"

"Oh, the marriages I've seen," she quipped. "I could tell you some horror stories from the Light Keepers. Getting married, for a woman, is basically signing away your right to make decisions for yourself. It's agreeing to always obey, always defer. Basically, it would never suit me."

"THAT'S YOUR EXAMPLE? The Light Keepers?"

Her smile dropped away. "Not only them, no. My biggest fear is being like my father and stepmother. My father changed so much after he married Lilith. He wanted to be what she needed, what she wanted. We moved to the Light Keepers because she wanted that kind of lifestyle. I watched it happen and I just wanted to scream, 'where are you, Dad, *who* are you'? But nothing I said mattered, and..."

She went silent, while he waited patiently for more. But she shook off the seriousness of the moment with a shrug.

"I guess I'm not marriage material either. We're more alike than it seems, the art history prof and the soldier."

She clicked her coffee mug against his again.

This time it didn't feel so amusing. If she wasn't marriage material, and he wasn't marriage material, that took marriage off the table. Which was...fine, right? Marriage had never been on his radar.

But still, it didn't sit right. A guy could change. With the right inspiration. But she didn't seem to want him to. And that...well, that kind of hurt. It was all coming clear now.

She wasn't interested in anything beyond sex.

A little rattled by that revelation, he gestured toward the maple syrup on her plate. "Guess we have a sweet tooth in common too. How many packets of sugar did you add to your maple syrup?"

She laughed and drew her finger through the syrup. "It's the stress. When I think about the Light Keepers, I go for the sweet stuff."

He tracked her tongue as she curled it around the tip of her finger. "Next time I'll dip my cock in maple syrup."

She nearly choked, her face turning pink, her pupils dilating. Aroused. "You really are crazy."

"The crazier, the better, right?" But he felt his heart contracting, withdrawing back behind his usual fierce facade. He'd pegged this right. She didn't want *him*. Not really. Just his hard cock—to be brutally frank about it.

The question now—was he okay with that?

THE DAY after their breakfast at the Milky Way, Carolyn stopped by the *News-Gazette*, where she found Merry tearing her hair out over an upcoming story about the new director of the observatory. "It's like he speaks another language. No one is going to understand this interview. I need a star geek translator!"

"This town is full of star geeks, isn't it?"

"Yes, but my deadline is *tonight*. Never mind. You're right. You're brilliant. This town is full of star geeks who will understand exactly what he's talking about. All I have to do is get the spelling right." Pleased, she sat back in her chair and stuck a pencil in her dark halo of curls. "So what's up? You solved my problem, now let me solve yours."

"It's...well, it's Tobias."

"Ah. Boy trouble. Not just boy trouble, *Knight* boy trouble. My specialty." She rubbed her hands together in glee. "I know he's a handful, but don't despair. His brothers say they've never seen him behave like this with another woman. They think he's a smitten kitten."

She bit her lip. "Smitten? No, I don't think it's like that. We're just two grown-ups enjoying ourselves."

Merry lifted one eyebrow. "I see."

Carolyn's gaze strayed to the sparkling engagement ring on her finger. "Neither of us is the marrying kind."

"I didn't think I was either," said Merry. "I was just fine on my own. Then I fell for Will. I guess I should say that I finally *admitted* I'd fallen for him. Anyway, this isn't about me. It's about you and Tobias. What do you mean, you're not the marrying kind?"

"Well, doesn't it scare you to think of losing your independence?"

Merry tilted her head, a dreamy look in her amber-brown eyes.

But before she could answer, Carolyn added, "Not that we're talking about marriage, anyway. Neither of us wants to get married."

Merry frowned. "Is that really what Tobias says?"

"Well, not exactly. He said women have told him he wasn't marriage material."

"Whoever that was didn't know what they were talking about. Tobias just needs the right person." Her phone rang. "Sorry, I have to take this. It's my brother Chase. He came to visit and Ben totally claimed him as his laborer repainting lines on the tarmac. I have to make sure he isn't traumatized. But Caro, don't write Tobias off like that. Promise me."

She was already into her phone call when Carolyn left, more confused than ever.

THE TOPIC of marriage didn't come up again after that conversation in the Milky Way. And Tobias seemed...different. Some of his fire was gone, as if his heart wasn't quite in it anymore. It shouldn't matter, if they were going to just stick to sex. But somehow, it did. She wished they'd never even talked about marriage. Had that conversation ruined things between them?

She threw herself into making love to him. Again and again, until they both dropped to sleep, exhausted but not quite...satisfied.

After too few hours of sleep, her door bell buzzed.

It seemed so out of place that for a moment she didn't realize what it was. Then she sat up, holding her sheet against her chest. "That's the doorbell," she said blankly. "Someone's at the door. What time is it?"

Tobias reached for his phone and squinted to check the time. "Six-thirty?"

"At night?"

"No, morning. It's the morning, sweetheart. Did I fuck your sense of time right out of you?"

She rubbed her eyes, truly shocked that she'd lost track of time through an entire night. "Did we sleep?"

"Yup. Here and there." He ran his hand along her spine. "Want me to get it?"

"What? No, no, that's okay. That might confuse people. Hang on."

She scrambled out of bed and pulled on her pajamas and a bathrobe. She smoothed her hair with her fingers as best she could, then hurried to the door. The buzzer was ringing again as she peered through the fisheye peephole.

Agent Maia Turner. From the FBI. The FBI was on her doorstep at six-thirty in the morning.

A shaft of fear shot through her. Her family? The compound? Something terrible? Why else would they be here at such a crazy time?

"Tobias," she called weakly. "Can you come here?"

In no time, he was at her side, in the midst of pulling his t-shirt over his head. In sweat pants and bare feet, he looked mouthwatering, despite the hard alertness in his expression. He looked battle-ready, as if he could pull out a gun at any moment.

"It's the FBI," she whispered. "The same agents I talked to at Evergreen."

He nodded and put a steady hand on her shoulder. "I'm right here, babe. Whatever you need. Go ahead and open it."

Her heart pounding with fear, she undid the deadbolt and opened the door.

"Happy New Year. Sorry to bother you so early," Agent Turner said. Despite the early hour, she looked as polished and competent as ever.

"We tried calling but you didn't answer your phone." Agent Jackson's gaze slid to Tobias, who stared back with an impassive expression.

"Can we come in?" Turner asked.

"Did something...is anyone..."

"No one's hurt," she said quickly. "But there's a situation we'd like to discuss with you."

"Of course." Numbly, Carolyn opened the door for them. She realized that she was wearing her fuzzy bathrobe with the adorable lambs that looked like something out of *Zootopia*. Just exactly what she wanted to wear while talking with the FBI.

They trooped into her living room. Luckily, she'd finally unpacked her boxes, but she did notice her bra dangling off the back of the armchair. She shot Tobias a glance. He discreetly stuck it in his back pocket.

"This is Tobias Knight," she told them. "Tobias, this is Agent Turner and Agent Jackson with the FBI. I spoke to them at Evergreen." She turned back to the agents. "Tobias actually witnessed one of the incidents, so he's aware of what was happening back there."

Turner sat on the edge of the couch and rested her elbows on her knees. "This is connected, most likely. And I gotta thank you for the head's up. It's a good thing we sent someone out there. As it is, we're playing catch up, but it could have been even worse."

Carolyn's stomach tightened. Obviously "out there" referred to the Light Keepers compound. "So what's going on?"

Turner handed over her phone. It showed a photo of a scrap of paper. In a child's handwriting, it read, "Pleez tell Carolin More to come get me. She iz my sister. I want to leev here. But I cant. Nun of us kids can. Im afraid. Sarah."

24

CAROLYN STARED AT THE IMAGE, SHIVERS ERUPTING ACROSS HER entire body. "What is this?"

"This is a note that was discovered on the fence that surrounds the property. One of the ranch neighbors found it and brought it to us. We're assuming that one of the children in the compound wrote it. If you hadn't called us in Evergreen, we wouldn't have made the connection to you. Do you have a sister named Sarah at the Light Keepers?"

She shook her head numbly. "Not that I'm aware of. I suppose it's possible that my father and stepmother had another baby."

She passed the phone to Tobias, whose eyebrows lifted as he read it. Without a word, he handed it back to Turner.

"What does she mean none of them can get out?" Agent Jackson asked. His sharp blue eyes seemed to have already memorized every bit of her decor.

"Well, the Light Keepers don't like people leaving. I'm proof of that. But she's obviously a child, so of course she can't leave without her parents. *My* parents. I guess." She touched her forehead, feeling a little lightheaded. "I can't believe I have a sister and they never told me. Can I see that again?"

Agent Turner passed the phone back to her. She read the note again, more carefully, now that the initial shock had worn off.

"She says she's afraid. What's going on?"

"We're not sure. They seem to be holing up. No one from the community has been spotted outside the property for weeks. Joseph Brown was the last, apparently. Since he went back, not a peep. And then this note was found."

Carolyn's stomach dropped in a sickening plunge. Ever since she left the group, she'd worried they might get even crazier. All those weapons, all that paranoia, all that training—someday, they might decide to use it.

"Can't you guys do something? Find out what's happening? Use satellites or something?"

"We did some old-fashioned surveillance. I managed to get onto the property, but I couldn't do much and I didn't find out anything useful. They had guards on me."

"You? Personally?" Her shock must have shown on her face, because Turner gave her a wry look.

"It turns out there's one kind of black person they allow on their property. They wanted their Internet fixed, and I was the only repair person available. Congratulations to me."

Caro's face flamed. She could well imagine the kind of treatment Agent Turner must have received. "I'm so sorry," she said, in a strangled tone. "That could not have been easy."

"Jackson here could have gone in, but I thought it might be useful to rile them up a bit. I took comfort in that."

"Did you wear that wedding ring?" Carolyn asked, glancing at her hand.

"Of course I did."

Tobias scratched at the back of his head. "How does the wedding ring figure in?"

"According to the Light Keepers, a single woman over the age of twenty-one is pretty much the devil," Carolyn explained, distractedly. "There's no way Agent Turner would have gotten in if she weren't married, I don't care how much they wanted their Internet back." She jumped to her feet and began pacing across the room. *She had a sister.* Maybe. A half-sister. Sarah. Who needed her. Who knew about her!

A frantic kind of emotion flooded her. The words from that note chanted through her mind—she could practically hear them spoken in a child's voice. *Tell her to come get me. I'm afraid. I can't leave. None of us kids can.*

Was Sarah just being dramatic with that phrasing—"none of us kids can"? It sounded as if they were being held against their will. Even more so than the Light Keepers usually mandated.

She wheeled on the two FBI agents. "So what's next? What happens now?"

"We're investigating. That's why we're here." Agent Jackson sounded irritated. "Has this sister tried to contact you in any other way? Email? Phone?"

"No! I didn't even know she existed. Kids there don't get access to email or phone." She wrung her hands together as she paced. Her sister—Sarah—couldn't be more than nine or ten. Maybe younger, judging by the writing on that note. She was just a little kid! A scared little kid hoping some big sister she'd never met would come save her.

"We thought that you could try to call your father," Agent Turner said. "Maybe you can get a hint about what's going on in there, read between the lines kind of thing."

Carolyn shook her head. "It won't work. He won't take a call from me."

The agents exchanged a glance.

"I can try," she said quickly. "But you'll need a plan B. What if the kids are being held prisoner somehow?"

"We don't know that. The neighbors say they're never any trouble. We have no probable cause to go in there except this note."

"Isn't that enough?" Carolyn waved at the phone. "That note's pretty damn clear."

"No it isn't. The kids are with their parents. We have no evidence that they're not safe. For all we know, this note is a joke. It could be from last month, or it could have flown against the fence in the wind. Maybe it's a fucking art project, who knows?"

"Are you kidding? Does that look like an art project to you? I don't see a single stick figure human or...or sun with rays coming out. And I'm an art history teacher."

That didn't make much sense. She plunged her hands into her hair, feeling her temples throb with an oncoming headache. Sarah aside, she didn't even know the kids at the compound now. Depending on their ages, they might have been babies when she left. Or not yet born. It didn't matter. She felt a deep kinship with them no matter who they were. She knew how it felt to be trapped behind that fence, with every detail of your life dictated to you.

"Don't worry, we're not going to ignore the note. But we have to handle it delicately. We can't go in with guns blazing. The last thing we want is some kind of shootout. They'd probably like that. Those fringe groups with all that firepower..." Agent Jackson shook his head. "People would get killed. Innocent people."

Kids, he meant. Violent shivers racked Carolyn's body again. She could picture it, the brigade members with their machine guns and their bulletproof vests with the Light Keepers logo. The agent was right; they would relish the chance to put their training to work.

But Sarah...*Im afraid* ... Oh God, she had a sister ... a sister in danger...

A firm hand descended on her shoulder, interrupting her frenzied thought process. "Carolyn." Tobias. Tobias was still here? She'd forgotten about him.

She stared at him blankly. "What?"

"I need your help."

"Help? What are you talking about? This is a crisis. Did you hear what they're—"

"I heard. Come on. I need you in the kitchen. It's the crack of dawn, we need coffee."

He was already relentlessly guiding her toward the kitchen. "We'll be right back with coffee," Tobias told the agents. "Hang tight."

In the kitchen, he turned on the fan over the stove. Its droning hum masked the sound of his voice, which he pitched low as he got the coffeemaker going. "Take a breath, Caro."

"I'm fine. I mean, I can't believe I have a sister. A *sister*. And she's asking for me. But those agents—" She shook her head in frustration.

"They have to follow their procedures and it's a tricky situation. I have an idea. But they can't know about it. Get me?"

She stared at him, his intense eyes, his serious face. "What plan?"

"I'll tell you all about it. But we have to get rid of them first. If they get so much as a whiff of it, they might block it."

Her thoughts slowly cleared. She nodded, and did as he'd suggested at the beginning. Took a deep breath. To collect herself further, she gathered together cups and spoons, milk and sugar, and placed everything on an enameled tray that depicted a medieval Madonna and Child. The image soothed her, grounded her, got her feet back on familiar ground. She hadn't even gotten this rattled by the letters and the vandalism.

She had a sister.

When the coffee was done, Tobias followed her back to the living room with the coffeepot. But the agents were already on their feet. "Sorry, we just got a call. We need to get going." Agent Jackson gave the coffee a regretful glance.

"Thanks for coming by," Carolyn managed. It was a good thing they were leaving. Acting normal was beyond her reach right now. "Will you keep me posted?"

"Absolutely," Turner assured her.

She waited in an agony of suspense until they'd left her house, walked down her front walkway, and disappeared into their official federal vehicle. Then she turned on Tobias, who was in the midst of filling cups with coffee.

"Okay, what's your plan?"

He set the coffee carafe on the tray with a clatter. "Simple. I'm going in." He picked up a cup and blew on it, meeting her eyes calmly over the edge.

"Just like that? Not much of a plan. Why would they let you in?"

"Why wouldn't they? Don't I look like a paramilitary type with a lead on some black-market weapons?"

Her gaze traveled up and down his body. He wore a t-shirt and sweat pants and bulged with muscle. He was right. Tobias looked every inch the tough, soldierly, aggro male. She knew that his appearance didn't tell the whole story, but they wouldn't. In fact, he represented the *ideal* of what most of the men in the Light Keepers aspired to. Most didn't have his powerful presence or his incredibly honed physique, but they wished they did. He could be the *poster child* for the "Brigade" part of the Light Keepers.

Another poster child for the fringe group. She and Tobias had *so* much in common. "I guess you do. But you don't have a lead on any black-market weapons, do you?"

"I'll get one. I have some contacts I can lean on. It might take me a few days, and I have to find someone who can vouch for me, but I'll be prepared by the time I show up at their door."

"Their front gate. Which is about a mile from the actual compound."

"Front gate." He acknowledged her correction with a nod. "Obviously you'll have to brief me on everything you remember."

She pictured him driving up to the outer gate with its security cameras and barbed wire. Pressing the buzzer. Talking to the armed men guarding the gate. Always men. Women never guarded the gate. It was a man's world there. They really only wanted women for one thing...

Slowly but surely, she felt the mantle of "art history professor" slide away. It had always been a safe haven, a way to exist in the world without force or violence. Underneath, there was a different Carolyn Moore. A person who would battle for what she believed. A person who would never stand by and let kids pay some twisted price with their lives.

And just like that, a plan fell into place. Her own plan.

Strange chills passed through her body, down to her feet, back up to the crown of her head. It was almost like feeling trapped all over again, as if the relentless march of destiny had led her here, to this very moment.

"No," she said, then cleared her throat. "No." It came out more firmly this time. "We can't wait a few days. And there's too much you don't know about the place. It has to be me. I'm going back."

He scowled at her in clear shock. "You can't go back. You said you were banned from the property."

"Yes." She nodded, feeling a little like a bobblehead. "But there's one way I can get back in. It'll work, if we do it right."

His eyebrows shot up nearly to his hairline. "We?"

"Yes. We." She drew in a deep breath. This was the weird part. The part she had no idea how he'd react to. "We have to get married."

25

"*MARRIED?*" CAROLYN COULDN'T HAVE SURPRISED HIM MORE IF SHE'D told him they had to dig their way in with a spoon.

"I mean, pretend to be married," she said quickly. "Pretend to *want* to get married. I know, it's a stretch, given how we both feel about marriage. But that's why it might work. It'll be a total charade. An act."

"Back up, buttercup. Explain this to me step by step. Like I'm one of those non-professor types."

She tugged her fuzzy bathrobe tighter around her and perched on the edge of the couch. "Sacred vows like marriage are very important to the Light Keepers. All marital unions are supposed to be sanctioned by the father. Even though I've been named a pariah, they would most likely grant my request for my father's blessing. Especially if I go crawling back begging. Which I will do."

From her expression, he imagined that would be about as fun as crawling over broken glass. "It's too dangerous," he told her. "They banned you. It's not safe for you to go back." He shook his head, the whole idea setting off every alarm bell he had. There would be no way to guarantee her safety if she walked into a compound full of people who hated her. *Armed* people. He turned away, decision made, coffee halfway to his mouth. "Absolutely not."

Before he could get his coffee to his mouth, something hit him on the arm. Coffee splashed onto his shirt and his coffee cup vanished from his hand. He spun around to see Carolyn holding it, her blue eyes spitting fire.

"I just disarmed a Night Stalker," she pointed out. "I can take care of myself, and by the way, *it's not your decision.* It's mine."

"You stole my coffee." He stared at her, dumbfounded.

"To make a point." A tiny muscle flickered in her jaw as she took a sip of his coffee.

"A minute ago you were suggesting we get married. Now you're stealing my coffee?"

"*Pretend* to *intend* to get married. If you're not interested, I can find someone else." Cool as cucumber, she sipped again.

Fuck that. Fury simmered deep inside him at the thought of someone else taking on the Light Keepers in his place. "No. If anyone's going to pretend to marry you, it'll be me. But Caro—"

"*I am doing this.*" Her steely tone left no doubt about her determination. "If I have a little sister in there, and she needs me, I'm going in. The FBI obviously isn't going to do anything right away, so I will. Don't tell me you wouldn't do the same if it was one of your brothers."

He scrubbed a hand across the back of his neck. Damn, she'd found the one argument he couldn't counter. Of course he would. He'd probably already be on his way, coming in hot, spoiling for a fight.

But this situation required more forethought and planning. They couldn't just barge in. "What happens if we find her? What then?"

"I don't know. Right now, I just want to talk to her. I want to make sure she's okay. Then we'll go from there."

"What's the risk to you? Will they want to punish you because you left?"

She held his gaze without flinching. "It's possible, but nothing I can't handle. I'm choosing this, Tobias. I'm willing to take that risk."

He paced around the living room, sorting through various scenarios. "We'll need backup. I'm not letting you go in there without someone standing by on the outside."

"The FBI? It's not like they can stop me from visiting my father."

He shook his head. "They'd find a way. We're civilians, especially you. I'd rather ask my brothers. Will was a deputy sheriff and Ben was in the Air Force. We can trust them, and they'd keep a lower profile."

"Agreed." She released a long breath. "Are we actually doing this then?"

He still wasn't entirely convinced. What if the Light Keepers got suspicious? What if he and Caro couldn't pull off looking like a blissfully engaged couple? "We need to make it look real. I'll get a wedding ring, we can use my grandmo—"

"*No.*"

Her sharp, almost desperate tone shocked him into silence.

"No grandmother's ring. We need a ring, but it has to be something with no sentimental attachment whatsoever. We can only do this if we both understand that *it means nothing.* It's not real. It's an act. We're not actually getting married. Ever."

He stared at her, trying to understand. "I get it. You don't want to marry me."

She turned away, the coffee cup shaking in her hand. She wasn't as cool as it had seemed at first. "I told you what marriage means for the Light Keepers. The only way I can handle going back there, pretending to be engaged, is if I know with *one hundred percent certainty* that it's not real and will never be real."

She set the cup on the tray. He watched her bend over in her fuzzy lamb bathrobe, feeling as if his heart was being ripped from his chest. If he agreed to help her, he'd be agreeing to never marry her.

Which shouldn't be a problem. He hadn't ever given much thought to marriage. Until recently. He could easily go back to not thinking about it. Couldn't he? She'd already given very clear signals that she was in this for the sex, not for some fairy tale ending. Nothing was changing. They were just making it official. Committing to never committing.

"Understood." He spoke the word coldly, professionally, like a soldier. "Hard pass on the wedding ring. We'll find something meaningless."

She nodded and drew in a long breath. "One more thing. You have to promise to do what I say in there. Promise to obey me, so to speak."

"Excuse me?" He scowled. "That's...uh...very old-fashioned of you. They don't usually put that in the vows anymore."

"If I'm going to go back, I need to know that you're going to do what I say. I need to be in control of the situation—at least our part of it."

"I'm not going to do anything you don't want, Caro. You know me better than that."

"Just promise me. Word of a Knight brother. To pull this off, I'm going to have to act...subservient. It'll make my skin crawl. I might want to throw up. If I know that you'll do what I say...it'll help me, that's all."

He turned it over in his mind. From the tense lines of her face, the clenching of her fists, this was going to be hell on her. As a man, he probably couldn't really imagine it. If she needed that assurance, he should give it to her.

"I promise," he said softly. "With one exception—if I think something is necessary for your safety, or *our* safety. I'm trained in infiltration, combat missions, surveillance. We have to use that to our advantage. Do you agree?"

She thought it over and finally nodded, a faint smile crossing her lips. "I do."

Oh, the irony of that "I do." Somehow, it didn't seem that funny to him.

"There's something I want to do before we go in," he told her. "I think it might help both of us."

"Bring it on. I trust you, my non-husband."

He gritted his teeth. *Better get used to it.* A non-husband was all he'd ever be.

TOBIAS HAD BEEN WANTING to take her up in the Cessna, but now he had an actual mission-critical reason to. The Light Keepers compound was located a couple hundred miles up the coast, easily within the range of the Cessna 206. An aerial overflight would help him understand its layout and potential escape routes. And it might be a good shakedown cruise for Carolyn.

He brought her to the Knight and Day reception office first, so he could enter the paperwork for this unplanned trip. He and Ben had decorated the place for Christmas, putting up sparkly tinsel around the door and windows. A Christmas tree in a planter, decorated with little toy airplanes, filled one corner.

Looking like a winter princess in a cream-colored wool coat and forest-green scarf, Carolyn clapped her hands in delight. "I love it! It's so Christmassy. And that sign is amazing. Who designed it?"

In the sign, a knight in shining armor rode a small plane bareback, like a horse. He held a banner that unfurled behind him with the words Knight and Day Flight Tours. "I don't know. Suzanne found it for us. It's perfect, right?"

"Completely. Whoever painted it is a genius. I'll have to pry the name out of Suzanne."

"Believe me, we tried. She said she's sworn to secrecy."

"Hm." She eyed him skeptically, but moved on to looking at

the photos they'd mounted on the walls. "These must come from Evie at the Sky View."

Tobias pulled out the ledger where they entered all the information for each trip. "That's right. The tourists love them. I'll just be a minute here." He did a quick weather check, and saw no problems to worry about. Clear skies all the way up the coast, wind at five knots, slight inversion layer farther up the coast.

After the paperwork came the preflight routine. "Want to come with me for the safety check? You can stay in here if you like. It takes about fifteen minutes."

"I'll come with you. I like seeing you do your thing. It's sexy." Even though her tone wasn't as flirty as usual, it was closer to their usual hot banter.

"I got to watch you teach a class, so it's only fair."

"Teaching a class isn't nearly as sexy as flying a plane."

"When you're teaching it?" He snorted and ushered her outside to the hangar where the two planes lived when they weren't in constant use. It gave him and Ben and a hopefully soon-to-be-hired mechanic a chance to maintain them in a protected space.

He quickly ran through the steps of the preflight check. Carolyn watched closely, asking questions now and then. It figured that she'd want to know everything about the process. In that way, she reminded him of Merry. No wonder they were friends. They both had such quick minds.

"Have you ever been up in a small plane?" he asked when he was done, and they were wheeling the plane out of the hangar.

"No, I haven't, and I can't say that I ever planned to. Merry didn't exactly give glowing reviews of her first trip. I had drinks with her afterwards, and she needed practically the entire pitcher of margaritas to recover."

"You can feel free to hold my hand." He grinned at her. "As long as I'm not doing anything important with the joystick at the moment."

"Gotcha."

They stationed the plane at the end of the tarmac. The windsock was barely lifting in the breeze, and the sun glinted off the sleek wings of the Cessna. The plane was a beauty and a workhorse, and Tobias had nicknamed it Lancelot. He brought over the step stool that helped shorter people board the plane, only to find that Carolyn had managed to climb in by herself.

She settled into the seat, found the seat belt and strapped herself in.

He closed the door and walked around the plane to the pilot's side. As he went, he stroked the Cessna's smooth metal curves and whispered his usual prayer for an uneventful flight. So far, Knight and Day had a perfect record, marred only by two cases of airsickness. He'd take a little stray vomit over wind shear any day.

Inside the plane, he switched on the radar, the onboard flight system, the gauges. He found a set of headphones for Carolyn and plugged the jack into the comms system.

"So this airstrip is remote enough that we aren't required to hook into an air traffic control system. The nearest tower is at the regional airport almost an hour away. But never fear, safety is absolutely our very first concern. So even though it might feel crazy rattling down this runway with no air traffic control tower, you don't have to worry. I got this."

"Tobias." Her voice sounded tinny through the headphones. "I'm not worried. I trust you completely. I let you lick chocolate off my nipples. If that's not trust, what is?"

His hand slipped slightly on the joystick. "Warning you right now, lady. That kind of thing is not going to fly up here."

"So to speak."

"So to speak," he agreed with a smile. "But seriously. I can't have you distracting me with talk of chocolate. You know how I am about sweets."

She laughed, then went quiet as he steered the plane to the far end of the tarmac. "Here we go," he told her. He increased the speed, feeling the powerful Continental O-520 engine respond like a beautiful thoroughbred. The Cessna sprinted down the tarmac, gaining speed, until it hit that perfect point when he could pull back on the yoke and feel the air current lift them off the ground.

It was always an incredible feeling, but especially in a small plane, when you could practically feel the air rushing past your face. He loved the illusion of having his own wings, of being one with the current, as if the plane itself was just a prop.

They rose over the little airstrip and its tarmac, which stretched for five thousand feet parallel to a length of coastline covered with beach grass and wild roses. To the west, the immense Pacific Ocean stretched like a hazy blue blanket and to the east rose the foothills, the higher ridges of the Sierra Nevadas revealed with each increase in altitude.

When they'd reached a cruising altitude of eleven thousand feet, he glanced over at Carolyn. Her lips were parted, her eyes shining with awe as she took in the incredible beauty below them, the pristine mountain peaks and endless stretches of cliffs.

"Wow," she said. "I know a few Renaissance masters who would have loved this."

"Didn't Leonardo da Vinci come up with an airplane design?"

"Yes." She smiled at him, looking pleased. "The ornithopter. We'd be lying face down cranking with our hand and feet in his version. It might have worked once it was in the air, but he never figured out how to get airborne without an internal combustion engine."

He liked the fact that she was the one doing the commentary on this flight, not him. It made for a nice break. "I do love my engines. You're riding on three hundred horses right now. It'll take us about an hour to get to the compound, so sit back and enjoy the ride."

She beamed at him, and settled back to watch the gorgeous West Coast shoreline slide past beneath them. The familiar sounds and sensations of flying took over. The engine droned, the plane quivered from the buffeting of the air currents.

He took a wide path out over the ocean so she could watch a pod of dolphins through the binoculars he'd brought. Then he did the same thing over the mountains. They spotted a white dot that slowly formed into a mountain goat, and a brown dot that may or may not have been a bear. They even noted a column of smoke from someone's campfire.

"In the spring we'll probably take the hotshots for some surveys of the snowpack, that sort of thing." He raised his voice to be heard over the engine noise. "Part of our mission is to help the local fire and rescue people. So far they haven't needed us, which is good because we didn't really have our act together. Plus, it's just good in general not to have any disasters. But we're ready if they need us."

"Once a hero, always a hero," she shouted back.

He gave her a thumb's up. If she wanted to think of him as a hero, he wasn't about to stop her.

The time flew by, and soon they were closing in on the compound. "How close can we get?" he asked her.

She was already getting tense, staring down at the ground, shoulders hunched, as if bracing for a blow. "We can fly right over. It's happened before, no one would be surprised. They won't shoot us down or anything. How low can you fly?"

"I can drop down a bit." He tilted the nose of the craft downwards, making sure to do it far enough ahead for a gradual descent. The forests became more differentiated, individual trees more identifiable. He watched the radar as they closed in on the Light Keepers' coordinates.

"I see it," she said suddenly. "I see the water tower. And the grain silo. And the chapel. They call it the Chapel of the Rays and there's a pattern cut into the wall so the light comes flowing in at dawn."

He peered down at the spread, taking note of distances and

the relative location of buildings. He was taking a logistical approach, but for her it must be an emotional experience, seeing the place she'd left behind at the age of eighteen. The place where her father still lived, where she might have a sister.

He checked on her. She huddled against the window of the plane, her light hair flowing in waves across the creamy wool of her coat, her headphones knocking against the hard clear Plexiglas. Every line of her body screamed alertness.

"I see the fence," she said. "The front gate. Everything looks pretty much the same so far."

"See any kids?"

"I can't tell. I don't see any people. But that doesn't really mean anything. They might be inside for a meal or a prayer service. I don't know. It's been ten years." Her voice was filled with worry, but when she turned back to face him, it was with clear eyes. "Let's head back, I don't think we're going to learn anything more like this. It's too far below, you know?"

He nodded. The property was already behind them anyway, and he didn't want to veer back and make any eyes on the ground suspicious. So he continued in a straight line north until the compound was out of sight. Then he made a wide turn toward the ocean.

"You okay?" he asked, taking her hand. She held on to it tightly.

"Yeah. Thanks for bringing me up here. It's really helpful. You know how you blow things up in your mind when you're away from them? I've been doing that for the past ten years. Now that I've seen the place again, I know I can handle this."

"I never doubted you could handle it, not for a second." And it was true. If he'd learned one thing about Carolyn Moore, it was that she was a warrior at heart.

As a warrior himself, he respected that. Along with all the other things he felt for her.

None of which would ever lead to marriage.

They spent the evening working out details of their plan with Will and Ben. This was a reconnaissance mission, they agreed. Their hope was to be in and out within a day, or maybe a night at the most. Their goal was to locate Sarah and ascertain her condition, then leave. But once they were inside, anything could happen. Ben would have the chopper standing by in case an air rescue was needed, whereas Will would drive up and hunker down in the nearest motel. If they hadn't heard anything within two days, they'd call the FBI.

After Will and Ben left, Carolyn filled Tobias in on as many logistical details as she remembered. He quizzed her on the leader of the group, its structure, its psychology. A clear picture formed in his mind of the image he'd have to present. An authoritarian, a swaggerer, a man who saw women as lesser, not equals.

That night they didn't make love. They were both too exhausted, physically and emotionally. Or maybe they would never make love again. Had they broken up? He wasn't completely sure. Carolyn snuggled her head into the notch between his shoulder and his chest and he stroked her feather-light hair as she drifted off to sleep.

And he realized something in that moment suspended between night and day. There was a chance he'd lose Caro for good tomorrow. Because in order to convince the Light Keepers that they were a couple, he'd have to bring to life her worst fear— losing her free will. What if she never looked at him the same after that?

26

CAROLYN'S STOMACH WAS IN KNOTS AS THEY DROVE UP TO THE GATE of the Light Keepers compound around mid-afternoon the next day. Tobias drove, of course. Anything else would look suspicious. They drove in Tobias's Land Rover, because it was guaranteed that the guards would check his license plate as soon as the surveillance camera took a picture of it. They would instantly know about Tobias—his military service, his father's murder, his recent departure from the Army.

Maybe they would see Tobias, with that background, as a good fit for the Light Keepers Brigade. That would make Carolyn and her would-be husband even more appealing to the group; at least that was their working theory.

He'd even put a few temporary tattoos on his arms and shoulders. Flames, a cross, a skull, a chain link. The sort of tattoos someone casting around for an identity might choose.

Every time she looked at him, she had to remind herself that Tobias *wasn't really like the men of the Light Keepers.*

He was strong, of course, the "alpha male" in appearance. But he didn't need to exert power over other people. He was confident in himself and he respected her. *Don't forget that.*

Besides, this was all an act. None of it was real. That was her mantra.

At the gate, the camera scanned their faces, then a voice came over the intercom. "This is a private organization. No entrance allowed."

Tobias gave Carolyn a glance, and she nodded. *Go time.* He addressed the intercom. "We're here to see Levi Moore. My name is Tobias Knight, and I'm here with Carolyn, Levi's daughter. We're here to request his blessing for our marriage. If you could let him know that, we'll wait."

Carolyn felt slightly nauseous at the word "marriage." This was real. Or at least pretend real. She kept her eyes down and her hands folded in her lap, the way women were supposed to at the compound. It felt so strange, after her time as an independent person in the outside world. And yet it came back to her so easily. Terrifyingly so.

After a long wait, another voice came over the intercom. Carolyn squeezed Tobias hand in the prearranged signal indicating this was the leader, known simply as Ray.

"Carolyn Moore is a pariah here. That means her father Levi has cast her out. She's no longer one of us."

Despite everything, that hurt. Carolyn dug her fingernails into the heels of her hands.

"I understand that. Since I've met her, we've spoken about it at length. Carolyn feels deep regret for the way she behaved back when she was a mere teenager. Now that we're together, she sees that she went down a wrong path. She's not expecting to be allowed back into the Light Keepers. All she's asking for is her father's blessing."

Another pause while the guards and Ray talked among themselves. Carolyn peered under her eyelashes at the high fence. Here at the entrance, the fence was fortified with barbed wire curling around the top edge. But at some points, she knew the perimeter of the property was less protected. "Carolyn Moore brought shame to her family and herself."

Carolyn tightened her hands into fists. *Shame*. She hated that word.

"Yeah, I get it. She's not after forgiveness. We know it's not going to happen. Just a blessing from her father, that's it. She says she won't marry me without it. It's part of why I fell for her, that old-fashioned quality. It's like a throwback to the way things ought to be. The man's the head of the household, and that's the way it should be."

Still Ray and the guards hesitated. Tobias had done his job—he'd sounded just as arrogant and "alpha" as the Light Keepers Brigade guys. Their request made sense. But would they bite?

She needed to do something to make it seem even more realistic. She needed to...

Swallowing down the taste of bile and defeat, she turned to Tobias and bowed to him, touching her hand to her forehead in the familiar Light Keeper gesture of female submission. It came back to her so easily, forehead lowered, the heel of her hand between her eyes, symbolizing the willingness of the woman to empty herself of all but what the man graced her.

She'd forgotten about that gesture until just now—probably blocked it out—which meant she hadn't taught it to Tobias. He flinched in surprise. "Put your hand over mind," she hissed in a whisper. "As if you're blessing me."

"Are you serious?" he muttered.

"*Do it*." It would look so suspicious if he didn't. "You promised to do what I say, remember?"

He placed his big palm on top of hers, all the while muttering something about how fucked up the whole thing was. She tried not to laugh at his reaction. But she found it incredibly reassuring. If he thought this was batshit crazy, she could probably trust him.

She did trust him. But damn, this was mortifying.

She completed the gesture by bringing her hands to her heart, whispering a quick prayer—"keep the light"—and placing her hands back in her lap.

There. That ought to do it. Now they'd see that she hadn't forgotten the old ways that had been drilled into her for eight years.

"You may enter," the guard finally said. "Leave your cell phones in your vehicle. No electronics allowed. Keep the light."

"Keep the light," Tobias muttered.

The gate slid open on its tracks, Tobias put his Land Rover in gear, and they drove into Light Keepers territory.

It felt surreal to Carolyn. She kept her eyes down in case anyone was watching them. But she had lots of practice in surveying her surroundings through lowered lashes. The heart of the compound was a former Grange Hall that had served the surrounding farmers. The Light Keepers had bought it nearly forty years ago and added many more buildings—the chapel, a longhouse, guest cabins, a barn, a solar power station, a grain silo. Each building sported the Light Keeper logo with its rays of sun. Fields of last season's wheat and corn extended as far as the eye could see, along with herds of alpaca and goats.

She was all too familiar with those alpaca. The women were responsible for shearing them and spinning their wool. The women did most things together, and even though she had chafed at the work, that sense of togetherness, of being part of a tribe, that was probably the one thing she truly missed.

"Ready for the next phase?" Tobias asked under his breath.

"Ready." Ready or not, they were approaching the meeting house, which was the old Grange Hall, the only building where visitors were allowed. This was where her father would meet with them. If they had any hope of seeing other parts of the compound, it would be through the grace of Levi Moore.

They were shown into the "atrium," which was where all contacts with the outside world happened. The computers and phones were located here, which meant no one under eighteen was permitted to enter. Carolyn glanced around curiously, since she'd never set foot inside this room before. On the whitewashed wall, big flowing letters read, "Keep the Light."

They sat for barely a moment before Levi Moore—her father—strode in, wearing the traditional white tunic of an Elder. Her heart squeezed at the sight of him. He showed every bit of the past ten years in the length of his graying beard and the sun wrinkles fanning from his eyes. In truth, she'd stopped thinking of him as her father long ago. At the compound, parental relationships weren't encouraged. Families were supposed to abandon all ties other than the spiritual one with the group. But she could still remember the time before the cult, when he'd been a distracted but generous father.

"Wow, you're an elder now," she said, forgetting for a moment the required protocol. "Congratulations, Dad."

He looked stunned at her break in etiquette.

Quickly, she kneeled on the floor, both hands held to her forehead instead of just one. That was the greeting reserved for elders.

But he didn't place his hands on hers to accept her gesture. Not a surprise—she was a pariah. No member of the group would ever greet her again in that way.

Instead, Levi Moore lifted his hand, palm open and swung it at her cheek.

She flinched, ready for the sting of his blow. It was what she "deserved," as one who had left. All she could do was brace for it and hope it didn't hurt too much.

But his blow never landed. Tobias stepped between them and caught her father's wrist. "No," he said simply. "She's my woman now. If anyone's going to hit her, it's my right and duty."

Carolyn cringed. Damn it, she should have warned Tobias this might happen. This was a potential disaster because he had it all wrong. According to the rules of the compound, she belonged to her father until she spoke her marital vows. Levi Moore had the right to hit her.

But maybe her father would let it slide, since Tobias didn't know the rules.

She peeked up through her lashes, trying to read his face. His beard made it difficult, but his body language told it all. Tobias was younger, stronger, and had that natural power-alpha presence. Her father never had possessed that kind of aura; he'd always feared weakness, especially his own.

With a sudden flash of insight, she wondered if that was why he'd joined the Light Keepers, so he could feed off the power of others.

"So you intend to marry my daughter," Levi finally said.

"I do. But it depends on you, sir. Carolyn believes it won't be a true marriage until you've blessed it."

"My daughter is correct. In order for her marriage to receive the blessing of the Light Keepers, she must bow before her father."

"So I understand. That's why we're here." Carolyn could hear the tension in his voice, though maybe to someone who didn't know him quite as well it sounded like toughness. "That's why she's kneeling here. Carolyn?"

Part of the drill was that women were supposed to wait to speak in formal situations like this. But now that her "husband" had given her permission, it was her turn. "Please, Father. I deeply regret my past actions. I'd like to move forward with my life in a manner that's as close to the Light Keeper way as possible. I beg you to grant me forgiveness and shed your light on me."

Out of the corner of her eyes, she saw Tobias's fist briefly close. She knew how this sounded, how totally embarrassing it was if you weren't used to it. Humiliation crept over her, sent blood into her cheeks. He was witnessing a grown woman, an educated professional, acting like a ridiculous child. Kneeling before the irresponsible man who'd dragged her here and abandoned his paternal obligations in order to play at being some sort of patriarch.

Then she took another look at Tobias's hand. He was lowering his middle finger ever so slightly. He was subtly, for her eyes only, flipping off her father.

And that one gesture sent renewed strength flooding through her. "I beg you, dear Father, to find the grace of forgiveness in your heart for your shamed daughter."

She was starting to feel the strain of keeping her hands at the level of her forehead. Maybe Levi was drawing out this moment in order to make her suffer physically. She wouldn't put it past him. He probably thought it would be proof that she was sincere.

Well, she *was* sincere. She sincerely hated every moment of this. But if she could do her part to find her sister, it was worth it.

Finally she felt a waft of air on her palms as he waved his hand across hers. "I will grant my blessing, on one condition."

Tobias spoke up, the way the "man of the family" should. "Anything you require, I stand ready to accept."

"You must spend a week here. We need to see you together, to confirm that you exhibit the proper deference to our way of life. How else can I, in good conscience, offer my blessing?"

Carolyn felt her gorge rise. *A week?* How the hell could she manage a week here? She couldn't! She wouldn't! She started to rise to her feet, to tell him that they had to discuss it. But Tobias put his hand on her shoulder, stopping her. "That would be a gift to us, and I accept your condition. I'm not as familiar with your way of life as Carolyn is, and I look forward to learning all I can."

Oh my God. *Seriously? One freaking week?* How dare he decide without even finding a way to consult with her? He was supposed to *obey her*, not the other way around. He'd done exactly what she'd asked him not to. She gave a little twitch of her shoulder to communicate her fury. He got it, and moved his hand away.

"Good, good. Another thing," said Levi Moore. "I want to see your marriage license."

Marriage license? Her blood ran cold. They hadn't gone that far with their charade. But Tobias was pulling something from his pocket. A piece of paper.

"This is our application. Obviously we're waiting for your blessing before we sign."

Levi looked it over, then handed it back without another word.

"We're a little tired from the drive," Tobias said. "Where will we be staying?"

"I'm afraid I can't allow you to stay with the members of Light Keepers, so you'll stay in a guest cabin while you're here. You are required to refrain from all marital contact."

No problem. Right now she was so frustrated the only contact she wanted was between her fist and something inanimate. A *week?* She was going to lose her mind. She already *was* losing her mind.

Her father bowed slightly. "Someone will show you to your quarters. Keep the light."

"Keep the light," Tobias answered. She made some kind of sound that hopefully passed for "keep the light."

The door clicked shut. Painfully, she rose to her feet. Tobias offered his hand to help, but she pushed it away. "You should have waited."

"I couldn't," he whispered back. He said that with a tender smile, the kind a man in love might give to his future bride. She wanted to wipe it right off his face.

But she lowered her lashes and folded her hands together. How many times had she stood like this, steaming on the inside?

A woman opened the door and came inside. Carolyn didn't recognize her, but she looked much like every other woman at the place in her floor-length dress and her hair in the traditional long braid. She bowed to Tobias and shot Carolyn a nasty "pariah" look.

"I'll show you to your cabin," she told them. They followed her outside. Carolyn stayed a half step behind Tobias, as was expected. *None of this is real. None of this is real.* She chanted it over and over in her mind. If she didn't hang onto that thought, she might not have a mind left to lose. *Focus. Observe,* she told herself.

They walked down a pea gravel path to a small A-frame cabin under a grove of pine trees. Carolyn did as much surreptitious surveillance as she could while keeping her eyes downcast. They passed a few other women in long dresses, but no one under eighteen.

That seemed odd, to the best of her memory. Something was definitely off here at the Light Keepers.

27

ONCE THEY WERE INSIDE THE CABIN AND ALONE, TOBIAS PUT A finger to his lips. "Bugs," he mouthed. She nodded and watched as he methodically searched the tiny cabin.

"Clear," he finally said.

Released from the need for restraint, Carolyn did what every muscle in her body had been screaming for since she'd stepped out of the car. She shook her entire body out, rolling her neck, flapping her hands. Reclaimed her physical self from the strict constraints of the bowing and head-lowering.

Then she turned on Tobias. "One fucking *week*?"

His expression tightened. "I had to improvise, Caro. We don't have to stay that long. But if I didn't say yes, I was afraid he would kick us out. "

"What happened to doing what I say?"

"Unless it's a safety issue, remember? I didn't want to set off any alarms. We haven't seen any kids yet. This whole mission would be wasted and they'd never let us back in."

"And that license? Where did that come from?"

"I pulled some strings at City Hall and they rushed me something official."

"Why didn't you tell me?"

"I didn't want you to freak out. Like you are." A smile dragged at one corner of his mouth.

"Aaahhhh!!!" Because he was right and she *still* couldn't stand it, she stomped her feet and dug her hands into her hair. "I hate this. I hate being here. It makes me crazy. It makes me want to... rage and scream and...gahhhh!!!"

He thumped on his chest. "Come on. Do it. Hit me."

"*What?* I'm not going to hit you."

"Yeah you are. You won't hurt me. I'm tough. What are you, some kind of weak helpless *female*?" He was goading her, blatantly; she knew it, but it still worked.

"Damn you, Tobias." She stepped close to him and pounded her fists on his hard chest, pouring out her frustration. He wrapped his hands around her wrists, not stopping her, just slowing her blows. And that touch, the warmth of his flesh, the solid bone structure of his chest, changed everything. It instantly grounded her in her real life, her grown up, independent life in which she'd been having wild hot sex with this man since Christmas Eve.

She stopped her rain of blows.

"Tobias," she whispered. "I'm so sorry."

"Don't be sorry. I offered. Feel better?"

She saw the concern in his eyes, the alertness. "Being here is a nightmare for me."

"I know. Don't worry about it, Carolyn. Just like you said, nothing that happens here is real. That includes your failed attempt to beat me up." He flashed a one-sided smile at her.

"Do you promise? After we leave, will you swear to forget everything we do here? Will you forget that I knelt on the floor to beg my so-called father to bless me?"

"Carolyn. Listen to me." He cradled her face in his hands. "You're here for your sister and any other kids who are in danger here. That's it. You're like a soldier, doing what you have to do.

You worry about finding your sister. You sure as hell don't have to worry about me."

The heat from his hands warmed her blood, made her feel alive again. Like a woman, not a possession. A real full-fledged human, not a second-class citizen.

"Make love to me, Tobias," she whispered.

His gaze intensified to a deep midnight, full of questions instead of stars.

"Please. Remind me who I really am. I'm not this...this...*thing*. This servant. This lesser being."

"Lesser? Never." He captured her mouth with his, pulling her into a deep kiss that she felt all the way down to her soul. She responded to him desperately. "You're a goddess," he murmured against her lips. "My goddess. I'd kneel before you right now if you wanted."

"No. No more kneeling. Not for either of us." She worked at his belt buckle, craving the touch of his flesh. When it wouldn't give way immediately, she plunged her hand into his pants. Hot skin greeted her, then the rough tickle of hair. Below that, the soft lump of his penis, already responding to her touch.

"Lift me up," she said in his ear. "I want to ride you like a cowboy."

"You got it." He put his hands under her ass and slid her up along his body until she could wrap her legs around his waist. She ground her sex against the growing bulge of his erection. For her return to the compound, she'd worn a very simple cotton sweater and a long jersey skirt in navy blue, with a pair of high boots underneath. It was the plainest, most utilitarian outfit she could come up with.

Tobias pushed the fabric up her thighs as he nested her against his groin. She felt his belt buckle press into her, just above her sex, and somehow that pressure made her nearly delirious. He found her ass under the skirt and rotated her slowly against him, his strong hands gripping her so tightly she saw stars.

"Fuck me, Tobias," she hissed. That was what she wanted. Not 'making love.' Not 'having sex.' No, she wanted the down-and-dirtiest, baddest, meanest sex any two people could have, the kind of sex where you don't care what you look like or sound like.

He growled and nipped at her neck, right under her ear, which happened to be one of her most sensitive spots. Then he bit his way down the tendon of her neck. Her nipples immediately went rock hard as if they were little soldiers at his command. He swirled his tongue across her throat, causing it to tilt backwards in sheer delight. She moaned loudly and swore again, brazen and foul-mouthed, craving that rebellion and freedom.

She couldn't act this way with anyone but Tobias. Couldn't even imagine it.

He marched over to the bed, a modest double with a rolled up blanket carefully placed down the middle. He sat down on the edge, so she was on his lap then reached back and shoved aside the bedroll.

"They said no marital contact," she reminded him, her voice ragged.

"We're not married. Not getting married. They didn't say anything about premarital contact."

"You are bad." And she loved it. "So bad."

"Damn right." He jerked her sex against his cock, which was now fully aroused. "You want a taste of this bad boy?"

"Yes. Oh hell yes." She pushed him back onto the bed. He spread-eagled his arms, a movement that put his magnificent chest on display. She unbuttoned his shirt, a plaid lumberjack flannel that fit the look of the younger guys at the compound. Her impulse was to rip it off, send those buttons flying, but he hadn't brought another one. So she stuck with slipping each button through its hole, her hands shaking with need.

He wore a clean white t-shirt underneath. She leaned forward to inhale the scent of fresh laundry and honorable man. God, he smelled good. If she could bottle this scent and keep it in a vial, she'd never feel lonely.

She shook off the weird thought. Obviously, she still wasn't thinking straight. But at least she wasn't having a meltdown. Unless it was a lust meltdown—that, she wouldn't even try to deny. She ran her hands underneath his shirt, savoring the ripple of muscle and hard curves of bone before stripping the shirt off him. "Well hello, Michelangelo," she crooned.

He grimaced. "I saw the statue of David, you know. I was in Italy during a short leave. I didn't have enough time to get to Cali, so I stayed and went to museums. I thought he had a small dick."

"You're so cultured."

"Right? And I was twenty-two, I really had no excuse."

"You're forgiven. This," she reached inside his pants and circled his penis, "makes up for any lack of aesthetic sophistication."

"I see what's going on here. You want me for my raw manliness. My stiff cock. You have your priorities."

Her sex jumped at his mention of 'stiff cock.' God, what was it about his blunt words that got her so fired up?

"I'll take your stiff cock and raise you a wet pussy," she told him. *That* got her even more turned on and she flexed her hips, seeking that hot friction against her clit. "Remember how you said you'd obey me?"

"Yup."

"You already screwed up on that one. So now you get another chance. Touch my clit," she ordered him.

His gaze flew to meet hers, so smoldering and intense it brought a flood of heat to her sex. "Yes, ma'am," he said. He danced his fingers up her thighs with delicate touches, pushing her skirt to her waist. He pulled aside the fabric of her panties and touched the pad of his index finger against her clit.

She tilted her head back and sighed, endorphins flooding her brain with happiness. Crazy how feeling him press the one tiny bit of flesh completely changed her mood. A sense of lightness expanded in her chest. She felt languid, relaxed, at one with the world.

And that was before he started to rub. With long, skilled fingers he spread her own juices over the seam of her lips. Then he rubbed again, adding more pressure, making sparks fly along her nerve endings. She rocked her hips against the rhythm of his strokes, seeking the bone of his knuckle, the stubborn weight of his hand, loving how it intruded between her legs.

Suddenly frantic, she jammed her sex against him. She wanted to explode, to be obliterated. She wanted everything else to disappear—the compound, her father, the weirdness of being back, the confusion, the doubt...

A blinding white nuclear blast of a climax splintered her vision, shattered her into a thousand pieces of free-floating joy. She rode wave after wave of an orgasm that never seemed to end. She didn't want it to end, because then she'd be back to reality. Back in the place she'd never intended to see again.

When her heartbeat slowed and she reluctantly opened her eyes, her vision filled with Tobias's dark blue gaze and naked, rippling chest. He blocked out everything else, whether he intended to or not.

His need was still obvious and urgent, judging by the rock-hard erection that pressed against her rear. She rose onto her knees and found him with her hand. Thick and solid, it responded to her touch by swelling even more.

Swiftly, they both stripped off the rest of their clothes and moved further onto the bed. Tobias snagged a condom from the back pocket of his jeans. "It's a good thing they didn't search us," he said as he tore it open.

"I can't believe you brought one in here. It's like a middle finger in condom form."

"Exactly." He grinned. "I've always been the rebellious one. Any chance to bring out the middle finger, I'm there."

He rolled the condom onto his erection. She helped him slide the latex down, as a sudden wave of sadness washed over her. When she'd lived at the compound, all the girls had dreamed of who they might marry, and how quickly they might have a baby, how many babies. The thought of sex with no chance of getting pregnant had never occurred to them.

To be honest, she hadn't known it was possible.

Now, she knew all about the facts of life. She also knew about the facts of *her* life. She'd chosen a different path, an independent one. A life without a husband—current situation aside. So why was she sad about protected sex with Tobias? Sex with no chance of a baby? Why were tears forming in her eyes? Why was her throat closing tight?

Why was Tobias blurring underneath her, overlaid with images of him carrying Faith on his shoulders, talking to the boy with the crutches, slinging his arm over Aiden's shoulder? Tobias would be an overprotective, but endlessly caring father and husband.

Savagely, she shoved all those crazy thoughts aside. This place was making her nuts. *Just have sex. Put him inside you. Fuck him.* That's what this was about, not some sentimental fantasy left over from her time with the Light Keepers. She was here on a mission. Nothing more.

Still, a sob broke through as she positioned the tip of his condom-covered penis at her slick opening.

"What's the matter?" Tobias asked sharply. "You're crying."

"I'm *not crying*. I'm not. I just want to have sex." She pushed down, lowering inch by inch onto his powerful cock. A tear ran down her cheek.

"Yes, you are. I can see a tear. You're crying."

"Just fuck me, Tobias. Please. Just fuck my brains out."

She felt him hesitate, and squeezed her eyes shut. More warm tears slid down her cheeks. Right now, she didn't want him to be sensitive and aware of her feelings. Using the strength of her thighs, she lifted herself up, then lowered down, using the hot grip of her body to make him forget everything except pleasure and need.

It must have worked. He stopped asking questions and followed her rhythm. He put his hands on her hips to add more force to his thrusts. They stopped talking and moved into a world of grunts and sighs and slapping flesh. She shifted into a state of floating bliss in which nothing in the outside world could affect her.

Such a happy place, so safe and above it all. If only she could stay here, filled with bliss and oblivion and Tobias's stiff cock, everything would be okay. No one but Tobias ever made her feel this way. This was the Tobias-state. Utter safety, utter freedom. She could rest easy in his arms, no matter where she was.

He touched her cheek, thumbing the tears off her skin. Even with her eyes closed, she knew he was about to come. His body went rigid under hers, his cock pulsed, and he was saying something, over and over...a murmur of words like a river sweeping her away...

Her eyes snapped open. "What did you say?"

Spent from his orgasm, he lay back against the pillows, his hair damp with sweat. His hand dropped away from her face, and his expression, which had been one of deep tenderness, went wary.

"I said I love you."

Ripples of shock traveled through her, as if she'd touched the electric fence around the alpaca pen.

Love?

No. This was sex. Not love. Not softness. Not tenderness.

"You can't say that. Not here." She tried to scramble off his body, but he clamped a hand around her upper arm.

"Why not?"

"Let me go." Her fierceness made him snatch his hand away in an instant. She threw herself off the bed and searched for her clothes.

"Caro, what the fuck?" He sat up, a blur at the corner of her eye. *Everything* was a blur. Wild emotions were tumbling through her. *This place was making her crazy.*

"None of this is real." She repeated her mantra. "This is all an act. Everything we do and say here is a lie."

"Not this." His deep voice vibrated across the space between them. Goose bumps rose on her skin. She couldn't think about what he was saying—it was funhouse mirrors, through the looking glass, down the rabbit hole...it was a dream turned nightmare, or a nightmare turned dream, she didn't know which... couldn't deal with it now...

"You promised." She stepped into her skirt, her voice trembling. "You promised to do what I say. Right?"

He nodded, a muscle ticking in his jaw, his eyes the deep dark of a thundercloud.

"Then stop talking like that."

They stared at each other for what seemed like forever. She had the sense of traveling at high speed, being pulled down a long wind tunnel, away from Tobias. Another funhouse delusion.

Finally he spoke, almost formal in his tone. "Agreed. I won't bother you again."

Before she could answer, or try to explain—not that she could have, the way her thoughts were spinning—he put a finger to his lips and cocked his head. Listening.

A rustling sound came from just under the window. Someone was out there.

28

GREAT FUCKING TIMING. TOBIAS PEELED OFF HIS CONDOM IN record time, then yanked on his pants, cursing himself six ways to Sunday. Why'd he have to choose that moment to blurt out what was in his heart? He knew Carolyn was under incredible strain from being back at the Light Keepers. Her stress level screamed from every tense line of her body. Why couldn't he just keep his mouth shut?

And now they didn't have time to finish the damn conversation because they had an eavesdropper.

Time to shove all their personal issues away and focus on the mission.

Softly, He stepped to the window and opened the curtain the tiniest crack. A little girl stared back at him. Dressed in a pinafore-type dress, her white-blond hair in two pigtails, her blue eyes big as saucers, she was the spitting image of Carolyn—at the age of eight or so.

"It's a little girl," he whispered to Carolyn, who was busy buttoning her sweater, color still coming and going in her cheeks. "It might be your mystery sister."

She hurried to his side. "Open the window and get her inside before someone spots her."

He unlocked the window, reached down and hauled the girl in by the armpits. He planted her on the floor, where she blinked at him as if he were Superman. He gave a quick check to make sure no one was chasing after her. The sun was just sinking below the horizon, bathing the fields and all the Light Keeper buildings in a luminous orange glow. He saw no one in the vicinity, so he closed the window and the curtains.

Carolyn was staring at the little girl as if she were a ghost.

The girl stared back. "Are you my sister?"

"I'm Carolyn Moore. My father is Levi Moore. Who are you?"

"Sarah!" the girl said ebulliently. "My daddy is Levi too. My mamma was Lilith but she died when she had me. The midwife couldn't save her."

Carolyn's expression shifted. "I'm sorry. I know how sad it is when your mommy dies."

Sarah looked her up and down, a frown on her little dimpled face. "Pariahs don't look so scary."

Looking self-conscious, Carolyn tucked the loose strands of her hair back into her ponytail.

"I don't mind if you're a pariah," Sarah added cheerfully. "It's okay. They say I'm going to be one too when I grow up, if I don't behave. But I don't *like* behaving."

Carolyn shot a quick amused glance at Tobias. His tension eased a bit; that was the first normal interaction they'd had since setting foot on Light Keeper property. "I know just what you mean," she said seriously. "I'm very happy to meet you. I didn't know I had a sister."

"I did," the little girl said proudly. "I knew you'd come some-day. Even though you're a bad person, I still like you. I don't have any other sisters, and the other girls are mean to me sometimes."

Tobias stiffened at the phrase "bad person," but Carolyn gave him a little head shake to warn him off.

"I'm sorry to hear about that. I know how it feels, but you can't let it get you down." To Tobias, Sarah didn't seem the kind to let anything get her down. "Sarah, do you mind telling me something? Do you live in the longhouse with the others?"

The girl interlaced her hands behind her back and rocked on her heels. "I'm not supposed to tell you anything or even talk to you. If they catch me, I'll be in biiiig trouble." She pulled her lower lip between her teeth, looking extremely anxious all of a sudden.

"We don't want to get you in trouble," said Carolyn quickly. "I just want to know where to find you if I come and visit."

"You can't visit. It's not allowed." Sarah glared at her sternly. "Besides, I'm not going back there. I'm coming with you."

Carolyn's gaze flew to meet Tobias's quickly. He shrugged, just as caught off-guard as she was. "What are you talking about?"

"We have to sneak away. I'm scared, sister Carolyn. They put us in the bunker and said we can't come out. None of the kids can. We don't like it and we're scared. Then Mark heard one of the Elders talking and he said your name and that you were here. That's why I came to find you."

Tobias jammed his hands in his pockets. So all the kids were being held in a bunker of some kind? This was worse than he'd imagined.

"Who's Mark?" he asked her.

She cast her eyes downwards, obviously unused to talking to male strangers.

"This is Tobias," Carolyn said. "He's my friend. You can trust him."

Sarah turned and gave him a skeptical up-and-down glance. "You're very tall and kind of scary," she declared.

"You don't look scared."

"I'm not scared of things, not like the little kids. Except for spiders. I really, really don't like spiders."

"I'm with you there," he said seriously. "Except Spiderman. I like him."

She looked at him blankly. Of course--they didn't have movies and TV here. She had no idea who Spiderman was.

Carolyn smiled at the little girl. "Sarah, I need to talk to Tobias for a second, okay?"

They stepped a few feet away, out of the girl's earshot. "What can we do, Tobias? They're being held in a bunker!"

"Do you know anything about it? Where it is?"

"No, there was nothing like that when I was here. I think they've gotten crazier since I left."

He eyed Sarah, who was now curiously poking around the little guesthouse. "It's hard to believe she's spent her life here. Why isn't she meek and obedient? Isn't that how the kids here are supposed to be?"

"*Supposed* to be, sure, at least around adults. But one good thing about living on a farm is there's freedom to run around and play. So she obviously has that side too." A certain softness came over her as she watched her sister. " She reminds me so much of myself."

"I can see the family resemblance, that's for sure." Sarah was now bouncing on the bed, her face bright with joy.

"We can't leave her here," Carolyn said firmly.

"But how can we take her? They'll never let her past the gate. We're unarmed, we have no backup, no standing to take her."

"But they're *being held in a bunker.* That's abuse. You're a Night Stalker. Are you telling me you can't figure out a way to get her out?"

He spun away from her and scrubbed a hand through his hair. He forced himself to think logistically about the situation. The element of surprise would be crucial. They'd have to act fast. And they'd need backup. Even if they managed to get beyond the fence, they'd need help on the other side. He'd have to contact Will, and probably the authorities, too.

"We'd have to leave tonight," he said, almost to himself. "They're up to something with that ploy to make us stay for a week. The faster we act, the better."

"Yes. Thank God you agree. Let's get out of here asap."

Tobias scowled and paced the floor, running through various scenarios. Would it be legal to help all the kids escape? They were here with their parents, after all. He went back to the little girl and crouched next to her. "I need to ask you a few questions. Do you mind?"

She nodded solemnly.

"Where is this bunker?"

"It's behind the barn," she whispered conspiratorially. "But it's supposed to be a secret."

"Did you leave the note on the fence, the one for Carolyn?"

"Yes, but Mark helped me put it there. He wants to leave because he thinks we're going to die. But I heard the Elders talking and they didn't say that."

"What'd they say?"

"They said we're going to do a standoff. That's not the same as dying, is it?"

Sometimes it was, but Tobias didn't want to scare her. "No, it's not the same as dying. But it could be dangerous." Was that why they were keeping the kids in the bunker, to protect them from this "standoff?" Maybe. But he didn't know enough about these people to be sure. "Coming with us means leaving your dad, and the bunker, which might be the safest place for you to be."

Sarah shook her head vigorously, eyes filling with tears. "I hate it there. I like to run and play and practice cartwheels, even though I'm not supposed to. In the bunker we can't do anything fun."

His fury grew. How could anyone choose a course of action that required kids to be kept in a bunker? If this crazy group wanted a standoff, they could have one. But they shouldn't be allowed to drag kids into the middle of it.

"How did you get out of the bunker?" he asked her. "To come and find us?"

"Mark showed me a tunnel."

"A tunnel? What kind of tunnel?"

"It's under the ground, and it has wires and pipes and stuff. Mark found a way to crawl into it."

Tobias looked up at Carolyn. "A utilidor. They found their way into a utilidor."

"What's that?"

"It's an underground corridor to bring in utilities, power, water and so forth. Maybe sewer. They're usually big enough for workers to access them." He turned back to Sarah. "How wide is the tunnel? Can an adult crawl through it?"

She surveyed him dubiously. "Maybe my sister can, but you're much too big."

Ah. There went that idea. "Do you know where else the tunnel goes?"

She squinted into the distance, as if trying to picture it, or remember. "No," she confessed. "Mark knows. He told me how to get here."

Carolyn cleared her throat. "It probably goes to the power station, which is at the western edge of the property, near the solar array. There's no other source of power out here."

Yes. That made complete sense. An idea began to form in Tobias's mind. A daring, terrifying idea. One in which a lot would depend on Carolyn.

Carolyn was asking Sarah about Mark. "Is he a good friend? He seems to know a lot of things."

"He's really smart. I wish he could leave with us, but he said I should ask for help after we leave. We can do that, right?" She gave Carolyn an enchanting smile and twined her hand in hers. "I hope we can because he's really nice. I hope we can help him find his mommy."

Tobias froze as her words sank in. Find his mommy? Did that

mean his mother wasn't part of the compound?

He shot a glance at Carolyn, who looked just as thunder-struck as he was. She sat down on the edge of the bed, still holding the little girl's hand. "Is his mommy missing?"

She laughed merrily. "No, silly. He was rescued from his mommy, except he says he was stolen. Just like Charity and Grace were. They cry at night. Sometimes I cry with them because they're so sad. My mommy's missing too but I don't remember her. And now I have a sister." She beamed with such joy that it practically lit up the room. The resemblance between her and Carolyn did something to his heart, as if it was being wrapped with golden ribbons.

"Yes, you do," Carolyn said firmly. "And I think all those kids ought to have sisters and mothers and families too. Tobias and I need to talk a little bit more to figure out a good plan, okay? Is someone going to notice you're gone?"

"Nope, Mark said not to worry."

Carolyn gave her a last squeeze on the shoulder and hurried over to Tobias. They huddled their heads together. "They're kidnapping kids!" she said fiercely. "Why would they do that?"

"Does it matter why? This changes everything. If it's true, we need to call in the FBI."

"But what if that's what they want? She mentioned a standoff. Defying the feds, maybe that's their goal. They'll get famous, they'll be on TV. All the other fringe groups will love them. We can't play into their hands."

He cupped his hands around her face, feeling the pulse fluttering in her throat, a frantic beat of worry. "We can't do this on our own. But I have a plan. Want to hear it?"

Her eyes widened, the trust in them like a shot to the heart. How could she trust him in some ways—but not the most crucial?

"One of us has to get word to the FBI," he said. "Which means leaving the property."

"It has to be you," she said right away. "It wouldn't make sense for you to stay and me to go."

"I can pretend that I want to join the group."

"But you can't fit through the utilidor. And you'd be surrounded by Light Keeper men the entire time. That's *if* they agreed to let you join. They might not want new members right now."

Good point. The Light Keepers were preparing for a big showdown. They might not want a new, unproven, unfamiliar member.

His heart sank. Caro was right. He had to be the one to leave. Which meant she had to stay.

In the place of her worst nightmares. The place where her father had just tried to hit her.

He ground his teeth together. It went against every protective principle he had to leave her here. He opened his mouth to object, then caught her fierce, resolute gaze. This was Caro, the woman who had knocked him off his feet in her borrowed office. She deserved his respect along with his protectiveness.

"Okay then. Here's the plan," he told her tightly. "We'll stage a big fight, a breakup. I'll leave in the Land Rover, with my cell phone. I'll contact Will and Ben and we'll handle everything on the outside. You'll make a big show of being heartbroken. You'll ask to stay in the comfort of your old home, where you grew up. You'll find your way to the kids, and locate Mark. He obviously knows the tunnels. You get Sarah to the power station, through the utility corridor."

She nodded, listening closely to every word. She was in warrior mode; he recognized it, that alertness, the determination.

"We'll meet you at the fence closest to the power station. I'll be out there as soon as I make contact with my brothers and the FBI, and I'll wait until you show up. If it's not tonight, then I'll keep waiting. But the FBI will probably want to make a move before long, so sooner is better."

A fierce light gleamed in her eyes. "It'll be tonight. Count on it."

He certainly wouldn't bet against her.

Carolyn glanced at her little sister, fear finally making an appearance. "They have all those guns, all that ammo. I don't even have a knife."

"It's better that way. You don't want a fight. If you run into trouble, tell them the FBI knows exactly what's going on. Tell them if anything happens to you they'll be in so much legal trouble that the entire place will have to shut down. If anything happens to a single child, the group is done. They know that. They're not stupid. You're smart and skilled, Carolyn. You're a warrior queen disguised as an art history professor. You can do this."

A slight smile brought that little dimple to life.

He couldn't help it; he touched her cheek. "Damn, I wish I could be the one to stay. You're getting the dangerous end of this."

She shook her head. "It wouldn't work, and you know it. They'd never allow you near the kids, for one thing."

A silence fell between them, a silence filled with the immensity of what they were about to attempt. He dropped his hand from her cheek, but she caught it before it got too far. Her gaze softened as she held his hand in both of hers. "Tobias...about before..." She trailed off. In her eyes he read regret, worry, gratitude.

But did that add up to love?

"Forget it." He turned away from her, toward Sarah, who was bouncing toward them.

"I just heard the bell for prayers before dinner," she said. "I have to crawl back, really quick!"

"I think it's go-time all-around," he said gruffly. "Ready for a fake fight with your fake fiancé, Caro?"

"Ready."

29

THEIR PLAN WORKED PERFECTLY...UNTIL IT ALL FELL APART. THEY waited until Sarah had disappeared, then Tobias stormed out of the guesthouse, ranting about crazy impossible women. He demanded to be able to leave immediately—the hell with Carolyn Moore. She could find her own ride back. He drove off in a rooster tail of gravel while the guards laughed their asses off.

Carolyn ran into the longhouse kitchen, sobbing. The women, who were busy serving the night's meal, clustered around her to offer comfort. She remembered a few of them, but others were new. Even though she was technically a pariah, the fact that she'd come back for her father's blessing softened them toward her. Everyone liked drama, after all. The women jumped at the chance to lecture her on the dangers of marrying godless men.

"You should find a suitable partner here," they told her. "Once your father has forgiven you and received you back into the fold, you'll have no shortage of offers, even though you're so far past your prime."

Carolyn didn't argue. She accepted all advice and lectures

eagerly. If it helped her find the children, she'd volunteer for a thousand scoldings.

And it worked. At the Light Keepers, the children always ate separately from the adults. When it was time to bring them their food, she volunteered to help out. "I can't possibly accept your hospitality without pulling my weight. That's against the Third Principle." Thank goodness the old jargon came back to her so easily.

The women smiled kindly at her and accepted the offer. Following their instructions, she piled trays of baked chicken and biscuits and gravy onto a rolling cart. The entire time, she made sure to sob occasionally, or drop her head into her hands, as if her heartbreak blinded her to everything else.

She followed Patience, a sour older woman she'd always detested, to the barn. Behind it, a large aluminum hatch door opened onto a short set of stairs that led down into darkness.

It occurred to her, with a jolt, that she should pretend to be surprised. "What is this place?"

"It's for the children's safety. That's all you need to know."

Carolyn accepted that with a bowed head, and carried a tray down the stairs. A motion sensor light went on, illuminating another door at the bottom of the staircase. Patience unlocked it —these kids really were prisoners!—and let her into a big open room filled with cots and about a dozen children from the ages of seven to fourteen.

Sarah's face lit up at the sight of her. Carolyn gave her a surreptitious "quiet" gesture behind her back. A boy of about fourteen whispered something in her ear and she snapped her mouth shut. That must be Mark.

Patience directed her to put the trays on the table and dish food into the bowls that had already been set out. Carolyn did so, thinking quickly. She had to find a reason to stay back here, something that wouldn't make Patience suspicious.

After they'd served all the food, the children sat obediently around the table and Patience delivered the blessing. Carolyn lowered her head along with the others, though her own silent prayer was slightly different. *Please, Lord, help me get these children to safety.*

Patience finished with a sharp clap of her hands. "I expect all the dishes to be piled on the trays when we return in one hour. Older kids, you're responsible."

"Yes, ma'am," they answered, mouths already full of biscuit and chicken. She turned to go, her floor-length skirt swinging wide. Carolyn remembered the feeling of those long skirts always dragging at her legs, of never feeling free to run and climb and dance. Of the many times she'd gotten her skirts tangled between her legs and fallen flat.

And that gave her an idea.

Following behind the older woman, she snagged her foot in the leg of a chair. She went crashing down, face first. She landed on her side, her face and shoulder slamming into the concrete floor. Pain lanced through her. The older woman whirled around with a scowl.

Carolyn sat up and grabbed her ankle with an expression of agony. Her ankle was fine, but she didn't have to fake the pain, with her shoulder and cheekbone throbbing. "I twisted my ankle. Oh sweet mother, it hurts." She moaned and rocked back and forth. The kids all turned to stare at her. Sarah jumped out of her chair and came running to her side.

"Oh miss, are you okay?"

Carolyn winked at her so she didn't worry too much. Sarah got the hint and dropped down next to her. She peered at her ankle.

"Ma'am Patience, it looks terrible. I don't think she can walk!"

"I'll be fine," Carolyn said with a gasp. "I just need a few minutes. You go on, Patience. I know you have a million things to do. By the time you get back I'll be up and ready to tackle those stairs." She put on a brave smile. She made a show of trying to get to her feet, then collapsing back down from the pain. "Just a little rest, that's all I need," she repeated faintly.

Patience let out a disapproving snort. "I suppose bad things happen to bad people. That'll teach you to leave the path of the Light Keepers."

"You're so right, Patience. That lesson has been brought home to me in so many ways since I came back. I'm truly grateful for your forbearance."

"I have to lock the door. The Elders require it. You won't be able to leave until I return."

"Of course you must do as the Elders say. Where would I go like this anyway?" She pretended to test her ankle again and winced.

With one last scornful glance, Patience bustled toward the stairs. She made a big show of locking the door. "One hour, children," she called as she left.

The sound of her footfalls echoed in the stairwell as she climbed toward the hatch. As soon as Carolyn heard it slam shut, she scrambled to her feet. Sarah jumped up and down and clapped her hands. "You're not hurt!"

"No, not much. A little." She rubbed her shoulder, then raised her voice to address all the kids. Most had stopped eating to watch the drama, though some of the younger ones were still focused on their food. She called on her best college professor voice—authoritative, friendly, calm, in charge. "Kids, my name is Carolyn Moore and I'm Sarah's half-sister. I used to live here, so you may have heard about me."

"You're the one from the poster," said a little girl. "But you're a pariah now!"

"Because I left when I was of legal age. Not because I sinned." Though she certainly had sinned plenty since then, and still would—if Tobias ever forgave her.

"I'm here because of Sarah. She wants to leave here and I'm going to help her."

Forks clattered onto plates and thirteen sets of hopeful eyes clung to her. Her heart twisted. How could she leave these kids here, with some unknown cataclysmic event about to occur?

"We want to go to," said a tall boy, the oldest in the group, as he rose his feet.

"Are you Mark?"

"Yes, and I know the tunnels so I can help." His eyes were snapping with excitement. "We all want to leave. We've already talked about it. We know how to get off the property, but we couldn't figure out what to do after that."

"*All* of you? Are you sure?" She surveyed the other children. Their expressions ranged from frightened to determined to thrilled—in Sarah's case.

"We all talked it over together. We only trust each other. The adults don't pay attention to us anymore. Even the kids with parents are freaking out because something weird's going on. We never had to stay underground before."

"Our parents never visit us anymore," piped up one small child.

Carolyn shoved aside her anger at the situation. Tobias would be expecting her and Sarah, no more. But how could she leave these kids behind? This might be their last chance. The prison would be locked that much tighter once one child escaped. And time was ticking away. *One hour.*

Tobias could handle it. Tobias could handle anything. *Decision made.*

"Okay then." She nodded. "Let's get moving. Mark, lead the way to that tunnel."

With a big grin, the kid hurried to the far corner of the room and moved aside a cot. Behind it lay a hatch door. Carolyn peered at the narrow opening—easy for the kids, tight for her. She couldn't imagine Tobias trying to squeeze in there.

"You go first, Mark, and lead the way. I'll bring up the rear and cover our tracks."

He nodded and beckoned to the other kids. They clearly saw him as their leader already, and easily followed after him, ducking into the tunnel one by one. Carolyn crawled in last and pulled the cot and the hatch door back in front of the hole.

She could barely manage to turn her body around in the narrow space. By the time she was pointed in the right direction, she was several yards behind the last child. The corridor was lit by dim utility lights at intervals so far apart that occasionally she found herself in total darkness. Ahead, she heard a few whimpers, and shushes, and an occasional whisper from one of the children. To her right, she felt the rough concrete of the tunnel, to the left the smooth surface of cords and pipes. A low hum seemed to fill the space.

They crawled, on and on. It seemed to last forever, this slow inching away from the bunker, toward uncertainty. Would Tobias find them? Would the FBI be there? Or would they be on their own?

Emotion welled inside her as she pictured Tobias waiting patiently at the fence line, all night if need be. *I said I love you.*

He loved her. It had shone from his eyes as he spoke those words. It was true. It was real. And she'd thrown it back in his face out of...what? Fear? Denial? Light Keeper-inspired craziness?

Maybe all of the above. But as she squirmed through the tunnel, those emotions didn't seem very important anymore. What mattered was Tobias, and the way he looked at her, the way he made her feel.

Of course she loved Tobias. Her love for Tobias sang through her heart, her soul, her mind, her cramped, crawling body. She loved him so deeply, so permanently. She'd fallen so fast and hard she hadn't even realized what was happening. Hot sex, she'd told herself. That was total crap, total self-delusion. She *loved* him. What if she never got a chance to tell him so?

Lost in thought, she didn't realize that something had gone wrong until she reached the end of the tunnel, where another hatch opened next to the power station. A fluorescent light illuminated the kids, huddled in a tight group against the wall of the station as an armed guard aimed a machine gun at them. He was speaking into his walkie-talkie, saying something about "stupid kids."

Which meant he didn't have a complete focus on his M15. And he probably didn't know she was with the kids.

Making a split-second decision, she crawled silently out of the hatch and lunged at him. She yanked his feet out from under him and he toppled to the ground, jarring his weapon loose. She pounced on him while he scrambled after the machine gun, then planted a knee in the small of his back, where he'd feel it in his kidney. She ripped the M15 out of his grasp. He was still fighting her, struggling to get away from the pressure of her knee. The walkie-talkie crackled. She had to finish this, now. Get the kids out of there. Hauling her arm back as far as she could, she rammed the gun against his temple. He slumped against the ground, unconscious. She grabbed the walkie-talkie from his hand and shut it off.

The kids watched, wide-eyed, as if she were some kind of Rambo. Sarah jumped up and down. "That's my sister," she crowed proudly.

Carolyn allowed herself a tiny smile. Adrenaline coursed through her as she slung the M15 over her back. "Come on, kids. We have to run. Go due west toward the fence. Someone will meet us there."

God, she hoped so.

The bigger kids took the smaller kids on their backs and they set off at the fastest pace they could manage through the stalks of last year's crops. She didn't know exactly how far the fence was from here. It was now full night, with the moon just beginning to rise. She walked backward, scanning for signs of pursuers from the compound. The station was silhouetted against ghostly silver light, like a scene from one of her favorite Rembrandt paintings, "The Night Watch."

The odd flashback to her real life disoriented her. Was it just a couple weeks ago that she'd been wrapping up finals at Evergreen? That she'd said a tearful goodbye to Dragon? Now she was back in the one place she'd never wanted to see again, jogging with a pack of kids towards freedom, hoping with all her heart that Tobias Knight would be there to save them. All of them.

30

As soon as Tobias could get a cell signal from the Land Rover, he called Agent Turner and filled her in. Naturally she was furious, but only yelled at him for a brief time until she hung up to mobilize a response.

Then he called Will and Ben. "I'm flying the chopper up," Ben said right away.

"No need. The FBI's got this."

"So at worst I get in some night flying practice. I'm coming." When Ben talked in that tone, there was no point arguing, so he didn't. Instead he scouted out a good landing site and sent Ben the coordinates.

When the brothers had purchased the Robinson helicopter for Knight and Day, they'd wanted it for ocean rescues, or natural disasters. Tobias certainly hadn't pictured it as the getaway vehicle from a fringe militia group. But so be it.

Will hopped in the big Ford Super Duty he'd borrowed from the Jupiter Point Hotshots and headed toward the compound. Knowing his brothers were on their way was a huge relief, but he wouldn't breathe easy until he laid eyes on Carolyn and Sarah.

After all that groundwork had been laid, Tobias parked his

Land Rover as close to the westernmost point of the Light Keepers property. He dug a pair of night vision goggles out of the bag of gear he kept in the back of his rig. In the greenish darkness they created, he hiked through the fields until he reached the fence line.

There, he watched and waited. He didn't have wire cutters, so he found a hole in the fence and gradually managed to widen it, relying on his hand strength for the job. At one point, he heard the *thunk-thunk* of the chopper setting down in the field. He'd instructed Ben to stay in the pilot's seat, ready for a quick escape.

He stayed still and watchful, a shadow in the night, and thought of his father. As an army sniper, how many hours had his father passed like this? Alert but still, waiting on a knife's edge? What did he think about? Robert Knight hadn't married and started a family until after he left the army. Had he wanted to? Did he dream of coming home to Jupiter Point? Was he already in love with Janine?

Tobias would never know these things. He could never ask his father. Because someone had reached out from the past and snuffed out his life. In that moment, an explosion of grief radiated through him, like a nuclear blast. *Oh Dad. You stubborn, upright, dedicated, strict, difficult, wonderful man. I loved you.*

A blinding flash of emotion lit up all the corners of his heart —the guilt, the penance, the grief. *And you knew that. I don't have to worry. I don't have to atone.*

Right. That's not your job. Your job is to live.

It sounded like his father's voice, the hushed whisper of a ghost. But it wasn't. It was him. All him. The deepest, wisest part of him.

Tobias shook himself back to attention, feeling as if he'd traveled a great distance in that brief moment. He checked the dark fields again, lit a garish green through his goggles.

Will appeared at his side, squeezing his shoulder as he crouched next to him. "Anything yet?"

"No."

"Should we go in?"

"Not yet, I don't want to set off any alarm bells. I don't know their cameras, their systems. If we hear anything that doesn't sound right, we'll go in."

"Roger that."

"Ben?"

"Standing by. About a quarter mile away, out of sight. He said the chopper flew like a dream on the way up."

Good man. Both of them.

They settled into silence. More time passed, but it had a different quality now that he had company. His brother's company, best of all.

And finally, there they were! A cluster of dark figures stumbled exhausted across the field. Wait—holy shit, that was more than just Carolyn and Sarah. Jesus, it was a whole group, ranging from little to nearly adult-size. What the hell had happened? Carolyn must have decided to spring all the children.

Good for her.

"That's a lot of kids," Will murmured.

"How many can the chopper carry?"

"I'll fit the rest in the Super Duty. It's a good thing I brought it. I had a feeling it would come in handy."

Tobias jumped up and waved to draw their attention to their location. The group veered their direction.

The first kid to reach the fence was a tall, gangly teenager carrying a smaller child. He was panting so hard Tobias could barely make out his words.

"Caro...Moore...back..."

"Carolyn?" he asked sharply. "Did something happen?" He scanned the group and didn't see her. More kids arrived, piling up behind the hole in the fence. He helped them through, one by one, until they were all on the other side. Little Sarah hugged his leg.

The first kid finally caught his breath. "They were following us. Carolyn stayed back to do something."

"*Do* something?" Shit, shit, shit ... she was putting herself in the line of fire...shit...

"Go," said Will. "I got this." He was already shepherding them in the direction of the chopper. "Follow me, everyone. Who's up for a ride in a helicopter?"

Tobias gripped the edges of the hole in the fence, using all his force to expand it enough so he could fit through. Damn, why'd he have to be such a big bastard?

When the hole was finally large enough, he squeezed through it, then double-checked on the .45 he'd stashed in the back of his jeans. Staying low to the ground, he ran in the direction the kids had come from.

After about five minutes, he heard voices, and dropped to the ground. On elbows and knees, silent as a snake, he made his way toward them.

And what he saw made his blood turn cold. Carolyn was with two Light Keeper men, one of whom had her in a headlock—with a knife at the side of her neck. The other had a shotgun aimed at her heart.

She had a weapon slung over her back, so they must have surprised her before she had a chance to grab it.

Caro spoke calmly, but her voice was thick with fear. "Don't make the kind of mistake you can't recover from, guys. The FBI is going to be here any minute. You can still survive this, if you don't do anything stupid like kill someone."

"Accidents happen." The man with the shotgun laughed. His voice sounded young—and weirdly familiar. "It's dark out here and you're trespassing. You attacked us."

"That's how it looks to me, too," said the Light Keeper with the knife. "And according to our code, we'll be forgiven because you're a pariah."

"The U.S. Government doesn't recognize your code, idiots,"

Carolyn gasped. She was staring at the gunman. "Joseph Brown, is that you?

A pause, then, "Yah, so what?"

"You're better than this. You went to college, you know there's a whole world out there. You don't have to do this."

"*Shut up,*" he hissed.

"The FBI knows about you. I talked to them myself."

"We're not afraid of the FBI. Let them come." The guard who was holding her shifted his grip, tilting her head back. The moonlight caught the long arch of her neck and gleamed on the knife's curving blade. And for one long, agonizing moment, Tobias teetered on the edge of madness. Visions of his father, throat slashed, attacked him like rabid bats, blinding him, blocking his vision. A kind of howl echoed through his brain.

He had to act—now—or Carolyn might be dead in the grass, bleeding out. But in the dark, even with his night vision goggles, he couldn't see where the Light Keeper ended and Carolyn began. He had to throw them off somehow. Gain an advantage.

"FBI," he called. "Put your weapons down. You're surrounded."

Joseph Brown swung around and fired in his direction. Something nicked Tobias's leg, but he made no sound. He couldn't allow the men to think he was hurt.

"You just earned yourself an assault on a federal officer charge," he said. He fired wide of the group, just to make sure they got the message. He pretended to speak into a comm. "Found them, about two hundred yards inside the fence line, due east. Hostage situation in progress, request—"

"Hey." Joseph took a step toward him—away from Carolyn. "She's not a hostage. We caught her trespassing and trying to kidnap a bunch of kids."

Savage triumph filled him. They believed he was the FBI. But he still had to get them away from Carolyn. "We can sort out the situation as soon as you step away from the woman. I'm going to need everyone to put their weapons down."

Joseph Brown followed his command, lowering the shotgun, but the other, the one with his knife still at Carolyn's throat, refused. "Let us go or I'll cut her."

"I don't think you understand how this works." Tobias had to work overtime to keep his voice calm. "If any harm comes to her, you'll answer for it to the fullest extent of the law. You have no leverage here. Your only good option is to disarm. Right now." He added an extra whiplash of authority to his voice.

"If I do, you're going to arrest me, aren't you? Once I let her go, I have no guarantee you won't."

That was true—or would have been if he'd actually been FBI.

"We'll be questioning all of you, including the woman. Now put down the knife and we can figure this out."

De-escalation. Get them to put down their arms, that was the first step. Maybe there was a way out of this without bloodshed.

Or maybe not.

The man moved again, turning Carolyn's body so she would shield him from any gunfire coming from Tobias's direction.

Carolyn's eyes flashed with terror. And Tobias couldn't wait another moment. Bullets be damned.

He launched himself toward Carolyn and her captor. Something brushed his arm—another bullet?—but he felt no pain. The only thing that mattered was keeping Caro whole and alive.

Everything moved in slow-motion, the way Tobias remembered from high-intensity combat situations. Carolyn stomped on the guard's foot and dropped to the ground, rolling away from him. Her attacker crouched to face Tobias, swinging the knife in one hand. Joseph fired again, but the bullets went high and wild.

With one part of his brain, he realized that Joseph didn't actually want to kill him. If he did, he'd probably be dead by now.

He saw the guard with the knife slash at him, Joseph lift his shotgun again. He had no plan to deal with them both, other than to disable the knife-wielder first, then tackle the other one, assuming he was still alive to do so.

Even that vague outline of a plan went out the window, as Carolyn darted around the knifeman and tackled Joseph at the knees, like some kind of pro football player. Tobias viciously chopped at the other guard's arm, choosing a spot that would stun his nerves. The knife dropped away, but the man didn't give up. He charged him like a raging bull, all fury and spittle.

That, Tobias could handle. They grappled for several intense moments, rolling back and forth in the grass, until finally Tobias got him pinned on his back. One last solid uppercut to the jaw knocked him out cold.

He rolled away, panting heavily, and found Carolyn kneeling next to him, patiently waiting for him to finish. He ripped the night vision goggles off his face. She was breathing hard, her hair a tangled mess down her back, a trickle of blood on her neck. But she was smiling brilliantly in the rising moonlight, and Joseph Brown was sprawled behind her, unconscious.

"How's that nonviolent communication working out for you?" Even though she said it lightly, her voice shook.

He sat up and wrapped his arms around her, burying his head in the soft skin at the crook of her neck. He breathed in the scent of her, the underlying sweetness mingled with the sharp scent of fear and the metallic smell of blood. So close. He'd come so close to losing Carolyn.

He felt her tremble in his arms. Those delicate bones, that soft skin, her caring heart and bright spirit—all wrapped up with the pure titanium toughness at Carolyn's core. She was it for him. Forevermore.

"You came for me," she whispered. "I was so terrified, I could feel how much they hated me. I thought they were going to kill me and bury me in the field somewhere. Then I heard your voice and it was like the sun coming up. I knew it would be okay."

He shook with full-body tremors as the past few moments of utter terror came back to him. "He had a knife on you. A fucking knife. He almost killed you."

"I'm fine." She put her hands on his cheeks, which he realized were wet with tears. Tears? When did he ever cry? He wasn't a crier, never had been. Not since he was little. "I'm fine. You saved me. Everything's going to be okay," she kept murmuring. Her voice was pitched low to soothe him, and it worked. Slowly, by gradual degrees, he relaxed and his head cleared.

He realized they were huddled together in an open moonlit field with two fallen armed guards nearby. And more possibly on the way.

"We need get the hell out of here before more crazies with guns come after us."

"Yes. Can you stand?"

He heaved himself to his feet, ignoring the pain. Blood dripped down his left arm and right leg.

"Oh my God, Tobias." Tears gleaming in her eyes, she came next to him and pulled his good arm over her shoulder. "Can you walk? That looks terrible."

"No walking. We have to run. Let's go."

Together they half-limped, half-ran toward the hole in the fence. In the distance, from the direction of the compound, voices shouted. Up ahead, he heard the *flap-flap* of the Knight and Day helicopter's blades. Ben was lifting off with his payload of kids. Hopefully Will was already on the road with the rest of them.

Just as they reached the fence, the gangly, ghostly silhouette of the helicopter rose over the treetops. Lights off, it briefly blocked the stars as it gained altitude. *Go, go,* he urged Ben silently. *Don't worry about us, we got this.*

He and Carolyn would survive this. Beyond that, he had no idea.

31

A TEAM OF FBI AGENTS SCOOPED THEM UP A FEW HUNDRED YARDS from the fence line. Thank God, because even though Tobias didn't utter a single complaint, Carolyn knew he was hurting. She could sense it in the way he held his body and the clenching of his jaw. And because every cell of her body was attuned to his right now.

He would have died for her.

Willingly.

He'd flung himself into certain gunfire. It had happened so fast she hadn't completely grasped it. One second the knife was pricking her throat, the next she was free and the other Light Keeper was trying to kill Tobias. A fury as fierce and pure as fire had propelled her through the air to tackle him. She'd felt superhuman, as if she could fly, and divert bullets, and fell bad guys without suffering a scratch. Like Wonder Woman without the headpiece.

But without Tobias, she could very well be dead by now. Her life, her beating pulse, her existence had meant nothing to that knife-wielding jerk. To him, she was less than human. A pariah. Someone whose death would mean nothing.

If they could feel that way toward a former "poster child," was anyone safe?

No.

She helped Tobias into the backseat of one of the FBI's sedans. He made noises about being fine, but the agent insisted he get checked out at the nearest hospital, fifty miles away. She snuggled next to him while he drowsed on her shoulder.

As the car raced down dark country roads, Carolyn's own road ahead became clear to her. She could no longer sit in her ivory tower art history class and pretend that she had nothing to do with the Light Keepers. Nope. From now on, she was going to speak out. She was going to shine a spotlight on the group and others like it. She was going to stand up and make some noise.

At the hospital, medical personnel whisked Tobias into an exam room. For a terrifying moment, she felt utterly alone in a place filled with strangers. If only Merry were here. A friendly face, someone who understood.

Then Will hurried into the hospital lobby.

"The FBI took charge of the kids and told me I'd find Tobias here," he told her. "How is he?"

Her eyes filled with tears. "F—fine."

With a quick look at her face, he pulled her in for a hug. "Hey, don't you worry. You should have seen some of his injuries growing up. This is barely a scratch."

She clung to the confidence in Will's voice like a lifeline in a storm.

When Agent Turner arrived at the hospital, she took Carolyn's statement in a deserted corner of the cafeteria. Carolyn carefully described everything she'd witnessed in the compound. The underground bunker, the stale air, the kids' pale faces. The overheard whispers.

"It sounds like they're preparing for some kind of dramatic standoff. And they've been kidnapping children. But I don't know why."

"From what we've picked up, it seems their leader, Ray, has gone off the deep end. The group wasn't growing fast enough. He made some bad decisions. But what happened tonight is going to change everything. It was a crazy thing y'all did, but it'll make a difference."

"Good. Even if I face some kind of charges, I'm still glad."

"We'll figure it out," Turner murmured as she scrawled notes on a pad.

"Did you find the two Light Keepers who attacked me?" She tested the cut on her neck, where the blood had dried.

"Yup. They're both alive and under arrest. One of them hasn't given us much, he's completely committed to the belief system. But Joseph Brown is talking. He admitted to the harassment incidents at Evergreen."

"Did he explain why he did those things?"

"He ranted a lot, but reading between the lines, he was angry that you escaped the group. He wanted to leave, but as a male pursuing a college degree, he was under tons of pressure to stay. He cracked, and took it out on you. Then the group ordered him back, probably to prepare for the standoff."

The standoff. She shuddered at the thought of armed warfare breaking out on the property. What if the kids had gotten trapped forever in that bunker? What if Sarah had?

"The kids. My sister. Where are they now?"

"Social Services is meeting the chopper at the closest Air Force base. I promise you'll see her, but they all have to be checked out first."

Carolyn nodded reluctantly. She'd only known Sarah for a matter of hours, but it might as well have been for the girl's entire short life. She would do anything—anything—to keep her safe.

Including...

Yes.

"I want to adopt her," she told Agent Turner. "Her mother's dead. My father can't be trusted with her. I'm her own family."

"Not my department. You'll have to work with Social Services on that."

"But she was kept underground like a prisoner! They all were. For I don't know how long. Can you imagine that?" She buried her head in her hands, the horror sweeping over her.

Turner put a hand on her arm, an oddly comforting gesture from the normally brusque agent. "I've seen all kinds of shitshows in this job. I've learned one thing that I try to keep in mind. People are resilient. Especially kids. If you doubt that, look at yourself."

Carolyn drew in a deep breath and thought about Sarah's bright smile. Even in the worst of circumstances, the little girl had found joy in bouncing on a bed. She pulled her hands away from her face and looked up at the agent. "You think they'll be okay? Based on your experience?"

"Those kids found that utility tunnel, Sarah found her way to you, now they're all on a helicopter riding to safety. They're resourceful, those kids. Hell yes, I think they'll be okay, with some help."

Some help. Absolutely. If anyone knew what the kids were going through, it was Carolyn. "I'll be their champion," she decided, out loud. "Their advocate. Their friend. Whatever they need. And I'm going to make sure Sarah ends up with me. I'll fight the Light Keepers for her if I have to."

"I sure wouldn't bet against you."

A nurse appeared next to them. "You can see Tobias Knight now. He's waiting for you."

Everything else fled her mind at that point.

TOBIAS'S left arm and right leg were covered in bandages, dirt and blood smeared his exhausted face. His eyes were closed, those incongruously long eyelashes blending with the deep shadows under his eyes.

He looked beautiful. And she loved him.

Carolyn crouched down next to his bed and stroked her fingers through his thick hair, which was now long enough that it actually had a wave. She remembered how he'd looked in her class—his buzz cut just starting to grow out, his wary expression. What would Tobias look like without the weight of the world on his shoulders?

"Carolyn," he murmured, his eyes opening just enough to reveal a sliver of deepest blue. "You're here."

"I'm here. And I love you. I love you, Tobias."

A slow smile spread across his face. "Good."

Now she *did* know what he looked like without the weight of the world. And it was a glorious sight.

"As soon as we get back to Jupiter Point we have to look for a house," he murmured.

Those painkillers must be doing a number on him. A house? What was he talking about? "Sweetie, just get some rest. We can talk more when you're feeling better."

"I feel great." His eyes opened all the way. "I'm alive. You're alive. I love you. You love me. And Will's going to find the person who actually killed our dad. Because it wasn't me. I found him, but it wasn't my fault."

"That's right, Tobias." Oh yes, he was definitely a little woozy from whatever meds they'd given him. "You found him, but it wasn't your fault. I'm really glad you see that. Now you should go back to sleep."

A glimmer of a smile lit up his face. "You think I'm babbling. I'm not, Caro. We're going to need a house because of Sarah."

She stared at him. "What are you—?"

"Sarah is going to live with us, of course. Other kids in the group might need a home too. So it's going to have to be a big house. Lots of outside space. No basement. A big farmhouse with room to play. A garden."

That image brought her such a powerful sense of joy that she couldn't form words.

Just then Will came in with a cardboard tray of coffees. He offered one to Carolyn, along with a look of gratitude that made her blush.

"I finally got the whole story from Tobias. He told me how you knocked out the asshole shooting at him. Don't be alarmed if we all start treating you like a queen."

Her face aflame, she hid behind the coffee. Queen? Nah. She was a red-blooded woman in love with an incredible man.

"Now what were you just saying about a farmhouse?" Will asked Tobias as he pulled up a chair next to the bed.

Tobias reached out and grabbed Will in a solid forearm grip. "We need something just like it, Caro and me. We're skipping right to the part where we already have kids. Way ahead of you, bro. Sorry. Guess you'll have to catch up later. Oh, and I'm going to talk her into marrying me if it's the last thing I do."

Carolyn's mouth fell open. Will looked as if he was trying very hard not to laugh. "You want to get married, big guy? Never thought this day would come."

"Shut the hell up. You knew it would." Tobias's grin flashed through the grime on his face. "When I'm wrong, I can admit it."

"Good to hear." Will leaned close so he could turn their arm-clench into full-on embrace. "Love you, brother. Damn glad you're okay."

When he released Tobias, his gray eyes were damp. Tobias fell back on the bed, looking happy but exhausted.

Will rose to his feet, swiping at his eyes. "I need to call Merry and give her an update. Caro, don't be surprised if you get a call from her. She's already working this story from the FBI angle, but she's hoping she can talk to you."

"Of course. I'm happy to tell her everything." A lot of it would be painful and embarrassing, but if she wanted to shine a light on the Light Keepers, it was necessary. And Merry was the perfect person for the job.

Maybe she'd ask for one thing in return—Will and Merry's help in locating Mira Ahmed. More than ever, she wanted to find her old friend.

After Will left, she snuggled up next to Tobias again. He put his good arm around her and hauled her onto the bed with him. His body heat warmed her. All the fear and tension of the past twenty-four hours drained away, until she felt boneless and content, like a cat by a fireplace.

"So. About my mission regarding marriage..." he murmured.

"You know how I feel about marriage." And yet those worries seemed so far away. So inconsequential compared to *losing Tobias*.

"Yes, I know. That's why I'm giving myself at least six months to talk you into it."

"Six months isn't very much time," she teased. "My reasons for fearing marriage are very well-thought out and logically sound."

His hand tightened on her shoulder. "And mine, professor, go beyond logic. They're about love. And magic. And a little girl who's going to need a family. And a man who thought he was going to spend his whole life alone, until he met you."

She buried her head in the crook of his shoulder. The steady beat of his heart was hypnotic.

"I would never want you to feel trapped or controlled," he said. "You need to have a panic button."

"What do you mean?"

"Like a one-way ticket to Italy sitting in your underwear drawer, so you can take a break if you want. Visit Michelangelo's penis statue."

She laughed into his warm skin. "Remind me once again to never let you guest lecture in my class."

His laugh vibrated deep inside his chest. "Are you sure? Because I can tell those kids all about *chiaroscuro*. You're the *chiaro* to my *scuro*, baby. You light me up."

That worked both ways. A sun seemed to burst to life inside her. Its light radiated through her, bringing intense joy to the deepest, most hidden parts of her heart. "You know something, Tobias?"

"What's that?"

"It took six minutes, not six months."

For a spellbound second he just looked at her. Then a huge grin took over his face. "Damn, I'm good."

32

Six weeks later, Tobias, Carolyn and Sarah set out on the most important mission of their new life. Sarah was so excited she kept spinning around like a top. Everyone they passed in Jupiter Point's quaint little historic downtown district smiled at the sight of the three of them. The story, of course, had spread through town like wildfire, especially after Merry's big exposé had been published and picked up by the national media.

A fringe throwback militia group, children held prisoner, some kidnapped, a big explosive standoff averted...it was astonishing that something like that had happened within a few hundred miles of Jupiter Point. And then the fact that the Knight brothers had been so key to rescuing the kids, and that *Carolyn* was raised in the group...it was all anyone had talked about for weeks.

The group itself was splintering under the pressure of the spotlight. The leader, Ray, had been arrested and charged with kidnapping. Some members had left, especially those parents who wanted to get their kids back.

That didn't include Levi Moore. He had enough legal issues

on his hands without worrying about Sarah. He'd agreed to the adoption without argument.

"Wait at the corner for us, Sarah!" Carolyn called to the little girl. Having lived her entire life off the grid, Sarah required close attention. She knew nothing about traffic or intersections or even strangers. Carolyn had taken the semester off from JPCC to help her get settled in.

Mark and the other kidnapped children had been reunited with their families. The rest had found temporary foster homes, a good number of them local. Carolyn had taken the lead on forming a support group to keep the kids in touch with each other. They'd gone through such an intense experience together. Every month, they planned to get together for a picnic, or for a potluck at someone's house. Carolyn and Tobias had hosted the first one at Will's farmhouse.

Which was now their farmhouse.

Will and Merry had decided they needed a smaller place that required less attention, since they were both such workaholics. They wanted to focus on their work and their relationship, not lawn mowing. So they'd bought a brand new duplex and turned one side into Will's new office. Jupiter Point's only private investigator needed his own office. He was also getting an intern—Chase Merriweather, Merry's half-brother, was moving to Jupiter Point to work with Will.

So Carolyn and Sarah moved into the farmhouse with Tobias. Even though they urged Ben to stay on with them, he refused, with many loud complaints about the epidemic of love breaking out all around him. He found his own bachelor pad in an apartment complex on the edge of town, as close as possible to Knight and Day Flight Tours.

And as far as possible from Julie, his ex-girlfriend, everyone noticed. But didn't mention out loud. Something was definitely going on with Ben and Julie, but any hint of a mention of her made Ben storm out of the room. So they all held their tongues and hoped for the best.

Carolyn and Tobias insisted that Aiden continue to stay at the farm when he was in town. Tobias and his youngest brother were closer than ever, and they all occasionally laughed their heads off about the angel tattoo and the smoking.

Sarah loved it when they laughed. While they chuckled, she'd bounce around the living room, dancing and hooting. Then she'd jump into Tobias's lap and tickle him until he cried. Sarah was a joy and an imp and a force of nature. Carolyn could barely remember life before her.

A sister, a husband, and now...

"We're here, we're here!" Sarah called, skipping to the entrance of Jupiter Point's pet shelter. The shelter had called this morning with the news that a Newfoundland puppy was up for adoption.

For weeks, Carolyn had been regaling Sarah with bedtime stories about her big guardian angel dog named Dragon. Now they were getting a Dragon of their own.

Carolyn's heart felt so full, she had to stop to take a deep breath before following Tobias and Sarah inside. She glanced at the simple gold ring on her left hand, the commitment she'd made to Tobias in a brief but tender ceremony at City Hall. In the end, marrying Tobias's was one of the easiest decisions she'd ever made. She wanted to be with him, that was that. She trusted him with all the secrets and fault lines of her innermost self. And he trusted her with that other side of himself, the vulnerable part that even years as a special forces Night Stalker hadn't erased.

She loved him for that. She loved him for so many things. All parts of him, shadows and light. And soon—amazingly, astonishingly—she was going to meet his mother and sister.

Will had found Cassie and Janine Knight. Soon, maybe even within a few weeks, a family reunion would take place.

In the meantime...her own little family—so new, so miraculous—was about to get bigger. Sarah burst out of the door before Carolyn even had a chance to step inside. A giant puppy almost as big as her capered behind her. The baby Newfie was fuzzy, long-eared, eager-eyed, the deep rich brown of hot cocoa.

"We got him! We got a dog! We have a dog! We have the best dog in the world!" Sarah jumped up and down, her pigtails shining in the sun. The dog ran circles around her, panting and awkward.

"That was so fast! I love him already." Carolyn laughed as the two youngsters, dog and kid, cavorted on the sidewalk. Tobias emerged from the shelter, putting his wallet back in his pocket. Even though he was dressed in black as he had been the first time she saw him, his expression was pure lighthearted joy. He grinned as he came to Carolyn's side and wrapped one arm around her.

"It was love at first sight. Couldn't stop her."

"Well, we are sisters." She leaned her head against his chest. "Count on us to know a good thing when we see one. Count on us to fight for it, too."

"Amen for that."

Carolyn expelled a long, happy sigh. Careful of Tobias's still-healing arm, she leaned against his solid warmth. Some moments were so perfect, they ought to live forever, preserved in indelible strokes of wonder. Wrapped up in their love, the two of them watched the girl and the puppy dance in the timeless winter sunlight, and rejoiced.

ABOUT THE AUTHOR

Jennifer Bernard is a *USA Today* bestselling author of contemporary romance. Her books have been called "an irresistible reading experience" full of "quick wit and sizzling love scenes." A graduate of Harvard and former news promo producer, she left big city life in Los Angeles for true love in Alaska, where she now lives with her husband and stepdaughters. She still hasn't adjusted to the cold, so most often she can be found cuddling with her laptop and a cup of tea. No stranger to book success, she also writes erotic novellas under a naughty secret name that she's happy to share with the curious. You can learn more about Jennifer and her books at JenniferBernard.net.

Connect with Jennifer online:

JenniferBernard.net

Jen@JenniferBernard.net

ACKNOWLEDGMENTS

Thank you to Miriam Matthews for sharing her expertise on small planes. To my editor Kelli Collins, artists Dana LaMothe and proofer Wendy Keel, thanks for all your great work. I'd also like to offer much love to the Hot Readers group. Jupiter Point would not be nearly so fun without you!

ALSO BY JENNIFER BERNARD

Jupiter Point ~ Firefighters

Set the Night on Fire ~ Book 1

Burn So Bright ~ Book 2

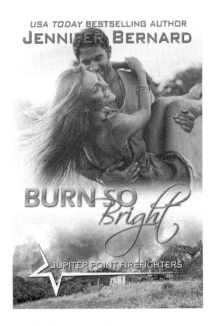

Into the Flames ~ Book 3

Setting Off Sparks ~ Book 4

Jupiter Point ~ The Knight Brothers

Hot Pursuit ~ Book 5

Seeing Stars

(Prequel and Hope Falls Kindle World Novella)

∼

The Bachelor Firemen of San Gabriel

The Fireman Who Loved Me

Hot for Fireman

Sex and the Single Fireman

How to Tame a Wild Fireman

Four Weddings and a Fireman

The Night Belongs to Fireman

∼

$ 11.99

63611856R00172

Made in the USA
Middletown, DE
03 February 2018